CHRISTOPHER J. STOCKWELL

The Complete City Attorney's Office Series

Book One Professional Camouflage: Book Two The Land of Lollipops and Suckers

*For all the attorneys I've hated before—each of you taught me how to smile at
someone while simultaneously stabbing them in the ribs.*

*And for Bubby, Nicholas, Laura, and Flingo I guess—each of you taught me
how much more important the people you love are than the people you hate.*

When dealing with people, remember you are not dealing with creatures of logic, but with creatures bristling with prejudice and motivated by pride and vanity.

— Dale Carnegie, *How to Win Friends & Influence People*

Preface

"Why do you write?" She asked me.

"Because I think it's time for everyone to get together and sing Kumbaya."

Maybe not, but it would be nice if we could stop devoting so much of our time and attention to tearing each other down. I don't expect everyone to like me, and I certainly dislike a lot of people myself, but somewhere along the way it got to be okay to just start hating mistreating people again because we don't agree with them or their lifestyles. I have a transgender kid in the midst of a second Trump administration, and the level of bigotry I've experienced in the past couple of years is worse then I experienced growing up in the 1980s. If you don't love me and mine, that's fine, but as a matter of common decency, it seems like it's time for everyone to, at a minimum, live and let live.

I'm a lawyer, a former prosecutor. Our profession is adversarial in nature. It's also toxic, and not an occupation fit for humans beings. In recent times cordial discourse has largely evaporated, and basic civil liberties like due process are on the brink of disappearing altogether. The legal system can certainly be a farce, and the criminal justice system in particular is deeply flawed. *City Attorney's Office* certainly pokes a lot of fun at that, but in all seriousness, when the legal process supporting your constitutional rights falls, so does your democracy.

Why do I write, because I was born free in a constitutional democracy, and if I have anything to say about it, I intend to die in one as well.

Acknowledgments

I would like to acknowledge and give my warmest thanks to Mr. Ice at Keithley Middle School. I never heard one thing a teacher ever said to me until that time you asked me if I wanted to flip burgers for the rest of my life. I did not, so thank you.

Prologue

It was the best of times, it was the worst of times. Wait that one might have been done already. Charles Dickens wasn't wrong though. If they were all the best of times, they wouldn't be. And if they were all the worst of times, you'd swallow a bullet. Dickens was right about there being two cities though. Unfortunately, the cities were Seattle and Tacoma, not Paris and London. And there was a tale.

Ben tried to read that fuckin' book so many times, but he never got past Chapter 8. It was so boring. "Hey Dickens, how about a chase scene every once in a while!" Back in high school, when Ben was assigned to read *A Tale of Two Cities*, he never really got it. The funny thing is that, written as a character in a story, Ben would have fit right into that book the way Mike Tyson's hand fits into a boxing glove. He never did go back and finished it as an adult. He did watch a poor movie adaptation of it with Maria one time, but they got bored and turned it off before Chris Sarandon got his head lopped off in the guillotine.

The wisdom that girls like Erin O'Connell got from literature, boys like Ben got from Hard Times and actually acting foolish. Sure Paris wasn't burning, neither was Seattle, but when disparate worlds and cultures collided, Ben walked the tightrope between belief and incredulity; Light and Darkness;

hope and despair. He came from the people who had nothing, but eventually made his way into the world of those who had everything.

Because Ben came from here and traveled to there, he ceased to be the one, but never became the other. He was neither here nor there, so he became an entirely new thing, a third option. He wasn't a drunkard in need of a moment of clarity, or a lost soul searching for redemption. He was the tool that a crucible alight with the competing flames of poverty and privilege forged.

I

Part One

Book One
Professional Camouflage

Chapter 1

He'd fallen ass-backwards into that job, just as he fell ass-backwards into most things. It wasn't that he'd ended up there accidently. He'd done everything quite intentionally. It's just that he'd seen the job announcement on the last day that it was open. It was also that a new city attorney had just been elected in Seattle. Pete Holmes had been only marginally to the left of the city attorney he defeated in the 2009 election, but a marginal ideology difference in Seattle politics often turned out to be an uncrossable chasm for many a politician. Welcome to Seattle, the place where political careers go to die. That change in leadership had opened up an opportunity—that is, the city attorney's office had suffered a mass exodus in December 2009 and January 2010.

Many who had feared new leadership left of their own accord. Others had been casualties of the ritual ideological herd culling by the new administration. Either way, there had been an opportunity for someone like Ben to slide into a job as a prosecutor at the city attorney's office. "I was punching way above my weight class landing that job, but I showed up and hoped that nobody would figure out that I didn't belong. I'd started putting on that professional camouflage way back in middle school. I always got thrown into the advance classes, but unfortunately that meant that I went from being the smartest person in a class full of dum-dums to the dumbest person in a class full of smart-ass overachievers."

Ben had been getting by in this manner most of his life, and one day at the city attorney's office convinced him that he'd be able to continue his mediocre string of successes by hiding in plain sight. This was mostly accomplished by not talking too much. Ben was smart, but he was usually surrounded by people who were more intelligent than he was. What he'd noticed long ago, however, was that people, smart and dumb alike, tended to talk too much when they became flustered. Women did it, men did it, kids definitely did it. "You can catch a kid red-handed, covered in red paint, standing next to the dog he just painted red, and he'll tell you that Sally did it. Plus, he won't stop at telling you Sally did it. He'll come up with a whole narrative about how he was in the house watching TV when he heard the dog growling, and how he came out to investigate. If you confront him about being covered in paint, he'll give you some other nervously constructed long-winded explanation that exculpates him from the crime."

Ben knew that lies should be simple, straightforward, and believable. That's common sense to any storyteller. An assertively told lie projects confidence and therefore credibility. A narrow scope and simple fact pattern provide as yet unused arterials from which to amend a story as needed to accommodate future circumstances. Anyway, the best lie is the one that stays loaded in the cylinder, dormant, never seeing the light of day. That lie stays pristine. As soon as you pull the trigger and fire it into the world, it picks up tarnish. No matter how masterfully it's crafted, that dreaded patina begins to form once it exits your brain and enters the world.

Staying quiet, on the other hand, never degraded cautious pretenders such as Ben. In fact, staying quiet made one appear wise. Looking engaged made one appear judicious. Physical posturing made one appear both calm and confident. When speaking became unavoidable, repackaging what was just said by another tended to work pretty well. "But that's the survey-level class; I got a whole fuckin' graduate-level course on surviving a professional jungle with limited talent."

You couldn't even say that most of what was said that first week at the city attorney's office went in one ear and out the other because that would have required Ben to have actually registered what had been said on some level. No, most of it went right over his head. The general criminal law course is the first class that every law school student takes. For the majority of law school students, it's also the last criminal law course they will ever take. Most law students take their first-year classes and then spend years two and three focusing on the practice areas they are actually interested in. For most, that's civil law courses.

Ben was no different. He passed his first-year criminal law course and didn't give the subject another thought until he was studying for the bar. Passing the bar required revisiting long-forgotten subjects like criminal law. That was it, no other criminal-focused coursework or internships, nothing. Most of the people at the city attorney's office had spent the entirety of their time in law school learning criminal law, doing summer internships at prosecutor's offices, and generally preparing for careers as prosecutors. Ben passed the bar, sent out a few résumés to downtown law firms, and gave up on finding work as an attorney altogether. It was safe to say that Ben was cut from lazier cloth than his University of Washington Law School peers.

Two years after getting a license to practice law, Ben was working as a night-shift stocker at the QFC inside Broadway Market. One day, he saw a job announcement pop up on his LinkedIn page for Assistant City Prosecutors. Ben had actually been wondering why he even had a LinkedIn page when he saw the announcement. The more on-point observation would have been why he bothered checking it every day, since he never applied for any of the jobs he saw.

On both of the job interviews he'd had at downtown law firms, back when he was still sending out résumés, he'd blown it. They were entry-level jobs, and they were looking for fresh law school grads who had done coursework and internships in employment and labor law. He was specifically qualified for both positions, but something about being qualified for a position, and prepared for an interview, seized up his personality. He was wooden. He couldn't convey information in an interesting fashion. He was like the kid at the school assembly, trembling hands clutching his prepared speech, reading it verbatim without looking up even once to acknowledge the bleachers full of students.

Applying for the Assistant City Prosecutor job was a goof.

He didn't take it seriously. He knew he wasn't qualified and didn't expect to get an interview. He knew people from law school who had done internships at prosecutors' offices. They'd graduated magna cum laude, and they still hadn't gotten the job at the city attorney's office. But that was 2008, and the city attorney's office was a very different place in 2010. When he saw the announcement, he didn't realize the city attorney's office was in flux. He didn't realize they were desperate for warm bodies. He didn't realize they would hire anyone with a license to practice law that would take the job. He did get an interview, and since he had no expectation about actually getting the job, he crushed it.

He did make an effort. He did show up as well as he could. It's just that when someone acknowledges and accepts inevitable defeat, their true abilities rise to the surface. At least, that's how it worked for Ben. Fighters shout at you to "leave it all on the mat"; runners say to "let it all hang out"; baseball players tell you to "swing for the fences." But simple is better, and skateboarders just say "gnarly" anytime someone accomplishes something that is apparently undoable on a skateboard. Simple is better, but they all say the same thing: a person excels best when they have nothing left to lose.

On the day of the interview, Ben ironed the better of his two suits, the navy blue one. The gray one had peaked lapels, and the fabric was flat, not textured like the navy blue one. In fact, at that time Ben had two of almost everything: two suits, two white shirts, two ties. There was two of everything needed to get a job as a lawyer, everything except shoes. Ben had one pair of dress shoes. They were pretty nice, a mid-to-high-end brand sold at Nordstrom. He couldn't remember the brand, and the gold-embossed company markings on the inside heel of the shoes had long since worn off, but they were more than good enough for his purposes.

It was a panel interview, but not his first—the two interviews he'd had back in 2008 were panel interviews as well. Both of those were three-person panels with a very similar composition: a managing partner who sat silently, clearly uninterested in the entire affair; a token minority or woman to explain the firm's, air quotes, "commitment to diversity"; and a whip cracker—a mean middle-aged white guy who was the junior partner in charge of humiliating and torturing new associates.

The city attorney's panel was different. There were seven people: the Trial Unit supervisor, a domestic violence victim's advocate, the new Criminal Division Chief, the new elected City Attorney, the new City Attorney's Chief of Staff, the office manager, and lastly Maria Deloera. Maria was a line prosecutor from the Domestic Violence Unit. She was someone to Ben; he couldn't quite place who, but she was someone to him.

It wasn't just that there were a lot of interviewers, but it was a hot panel too. They kept throwing questions at Ben, sometimes lumping them on before he'd had an opportunity to answer the one asked just prior. At that interview, he appeared unflappable. Even when he didn't have a great answer, he brushed it off and kept rolling. Two weeks later, he got a call from the Trial Unit supervisor. A few days after that, an offer letter arrived in his mailbox.

Chapter 2

Ben was twelve when his brother died in 1993. Ben had just mastered the kickflip on his new Rodney Mullen deck. He was obsessed with Plan B's *Questionable* video. Rodney Mullen seemed like an alien super soldier in that video. The tricks he pulled off during his sequence were feats beyond human ability. They were, in a word, gnarly. It was appropriate that the first kickflip that Ben ever landed was on a deck bearing the name of the inventor of the kickflip.

The last time he had seen his brother was when he had come over for Sunday dinner a few weeks before. Ben had barely been able to ollie properly at that time, but Mike had grabbed Ben's board and ollied onto a bench at the church down the street from their house. He had done a 180 kickflip off the bench. It had been the best thing Ben had ever seen a skater do in real life. Mike was no Rodney Mullen, but he was good, and if he had focused on skating, he probably could have been great.

Mike hadn't been focused on skating for quite a while at the time of his death. Ben was vaguely aware of crack, and his parents didn't shield him from their conversations about Mike's problem. Ben knew it was a drug. He didn't know how destructive it was, but he knew it had hollowed out his brother—hollowed him out both emotionally and physically.

The last time Ben saw him alive, at that Sunday dinner, he was a pale, gaunt caricature of himself. But not really a caricature. Caricatures exaggerate and poke fun in a good-natured way at someone's unique physical characteristics. A caricature of Mike at that point would have looked more like one of those Nazi Holocaust-era propaganda cartoons denoting Jews as dirty, sickly, and alien. There was nothing fun or light about Mike's appearance by that point. Mike's caricature could have been American government propaganda denoting the dangers of crack cocaine. And unlike the Nazi propaganda, the American propaganda would have been accurate.

It had only been a couple months before that when Ben had gotten the Rodney Mullen deck with the G-Bones wheels and Independent brand trucks. Mike and Ben's parents had given Mike $180 to get Ben a skateboard, his birthday present. They had also assumed there would be enough for lunch. There had been, but they hadn't gotten lunch that day.

Mike and Ben rode the bus over to Northwest Snowboards, and Mike had pointed toward the Rodney Mullen deck. He had pointed out the G-Bones wheels. He had strongly urged Ben to get the Independent brand trucks, not the Ventures. Ben actually preferred the Ventures later on, but at that time, Mike was his skate guru. To Ben it had seemed like a lot of money: forty-two dollars for a deck, thirty-five for wheels, forty for trucks, five for grip tape, and ten for bearings.

His parents had given him the new Airwalk Disaster shoes at the house before he and Mike left to go to the skate shop. His family wasn't rich, but his dad was a commercial electrician and a union member. Two hundred and change for a kid's birthday was a lot, but it certainly hadn't broken the budget.

After they left the skate shop, they'd gone over to Baker

Middle School by their house. Mike had spent the rest of the afternoon showing Ben the fundamentals of street skating. "After that, Mike and I walked back to the house. He didn't come in. He didn't say goodbye to our parents. He gave me a hug, wished me a happy birthday, and strolled off toward the bus stop. He stuffed the receipt from the skate shop into my pocket in case I had to return something. When my parents asked me what we'd had for lunch and looked at the receipt from the skate shop, it wasn't hard for them to figure out why Mike took off without saying goodbye, and why there was no change. My mom made me a grilled-cheese sandwich. After that, she went upstairs and cried for a long time. My dad just sat in his chair flipping through channels, watching nothing in particular for most of the evening."

Ben never wanted to be like Mike. His crew—Mike, his best friend Jack, and his other friends Todd and Ron—had been societal miscreants, drunk and stoned juvenile delinquents who easily transitioned into hardened adult criminals and drug addicts. Ben loved and idolized his brother, but he also knew that he was severely fucked up. He had known his brother would die too soon. He had known it before everyone else had. Every hour he had spent with Mike that year he had spent like it was the last time he was going to see him, because he knew that one of those times in the not-too-distant future it would be the last time.

Ben knew that Mike actually had talents, and he had them in greater supply than Ben ever would. Despite great effort over many years on Ben's part, his strung-out malnourished brother had managed greater marvels on a skateboard that afternoon at Baker Middle School than Ben ever would. Unfortunately, the world had also saddled Mike with equal portions of vices that ensured he would flame out early. Ben had known he was powerless to change the trajectory of his brother's life, so he had loved him as best he could for as long as he was around.

Then he really was gone. Mike was shot less than three blocks from the four-story house of horrors that he lived in. "We went over to his place to clean it out after he died, but there was nothing to clean out." There was a stained mattress on the floor and a chair with so many black eyes and bruises it was hardly recognizable as a chair at all. The door was wide open when we got there, and the dead bolt was gone altogether.

That dead bolt hadn't gone far. Mike had been carrying it in a filthy sock when they found him. "Why did he go up to the Lucky 7 with a dead bolt in a sock? No one will ever know for sure, but I've had a lot of years to think about it. Since it was the last thing in his possession that might have had even the tiniest bit of value, he probably took it up there where the crack dealers were to see if he could get a rock for it. The other possibility is that he put it in the sock to use as a weapon to mug one of the crack dealers. Everyone knows a crack dealer shot him. Nobody knows which one. After all this time, I don't think it much matters to me who actually did it. It was going to happen that night or some other night. The person who shot him is likely dead as well by now."

Whoever it was likely never rose higher in life than dealing crack on a lonely street corner in a gritty little city. It seems like their punishment was implicit. "I just hate thinking about it. It hurts because it makes me not want to think about Mike at all, and so I find myself actively forgetting him a large part of the time now."

There was a man lying on the stained mattress when they got

there. There weren't even any clothes except for a Circle Jerks shirt that had burn marks and holes all over it. Ben took it. He still has it. It's in a box in his parents' attic. Since there was nothing else to salvage, Ben and his parents left that place. They didn't even bother to wake the writhing withdrawal-ridden form occupying the mattress.

Going into Mike's building was scary, but the three of them had been steeled by their righteous cause of reclaiming the possessions of their fallen loved one. Leaving, on the other hand, was a demoralizing retreat from a hostile landscape. Ben had seen his dad stick the .45 he kept on the high shelf in his bedroom closet into the back of his waistband before they left the house. He saw him load a magazine into the empty slot in the grip.

Ben's dad was Ben Sr., but after little Ben was born, people always referred to him as Big Ben. It made sense; he was big and tall, with muscles, a beard, and scraggly hair. His dad was a monolith in their neighborhood, like the actual Big Ben was a monolith on the London skyline. Big Ben presided over less impressive versions of himself up and down South Eighty-Third Street, from South Yakima Avenue all the way to South I Street. Big Ben saw little Ben as he was pulling his T-shirt down over the exposed handle of the 1911. It wasn't something his dad necessarily wanted little Ben to see him doing, so Big Ben just winked and gave him a thumbs-up. Little Ben returned the thumbs-up. He'd never seen his dad take that gun out of the closet. He only knew it was there because he'd been snooping in there a year or two before. To Ben, there wasn't anything his dad couldn't handle, so Ben gave it no more thought.

"Right then, leaving that place, I caught a glimpse of my dad's face. It was as though the notion that he might actually have to use his gun to get his wife and only remaining child out of that place alive had just occurred to him." That swagger and cocksure attitude were gone. In that moment, Big Ben was the scared child whistling in the dark. "My dad was more scared than me and my mom. We so completely believed in my dad's ability to handle anything." It lasted only a minute or two, but in that short time, his mask had cracked. There was a person inside the brick tower. He cried when he lost a son, and the thought of losing another rattled his otherwise unshakable foundation.

Ben heard screams coming from the other side of the cinderblock walls, and he saw orphaned corners adopted by the hordes of homeless crackheads that used Mike's building as both a crack market and a flophouse. Then he smelled something odd. He looked around and saw someone smoking crack using tinfoil and a hollowed-out Bic pen. He figured it was the smell of the plastic pen melting. Years later, he realized that was just how crack smelled.

Seeing how scared his dad was at that moment scared Ben. They were from South Tacoma. The neighborhood was rough, and his dad was the mayor of their block, the guy with a skilled trade and a masculine build, not to be trifled with. A few months before Mike died, there had been these bikers staying at that one house on the block, the house everyone knew about.

Every block in a blue-collar neighborhood has that house. Little Ben hadn't slept more than a few hours in at least a week on account of the noise coming from that house. One night his dad got up and walked over to that house in his wife-beater and boxers, no shoes. He kicked over a very shiny Harley with a custom-painted gas tank. Three guys came out. One walked straight up to Big Ben. "They were all yelling, saying they were going to kick his ass, you know the sort of shit you expect to hear in a situation like that. Big Ben didn't say a word. When the biker closest to him leaned in to hurl more hollow threats, Big Ben drove himself forward and headbutted that biker across the bridge of his nose. That guy's face exploded, blood shooting every-fuckin'-where." Big Ben had made his point, but he never liked having to do things more than once.

Big Ben felt that an unreasonable level of retaliation was always a reasonable response to unprovoked provocation. The two bikers who had initially confronted Big Ben grabbed their bloody friend and retreated. Next, Big Ben gestured to the two guys who were on the porch, then he kicked over another motorcycle. After some more yelling and posturing by the guys on the porch, he kicked over the third one too. All of a sudden, the yelling stopped, and the block was so quiet you could hear the traffic on Eighty-Fourth Street. "Basically, if you started an argument with my dad, he felt justified in destroying you, your entire family, and everyone you ever knew. I think that's what they call a scorched-earth policy."

Someone called the police, and Big Ben got locked up that night, but no one ever saw those bikers again, and the renters at that house became as tame as beat dogs. "On our street, Big Ben was lauded as a working-class hero, but he was also someone who neighbors walked on eggshells around. What scares a person like that? The fact that he was scared that night at Mike's apartment building terrified me. How could we be in a situation that he might not be able to handle? There was a group of guys standing in front of the elevator doors, and I saw my dad actually reach into the back of his waistband. Right then, he saw the door to the stairwell and directed me and my mom to it."

Ben cried. He mourned. It hurt, but he'd made himself ready for it. His parents hadn't accepted that Mike was unsalvageable while he was alive, so they imploded when he died. Ben mostly raised himself after that. "Mike had shown me what not to do. My parents had shown me the wrong way to handle loss. I started looking forward. I started looking past my house, my upbringing, my family, and most importantly I started looking at Tacoma as a place to put in my rearview mirror as soon as I could manage it."

Chapter 3

Ben didn't pick up on much of what was going on those first couple of weeks on the job. What he did take notice of was Maria. She was his peer mentor. She was supposed to show him the more practical aspects of the job, things like how to locate case files, how to put together discovery disclosures for defense attorneys, and so on. Mostly, what she did was bring Ben up to speed on all the current office gossip. While Ben was certainly interested in the shenanigans of the people who worked there, it wasn't helping him get his arms around the job itself. Maria herself was a somewhat significant distraction already. Other than that first-day gossip session, Ben didn't see much of Maria, and he began to think she didn't take her role as his peer mentor very seriously. Ben was sure he knew her, but there was so much whizzing by him, he set it aside for the time being.

It was only Tuesday. Ben rolled out of bed to the sound of his alarm clock. He was twenty-nine. People thought he was twenty-one. He felt like he was fifty. Skateboarding had not been kind to his body. When he sat in one position for more than an hour, his lower back tightened up and he had spasms. His knees were shot. When he was working as a night stocker at QFC, his knees were so painful that when he got home in the morning, he would take the store-brand Ibuprofen bottle out of his medicine chest and turn it upside down over his mouth, like he was chugging a beer. He didn't even bother to count them. There was a certain feeling he got in his mouth when there were six or seven of them in there. That feeling was his only guidepost. He'd chase them with one of the two Rainier tall boys he always brought home from work. Once he had a shower, he'd drink the other Rainier with the fried chicken and jojos he got at the QFC deli. Most mornings, he was so beat he'd just pass out in his chair. Sometime around ten or eleven in the morning, he'd wake up with a violent urge to piss. After that is when he would typically migrate to his bed.

But that was then and this was Tuesday, and Ben was waking up to put on one of his now three suits to start his third week at the city attorney's office. Stocking shelves on busted knees was hard, but to Ben, this was harder. Every morning he'd wake up at six. That, in and of itself, was miraculous. Ben had never once in his entire life woken up excited about the day to come. Even when he was little, even on Christmas morning, he wanted to be left alone to sleep. While everyone opened presents, he'd sit on the couch and wonder how much more he'd have to endure before he could go upstairs and go back to sleep. It was all he ever wanted, but it was also something that had eluded him his entire life. He never felt rested. In reality, he was never actually fully asleep. He always needed more because he never got any sleep worth having in the first place.

He'd gotten his first paycheck the previous Friday, and he went down to Nordstrom after work that evening and bought a pretty nice off-the-rack suit, and a couple more shirts and ties. The alterations were done on Monday, and Ben was now able to add a third suit to the weekly rotation. For his first two weeks, he'd been doing the navy blue on Monday, Wednesday, and Friday. He was wearing the dark gray one on Tuesdays and Thursdays. It made the most sense to wear the navy blue three times a week. It was the de facto uniform of a prosecutor, really of all lawyers who went to court on a regular basis. It was easy to assume that he, or any of the other male prosecutors in the office, had several dark blue suits. If you changed up the tie, nobody was the wiser. Still, getting the new light gray one and a few new ties into the rotation that week would make Ben feel less self-conscious.

Tuesday morning hurt. It hurt more than Monday morning. He expected to be miserable on Monday. Tuesday just felt like an extension of Monday, and the weekend seemed no closer to Ben than it had the day prior. He showered. He brushed his teeth. He parted his now clean-cut brown hair on the left side.

Getting dressed took at least ten minutes. He hadn't been wearing a suit long enough to be comfortable in one. The new light gray one was stiffer than the other two, and he constantly felt like the ass was going to tear open anytime he had to bend over for any reason. Tying his shoes hurt his knees. Tying his tie hurt his pride. Ben had fallen victim to the pattern that all men who had just started wearing a suit every day fell into. Every detail had to be perfect. He'd tie the tie four or five times to get the correct shape, size, and symmetry in the knot. He'd tuck and re-tuck his shirt constantly, trying to get the shirt to look flush with his pants. He'd push the belt buckle to the front of his pants. He'd pull his socks up over and over, trying to make the spandex-feeling fuckers hit the same point on each calf.

He was yet to realize that the tie knot was going to loosen

no matter how well he tied it, and the shirt was going to come largely untucked the second he sat down in his car. Everyone figures out how to get comfortable in uncomfortable constrictions given enough time. Also, nobody was even paying attention to the details. All anyone saw was some white guy with a dorky haircut in a boring-ass suit. "One day I did figure it out, and that day I added another arrow to my quiver full of professional camouflage arrows."

Seattle Municipal Tower—"SMT is what we called it"—was a huge biracial penis penetrating the Seattle skyline. It was clearly biracial because it was too dark to be a white guy, too light to be a Black guy. Maybe it could be Middle Eastern, Latino, Asian, who knows. Maybe it was a testament to Seattle's newfound commitment to racial diversity in the city's ruling white patriarchy. Unfortunately for the ladies, there were no gigantic vaginas of any skin tone in the city until the new football stadium was completed in 2002. That day the city gained a gigantic vagina. Unfortunately, they demolished the Kingdome to build it, so in gaining a vagina, the city also simultaneously lost a gigantic boob. Sorry ladies. Anyway, whatever SMT wasn't, it was clearly a huge penis. If it had been shaped any more like a penis, they would have had to dip it in gold and hide it in the background of *The Little Mermaid*'s movie poster. That little stunt was a beautiful little act of resistance by an underappreciated white-collar guerilla terrorist. Needless to say, any skyline, Seattle included, was choked with phalluses, but SMT was a throbbing cock among less ambitious phallic pretenders.

The Criminal Division of the Seattle City Attorney's Office was on the fifty-third floor of SMT, somewhere on the shaft slightly below the head, but well above the balls. Every morning as Ben and an elevator full of random city employees shot skyward in their little steel sperm, he felt as though they were traveling up SMT's main vein, about to be ejaculated out to impregnate the city sky. That exciting proposition was always smashed when Ben heard the telltale ding of the elevator arriving on fifty-three.

His key card—proof actual, as well as symbolic, that he was a preapproved member of this tribe—hung on a lanyard around his neck. He had been anointed as such by the chief of their tribe. "That shit cracked me up. It was fuckin' funny because that place really was like a tribe, and my boss was actually a chief—Criminal Division Chief. That was his actual job title. Plus, the city's logo is Chief Seattle. It was hard not to see the parallels everywhere. Walking into the office on any morning meant going to war with our rival tribe, the Department of Public Defense. The DPD was actually more like a coalition of several tribes. They squabbled among themselves, but they had one thing in common: they wanted to shoot an arrow through the heart of anyone under Chief Seattle's flag.

Chapter 4

When Ben was eight, NBC replayed both the original *V* miniseries and *V: The Final Battle*, the follow-up miniseries. There was a TV show that came after, but the network killed it after one season. Ben was obsessed from the opening scene. Fascist aliens use aspirational rhetoric and hollow promises to gain control of every lever of power on the planet without firing a shot. V was an entertaining and clever tool to show young people how powerful propaganda and rhetoric can be.

It could almost be seen as a piece of informative propaganda designed to expose corrosive propaganda for the smoke screen it was. Perhaps it was a form of Hollywood-inspired counterpropaganda. How it ever got green-lighted is a mystery to this day. Giving people a look behind the curtain at how vulnerable and thin human institutions really are was certainly not something the Reagan administration would have wanted. Exposing the bag of tricks that every propagandist has used since the first caveman stood on a tall rock and spoke from on high to the peons below is not anything anybody with fascist aspirations would ever want.

There were themes that were immediately clear to young Ben. Resist all forms of oppression, inequality, and domination.

Question everything you're told. Truth is an empirical process and the enemy of the powerful. He'd taken to carrying a can of red spray paint in his backpack that summer. He spray-painted his first "V" on the back of his house, in a place where there was a bush to cover his handiwork.

After that, he branched out to the Catholic church down the road, his school, the strip mall where the Korean lady's candy store was, the post office, and anywhere else there was a secluded wall. Little Ben knew, V doesn't stand for visitors. It stands for victory. "You understand? For victory. Go tell your friends." The words of the old Holocaust survivor from the miniseries, so powerful, ringing in young Ben's ears. He said it over and over again to anyone who would listen. When Big Ben found the "V" on the house, little Ben told his dad it was his birthright as a human being to resist all forms of oppression, inequality, and domination. Big Ben just laughed and told him their family was already part of the resistance and that he should go after the symbols of oppression. Little Ben assured Big Ben that he'd already gotten the church, strip mall, school, and post office.

Big Ben said, "Don't get caught, but if you do, I'll sort it out. Now get lost. I got to paint over this before your mother sees it and has a fit."

With that, Ben departed. He'd already gone full outlaw, but it was in the pursuit of justice. Outlaw yes, but he was a freedom fighter as well, saving humanity from itself, and possibly lizard aliens. Now he had the support of a higher authority. Ben's dad was camouflaged in plain sight. Union strong, malcontent, miscreant, he kept an aluminum baseball bat behind the bench seat of his Ford F-250 even though he never played baseball. If you knew the secret language, you could understand what he was really telling you. Ben understood. If you had the secret glasses, you could see what he saw, just like Rowdy Roddy Piper. If you tuned into the right pirate radio station, you could hear all of them broadcasting subtle defiance out on radio waves to an empty night sky.

From that day forward, Ben sought out the enemy like never before. He looked for those symbols of oppression, inequality, and domination everywhere, in every context. Practically every day, he rode his bike to the Fred Meyer on Seventy-Second Street. Nearly every day, he stole baseball cards, G.I. Joes, Star Wars action figures, and candy. And of course, Fred Meyer kept him well supplied with red spray paint.

These were the spoils of a campaign of resistance. At first, he kept his booty in his room, but hiding all those new toys became cumbersome. He started giving some of his stolen toys to other kids on the block. He had duplicates of dozens of figures, and he enjoyed stealing them more than he enjoyed playing with them, so he didn't mind just giving them away.

That summer, construction sites suffered as well. Late at night, Ben would sneak out of his house. There were houses being built two blocks over. Those construction sites had all sorts of useful things lying around. Carpenters would leave hammers, nails, even power tools. Everything that a kid might need to build a fort was sitting there for the taking. Ben took only what wouldn't be missed, or could easily be chalked up to misplacement. He got his first hammer there. A few nights later, he found a couple of screwdrivers. The next night, he took a box of nails. Every night after that for a couple of weeks, he hauled home one or two small scrapped two-by-fours or sheets of plywood. During the day, while his parents were at work, he'd build. Little by little a form took shape on the horizon. No one could say exactly what shape that form was, since Ben had never built anything, and he built unencumbered by the yolk of silly things like building plans and carpentry skills.

Ben's mother asked Big Ben multiple times where little Ben had acquired the building materials. He always told her that it was scrap material from his job sites. After a while, Big Ben started really looking at what little Ben was building, and after that, he actually did start bringing home scrap material from job sites. It was good timing, too, because the construction sites up the road had mostly finished with the building portion of the construction, and materials over there were becoming hard to come by.

Eventually, the fort in the backyard would span two rooms on the ground level and a crow's-nest type upper level. He'd built himself an outlaw's lair, or a resistance cell safe house. Maybe both. He wasn't really sure. He finally had a place to keep the piles of candy, action figures, and hundreds of other ill-gotten consumer goods he'd pilfered that year.

By the time he'd completed it, most of the summer had gone by, but he spent a solid two weeks sleeping in his fort. He took his meals out there and had a few epic sleepovers in the weeks before fourth grade started. That fort would stand for four years, before he deconstructed it the summer before he started eighth grade and built a half-pipe there. And of course, the front door of that fort, his nerve center, was adorned with a red "V" for victory.

Chapter 5

Maria was sitting in the driver's seat of her BMW in a haze of gray smoke. She had that Jawbreaker CD playing. The one that all the girls loved in 1995, *Dear You*. Guys loved *24 Hour Revenge Therapy*. It was seven in the morning, and getting baked in your car right on Level 2 of the SMT parking garage was probably not the wisest move. In prosecutorial terms, what she was doing was being in physical control of a vehicle while under the influence. It was a lesser included offense of driving under the influence, not that anybody was charging her. The Trial Unit prosecuted those, not the Domestic Violence Unit, where she worked. And as far as Maria was concerned, the DVU had a problem. His name was Alan Thorpe, her supervisor.

Alan Thorpe was a sleazy fucker by any metric, but the fact that he was the supervisor of the DVU made it even worse. The DVU's primary purpose and stated goal was to vindicate the interests of victims of domestic violence, almost exclusively women. Maria could tell by the way Alan interacted with the women in the office that he had no respect for them whatsoever.

Everybody knew about his current affair, and the prior one, and the one before that, everybody but his wife. Maria didn't really care that he was philandering piece of shit, but the fact that he bent over and spread his cheeks anytime a supervisor from DPD called to complain about their client being mistreated by one of the DVU prosecutors set her off every time. Alan was a lifer at that place, and to leadership, the line prosecutors were expendable. He was never going to go to bat for anyone like Maria. To him, it was more important to appease the judges and DPD supervisors.

A couple of days before, the defendant in one of her cases was released from jail. The court refused to put a no-contact order in place because, in the judge's opinion, the defendant currently lived in another county, did not own a car, and was not likely to encounter the victim. Therefore, the judge opined, a no-contact order was not the least restrictive means for ensuring public safety.

This particular defendant had two convictions in the last three years for violations of domestic violence no-contact orders. He also had two domestic violence assault convictions. He was there that day after being arrested for yet another assault against the same victim. The first two times, the victim had been too scared to assist the prosecution, but on this occasion, she was on board. That fell apart the second the court decided not to issue a no-contact order. The victim knew the defendant would be at her apartment the next day. If she was assisting the prosecutor's office, he would definitely kick the shit out of her. If she refused to assist the prosecutor's office, he might kick the shit out of her.

That's how things work at Seattle Municipal Court. At SMC, judges bow to the defendants and thank them for coming to court. On that day, Judge Derek Johanson delivered his well-worn ridiculous colloquy to the defendant.

"Thank you so much for appearing here in court this morning, Mr. Lewis. Now, I know how well you were doing after the last time I saw you at your sentencing. You were keeping in contact with your probation officer and had only missed three appointments with her. Now this happens. This is very serious, and I need you to promise that you will stay away from Ms. Thompson. Can you do that? Okay then, I'm going to release you on your promise to appear at your next hearing, and even though I'm not issuing a no-contact order, you might want to stay away from Ms. Thompson, at least until you two can work things out."

This was kangaroo court at its zenith.

Maria sat at counsel table watching the defendant vigorously nod his head, a tiny almost imperceptible grin curling up the corners of his mouth, a perfect example of a microexpression that people are powerless to control. What did his microexpression mean? That was a rhetorical question Maria silently asked herself. She'd been around long enough to know. It meant his victim would have a fat lip an hour after this scumbag was released. Meanwhile, she heard the victim in the gallery behind her sobbing and whimpering "no, no, no" over and over again. His defense attorney, some white Ivy League girl, who'd been in Seattle for about five minutes, went on about how the defendant only had two assault convictions and was trying "really, really hard" to be a good person, but as a person of color, things were extra difficult for him.

The DPD imported these newbie true believers largely from Harvard and Yale. "Who could graduate from an Ivy Leage law school, with hundreds of thousand of dollars in school debt, and then come out to Seattle to slum it at the DPD for $50,000 a year? Rich kids, that's who." The DPD's little army of true believers were the great white hope to all the downtrodden of Seattle. They came from the cosmopolitan Northeast to the provincial Northwest to spread the good word, just so long as they didn't have to live in Rainier Beach.

"Those fuckers never lived around here either, but they're only too eager to tell everyone who lives in the city how it should run so long as they have a nice little upper-middle-class enclave on the other side of Lake Washington to run to when the sun goes down." As a person of color, Maria was insulted by this dog and pony show these rich little cunts put on in front of the court. Having a privileged white girl sit there with a straight face and tell a white male judge about the adversity faced by people of color was tone-deaf entitlement on a scale few would ever witness, but it was just another day of any week at SMC.

Maria mumbled under her breath, "These uptight white bitches are the most racist people in Seattle."

Maria then addressed the court on the record: "While I'm sure that Yale Law School gave Ms. Spencer over there a great deal of firsthand experience with the sort of adversity that people of color face in the criminal justice system, I should remind the court that the victim in this case is a person of color, as am I. The victim doesn't have any assault convictions, but your whiteness—I mean your honor—and Ms. Karen Snobington Esquire over there are correct. Can we all just give the defendant a big hand for only being convicted of beating the shit out of his girlfriend twice!"

Maria was getting baked in her car before work instead of after, like usual, because she had to attend a meeting to discuss her conduct in court. They couldn't fire her. The city prosecutors had a union and what the law refers to as ownership rights in their public employment. The city continued to inappropriately label the Criminal Division prosecutors as "at will" employees, but in practice, the Civil Division attorneys charged with dealing with the termination of Criminal Division prosecutors knew they were "for cause" employees and proceeded appropriately. The result was an impotent system of progressive discipline.

On the rare occasion that a city department actually did follow through with terminating an employee, the city was always sued by that employee. Shortly thereafter, the Civil Division lawyers in the Employment Unit would roll over at the negotiating table, and the terminated employee would hit soft earth gently after descending on a parachute made of settlement money from the city. At least Seattle was consistent. There were no consequences for defendants and no consequences for city employees. Maria correctly assumed the most entertaining way to coast through a toothless inquiry by two middle-aged white men about her conduct was to do it baked.

Ben knocked on her window. She rolled it down, and a cloud of pot smoke hit him square in the face.

"Did you bring enough for the whole class?" he asked.

Chapter 6

Ben became a middle child around the same time that he became the oldest child. After Mike died, his mother's reaction to her pain was to get pregnant. His parents had met in high school and had stayed together all those years. Ben's mom, Barbara, had gotten pregnant in her senior year of high school. Big Ben and Barbara lived with his parents after high school. Barbara's parents hadn't disowned her or anything, but Big Ben's parents had a finished attic where Big Ben, Barbara, and baby Mike could stay. They stayed long enough for Big Ben to finish his electrician program at Bates Technical College. That was a fancy way of saying vocational or trade school.

Barbara was thirty-nine when she got pregnant with Lisa, Ben's little sister. She wasn't old, but she was pretty old for getting pregnant, especially in the early nineties. Lisa was the baby of a trio of children, the oldest of whom she would never meet. In death, and in her eyes, Mike was the best of big brothers. His story had already been inked. She accepted what was written, and she judged his existence on a rather brief record. Ben, on the other hand, was alive—and fallible.

Ben had been the forgotten child when Mike was alive. Mike took the oxygen out of every room he entered. No one could ever breathe because he had either just impressed you with a talent or skill he possessed or just shocked you with something he'd said or done. In death, Mike loomed large over their home. Ben was now in the middle, smashed between the lionized apple of his parents' eye and their new hope. It seemed unfair to Ben that he was now both the forgotten middle child and the eldest sibling. Eldest sibling came with specific expectations, and by and large, Ben fell short of those expectations.

While he never quite understood, or valued, his role as eldest sibling, he was an excellent forgotten middle child. Does a spare ever really want to be king? Ben never did fill those shoes, and eventually he was permitted to settle into the quiet obscurity he'd always enjoyed within the family unit. It wasn't that his parents neglected him. He knew his parents loved him, that much was clear. After Mike died, Ben mostly operated according to his own agenda. His parents tried to connect with him. They mostly failed, but they tried.

He was lucky because his parents were still married. Most of his friends' parents were divorced. And if they weren't divorced, they couldn't stand each other. Ben's parents were together, and wanted to be together. There wasn't violence, alcoholism, or drug addiction in the home. The family's experience with drug addiction was confined to Mike's crack addiction. If anything was going to drive a wedge between husband and wife, it was the death of a child. Ben's parents didn't split apart. They reinforced each other and propped each other up until they could both stand again.

Ben was effectively trusted to be on his own before Mike died because Mike required so much attention from their parents. Ben was free to be on his own after Mike died because his parents were lost in a fog, and it took some time for them to get their bearings and navigate out of it. Ben remained on his own after Lisa was born because his parents needed to devote their time to a new baby. Ben left the house on his own when he was financially able because he wanted to pursue something other than a blue-collar existence in a gritty little city. Ben was born with the cleverness to manage his own affairs from an early age, and the world obliged him by giving him a largely free hand in crafting his own reality.

He was fourteen, and the area of the backyard that used to be dominated by Ben's fort was now dominated by a four-foot half-pipe. His sophomore effort as a builder was executed with a great deal more precision than the fort. Ben had met this kid Josh earlier that year. They were skating the same spot at the Parkland Transit bus station parking lot. Josh was from Lakewood. Lakewood was effectively an overflow valve for GI housing. It sat right outside Fort Lewis Army Base and McChord Air Force Base. Later, the bases merged and became Joint Base Lewis McChord, but back then it was two separate bases. Every GI who didn't feel like living on base lived in Lakewood, but that wasn't important. Josh's dad had hired someone to build him a half-pipe, and when he was done, he'd given Josh the blueprints he'd drawn up. Josh hung that big piece of drafting paper on his bedroom wall. The first time Ben went to Josh's house, he knew he needed to have that blueprint.

Ben gave Josh twenty bucks for it. After that, he made a list of supplies he needed, went to the hardware store to price it all, and presented the plans and price quote to his dad. Big Ben showed up late from work that Friday evening, his truck loaded down with every item on Ben's price quote list. His dad took him to the garage and showed him where the drill, circular saw, and table saw were. Saturday morning, Ben deconstructed the fort. Sunday morning, Ben started building his ramp. Big Ben came out periodically and assisted on some of the trickier portions. Cutting the transition pieces was especially difficult. Harnessing the metal coping required drilling the steel pipe, and Big Ben mostly took care of that part too. The rest little Ben managed on his own. It was a monument that symbolized his own upward mobility, craftiness, and work ethic.

The first time he dropped in on that half-pipe, he fell flat on his face. For the rest of his life, Ben had the hint of a discolored little scar on his right cheek. The Masonite that covered the half-pipe had left it. It was like the road rash that bikers got when they fell off their motorcycles and the street devoured first their clothing, then their skin. It was a Masonite burn, and he wore it openly with pride. He hadn't been wearing a helmet. He was a street skater, and street skaters wore baseball caps, not helmets. He never started wearing one either. "That ramp had dealt me what I would someday realize was a concussion, but it wasn't my first. Hell, it wasn't my tenth. It certainly wasn't my fuckin' last. I'd been slamming my unprotected head into concrete since that day with Mike at Baker Middle School. By my early twenties, my back was constantly stiff, it hurt to fuckin' stand because my knees were so bad, and I'd had probably a hundred undiagnosed concussions. Honestly, my brain is likely pretty damaged from all the collisions, sort of like a punch-drunk boxer or pro wrestler. It's a wonder I got into any college at all. So what. Suffering ongoing mental issues from undiagnosed head trauma. Whatever. Everybody's carrying around some sort of damage."

Ben knew that people brought their damage to every situation that life presented them. Damage informs future decisions and courses of action. "Nobody can ever be one hundred percent, because to perform at your best means that you've roughed up your body so much that you are likely never better than eighty-five percent, but having the experience that comes from beating yourself to a pulp is what makes you ultimately perform at one hundred and twenty percent. If you're physically a hundred percent, you've never road-tested yourself, so as far as I'm concerned, you're actually sixty percent."

That first ramp concussion rang Ben's bell pretty good. He was dizzy every time he stood up, so he just lay down in the grass. Josh from Lakewood had come out to South Tacoma to give the new ramp a ride. He skated it for about an hour while Ben fell asleep in the grass. After a while, Josh woke Ben up and asked him if he wanted to get high. Ben had taken a couple of puffs off a joint before, but it was shake—just leaves, no buds. Josh held a sticky, smelly little green thing, which had left crystals and orange hairs all over the little dime baggy he pulled it out of. He loaded it into a little steel bowl atop the end of a small steel pipe.

They lay down on the ramp, where no one in the house would see them. After they smoked, they talked and they joked. For a long while they stared at the sky turning orange, then that twilight blue color, and then ultimately that purple that was almost black. Josh grabbed his board and ran off to catch a bus home. Barbara called for Ben to come to dinner sometime later, but he just stayed on the ramp for a while. His mom and dad didn't call for him again. Big Ben told Barbara to let him have fun with his new ramp. Despite the lack of telltale skate noises coming from the ramp, Ben's parents assumed he was out there skating.

Ben looked at his ramp. It was good. It was the product

of a defiant and determined personality. Building something required defiance. The temptation to acquiesce, to quit, to beg Big Ben to have somebody more capable come over and build the ramp for him, had dogged him at every turn. He liked Josh, but Ben loathed the idea of having a ramp in his backyard that someone else built.

Skating was great, and building a ramp made him feel good about himself, but the world was composed of much more impressive accomplishments. After he built the ramp, every time he walked to the front of his house, he'd look back and forth. He'd look up and down his little street. Every time he did it, it looked smaller to him. Every time he did it, it felt as if it were closing in on him. When it closed in enough, it would bind him up, tie him down, and ultimately dictate to him the terms of his surrender. It would squash him into that mosaic of pickups and forklifts. It would squash him into that city of socially undervalued vocational trade skills. It would squash him into that honest but limited view of the world.

He started wondering if he'd been hoodwinked. Ben never tried at school. He could be lazy when it suited his purposes, even more so when it would irritate someone. He'd thought that fucking around at school was defiance. Right then he became convinced that he'd been duped. School wasn't there for people like him to succeed. It was the appearance of social mobility, but there was no incentive for schools to produce upwardly mobile people in percentages greater than society's need for them. Society needed only a small percentage of people to be educated and capable. In fact, society needed most people to stay ignorant and lazy. His middle school needed him to stay right where society had placed him. His middle school needed to produce academic failures in much greater numbers than they did academic successes.

By fucking around in school, he was doing exactly what he was designed to do, which was to stay put. To leave the socioeconomic strata he'd been born into was society's nightmare. To succeed in spite of overwhelming opposition was true defiance. That Monday, Ben did something that he'd never done before. He went to school and turned in a homework assignment on time.

Chapter 7

Erin O'Connell worked for the DPD. More specifically, she worked for The Defender Association, a particularly zealous division of public defenders within the DPD. If you said TDA, everyone around there knew what you meant. Burning down every prosecutor's office in the county, along with the prosecutors inside, appeared to be TDA's sole purpose for existing. They were good at it, too, certainly the tip of the spear, or the green berets of the DPD. From Ben's perspective, they used their clients as battering rams and cannon fodder on the front lines of ideological legal campaigns designed to dismantle the system, brick by brick if necessary. But Ben was a prosecutor, so it's possible that his impression may have been a little less than objective.

Prior to working at TDA, Erin actually admired, even venerated, TDA and the DPD more generally for their steadfast determination to get justice for the most disadvantaged people in our society. After three years at TDA, she was a war-weary soldier who was just trying to keep her compass pointed to true north. Day after day she put on her armor, picked up her sword, and set out to slay the dragon. She was a good soldier too. If the DPD said to go take a hill, she took that hill, but she wasn't a true believer. A good soldier, yes, but in like-minded company, during interludes of momentary candor, she voiced her concerns.

DPD soldiers didn't typically spend three years in the misdemeanor trenches. By the time they had a year, they would promote out of municipal court. They would go to superior court, still rank and file but in charge of defending felony cases instead of the petty misdemeanors in muni court. Sometimes they'd become supervisors in muni court. More often than not, they'd end up as casualties, departing the battlefield altogether.

Erin was an aberration and, in all honesty, a thorn in the side of her division. That first year, all the newbie DPD attorneys were born into the practice as Kool-Aid drinkers. The DPD preferred to get fresh law school grads. They combed Ivy League job fairs looking for the perfect marks. Their meat was rich kids carrying around three tons of white guilt, charged up by the idea of bringing a superior brand of justice to the far-flung reaches of provincial nowhere cities such as Seattle. To that tune, they enlisted. Like the missionaries of old, they marched into the savage terrain of places like the Pacific Northwest to civilize the land with New England aristocratic values. They marched with a criminal code book in one hand, the new word of God—not a bible, just the new white law.

Like a new-model Christian soldier, Erin marched right out of Harvard Law and into the fray. She was a good Protestant girl from New England, so of course she marched. She was a WASP of the first order. Her parents were old money, New England proper, Dover. Of course she marched out of Harvard Law and not, say, BU Law. BU is where all the blue-collar lawyers went. They were the poor Catholics from Southie who crawled out of the grime and shit of the gutter to gain an inkling of respectability by becoming prosecutors in the Suffolk County District Attorney's Office. Erin rightly figured that nobody from BU Law ever left Boston. Most of them probably never even found work as lawyers at all. Certainly, nobody from Seattle was at their law school's job fairs trying to recruit them to their righteous cause.

Because of her pedigree, Erin never had a meaningful choice about where she would go to college. There was an expectation that it was going to be Harvard or Yale. The binary choice presented to her was about as interesting as the choice between Coke and Pepsi. Given the opportunity, she would have gone to the University of California at Berkeley. She could have gotten in, but it wasn't an option for her. In her family, going to a hippie school on the West Coast was strictly forbidden. That was especially true when talking about a state school. The only West Coast option in her family was Stanford, and Stanford would only have been an option for her if she were mentally slow.

Her parents spent thousands on SAT prep courses for her. They also hired a lawyer to harass the illustrious Groton School into changing three of Erin's B grades to A grades, so as not to besmirch her Harvard and Yale applications. Being captain of Groton's tennis team and volunteering at the local food bank rounded out her applications. Putting together those applications was just an assembly-line operation in her community. Everybody knew what needed to be there. Smarts, sports, and service—it was the holy trinity of Ivy League applications.

Since she planned to go to law school, she chose the easiest college major she could find: communications. The plan was to get the highest GPA possible, and that was most readily accomplished by taking the easiest classes offered. Surprisingly, getting great grades at an Ivy League school was not hard. Maybe they figured if you could pay the tuition, you were entitled to the grade. Much the same way, in times gone by, men assumed if they bought a woman dinner and took her to a movie, they'd essentially purchased use of the woman's body at the end of the evening.

Maybe these schools just didn't want to admit that their handpicked crops of spoiled silver-spoon whiners were largely nothing more than kids of average intellect with superior funding. "For Christ's sake, George W. Bush when to Yale. After that, he went to Harvard Business School when he couldn't get into a state law school. How hard can those curriculums be if a bonehead like W graduated from them?"

It wasn't even their fault, but most of them were truly nothing more than toy robots. Their parents would wind them up and point them toward their goals. Parents who didn't even bother to take a primary role in raising their children in the first place became very active when the discussion turned toward reaffirming their own narcissism by wedging their offspring into Ivy League schools. Erin was certainly used to the shuffle. Her prep school's tuition was more than the tuition at most private colleges. She lived in a dormitory all week long, and went home to Dover on the weekends and holidays. She didn't have to work hard to get good grades in high school, and her dad's lawyer fixed the ones she couldn't achieve herself. In similar fashion, Erin cruised through Yale's undergraduate curriculum as well.

After college, she took a whole year off just to study for the LSAT. Getting into Harvard or Yale required, in addition to an impeccable undergrad GPA, an LSAT score of at least 175 out of a possible 180. Her internship at the New Haven Legal Assistance Association and being on Yale's women's tennis team, coupled with her 177 LSAT score and 3.94 GPA, pretty well assured her acceptance to Harvard or Yale Law.

Harvard Law turned out to be just another link on the long chain of formality heavy but substance devoid activities. There was much to hear but little to learn. Erin's grades remained very good, though not 3.94 GPA good. By the end of her first semester, she realized that there was no school to get into after law school. She didn't have to engage in any extracurricular activities because there were no more school applications to be filled out. Even if she graduated dead last in her class, her future was assured. There would be a bar exam to pass, but the reality of the situation was that she would be a Harvard Law School graduate, and as such, there was nobody left to impress.

Jumping through the hoops set out by her family hadn't really bothered her. She was a good show pony, and she could perform ad nauseam. It bothered her that, at the end of it, she had done little more than attain the bare minimum expected by her family. Going to Harvard Law School, graduating near the top of her class, these things didn't set her apart. They only ensured her continued trajectory toward the upper class, the crown made from Ben Franklins, the only royalty the United States permitted: the Moneyarchy.

As soon as she realized there was nothing she could ever do to impress anyone in her orbit, she decided to take a summer internship with the DPD in Seattle. It wasn't California, but she had figured that a summer on the West Coast would be a welcome change of pace from buttoned-down and tied-up New England. "I used to think she meant 'tied up' like they were stitched into their lifestyle by money and class, but then she told me she always said 'buttoned-down and tied-up' because New England was full of closet BDSM freaks. I guess if you're that stifled in your normal life, the freaky shit's got to come out somewhere, and apparently that's it. Erin told me about all the sex-dungeon gear she'd found in her parents' private room, weird shit too: leather underwear, whips, ball gags, you know, normal uptight New Englander stuff."

After that first summer in Seattle, Erin came back after her 2L year, and accepted a job offer after graduation, pending passage of the Washington State bar exam, of course. Unlike every other standardized test she'd taken before, she wasn't shooting for the top 5 percent of scores. It was the first time in her life that the score really didn't matter as long as she passed. Nobody ever asked you what you scored on your bar exam. She took a bar prep course early that summer and passed the exam with ease.

Erin slayed many a dragon that first year at the DPD. By the end of it, she began to realize that many of her baby lawyer colleagues had disappeared from the DPD altogether. People with similar blue-chip pedigrees had abandoned the law as a profession after a brutal year at the DPD. New ones showed up by the dozens as soon as summer bar scores were posted. This ritual first-year massacre was not something widely talked about at the DPD, certainly not by the supervisors.

For the first time since being at the DPD, there was a chink in Erin's armor as she observed the smiling mask worn by her DPD minder, Tim Hathaway, absorb its first crack when she questioned him about this exodus. When Erin began voicing concerns about client outcomes versus superfluous litigation designed to thwart the courts and prosecutors' offices and change the political landscape through appellate litigation, the second crack in Tim's mask appeared. Water seeped in, and those cracks swelled over the ensuing two years to the point where Erin could see a much more sinister smile on the face of her mask-laden minder.

From that point on, she was a liability to her division and to the DPD as a whole. She took her orders and she executed them, but she was a dissident. She did the bare minimum of the political agenda pushing required by the DPD, and focused extra hours above and beyond what was required on client outcomes.

More importantly, she stopped viewing her clients as angels with dirty faces and started seeing them as they were. Sometimes they were people suffering from a mental health or substance use issue and committing petty crimes as a result of that affliction. Sometimes they were dumb, barely adult teenagers making bad decisions. Sometimes they were hardened criminals committing petty crimes as a matter of course, just an ongoing consequence of their being alive. Taking off the rose-colored glasses made her a much more effective public defender. She began seeking the appropriate resolution to her clients' criminal matters instead of fighting with the prosecutors and courts simply for the purpose of fighting.

She was a better lawyer, that much was indisputable. Her clients' outcomes were better and more appropriate in light of their circumstances. But as a dissident, she was a grotesque perversion and thus wished into the cornfield.

Chapter 8

On the other side of the bog, a young Benjamin Sullivan stared blankly at a blackboard with a string of numbers, letters, and symbols on it. It was an AP Calculus class at Mount Tahoma High School in South Tacoma. While he was staring at the blackboard, he decided to start calling the neighborhood Southie Tacoma. People from around there called it South T, but Ben thought his play on Southie in Boston was clever. He decided he would try to get it circulating through his group of friends. Hopefully, it would spread from there. The city as a whole was already pretty well supplied with good nicknames. There was T-Town and, of course, Tacomatose, aka the greatest nickname for a city ever. It had a slogan now, too: "Tacoma 185,000 Alcoholics Can't Be Wrong." That one had shown up on a T-shirt recently, and Ben kept meaning to get one but never did.

Right then, Ben's teacher called on him to provide an answer to the equation on the board. Ben was in the AP Calculus class because he had been planning on going into a math-based discipline in college. He was good at fixing things—cars, appliances, anything mechanical. He didn't want to be a mechanic, though. He thought he might become an engineer. He understood algebra. He was even good at it.

Geometry was practical, almost as practical as basic arithmetic. Normal people could use geometry to solve all sorts of everyday problems. Trigonometry was a little more esoteric, but he still got a B in it. He could see its usefulness for what he was interested in, even if it had a very diminished level of usefulness for most normal people.

It was day three of AP Calculus, and Ben had an epiphany in two parts when his teacher called on him that day. First, calculus was a necessary skill for any engineer to master. Second, Ben would never master it. "Basically, I just said I didn't feel well. My teacher moved on to some other poor student, this girl who looked as confused as I was. Too bad for her."

Getting into an engineering program at the University of Washington would be impossible without stellar grades in advanced math courses. "Trig was hard, but I gutted out a B. I would have passed AP calc, but I probably would have gotten a C, which would have put an end to my aspirations of going into a math-based discipline. Even if I had managed to get into an engineering program at some other university, with a C in AP calc, the college-level courses in any engineering program anywhere would have ground me out of college altogether. That, or I would have ended up with a bachelor's in something useless like communications."

A tall, goofy-looking motherfucker with a cartoonishly huge revolver once said, "A man's got to know his limitations." "That goofy-looking motherfucker was right about that. He was wrong about what revolver to carry—a .44 mag, seriously? A .357 mag has all the stopping power anyone could ever need, plus you can actually hit what you're aiming at. A .44 mag kicks like a fuckin' mule. You're lucky if you can hit the side of a moving van. No wonder he had to use all six shots in *Dirty Harry*. Whatever. Keep dreamin', Clint!"

It was the last semester of Ben's senior year, and he was within the drop window. Even with all the math classes, he'd managed to keep his GPA in the 3.8 neighborhood, and since he was dropping out of AP Calculus, he decided to take a class he genuinely wouldn't have to work hard at. In the school office, he looked at the list of classes that hadn't filled up. There were still two open spots in the drama class, so he signed up. Little did he know how useful the skills taught in that class would ultimately be to him in his adult profession.

Before that day, Ben had a clear direction. There had been a pinprick of light coming at him through the construction paper of life. All that had been required of him at any given moment was to continue to move toward that little point of light in whatever fashion he was able. Going to college was still the plan, and going to the University of Washington was his highest aspiration.

Applying anywhere else didn't even occur to Ben. Small-town thinking and a townie-centric mindset prevented Ben from thinking outside the part of the I-5 corridor that encapsulated Olympia to the south, Tacoma in the center, and Seattle to the north. And in that little snow globe of existence, one university sat high above the rest, U-dub. Ben's provincialism moved backward and forward through time, so much so that to say that he was born, lived, and would die within view of the Puget Sound would be more or less accurate.

When he did arrive at U-dub the following fall, he was amazed to discover that many of his fellow students were not just from all around the country but from all around the world. Similarly, the fact that many of his professors went to Ivy

League schools back east also came as a surprise. Up until that point, he had just assumed that the professors had gone to U-dub themselves.

Before that first day of class, he'd thought only presidents and Supreme Court justices went to Harvard or Yale. To him, they weren't even colleges, they were hidden realms. They were places that people talked about but nobody ever actually saw, much less attend. His family wasn't exactly the traveling to the east coast type. Even if they had gone to Boston or New Haven, they wouldn't have been meandering around an Ivy League university's campus. Either way, they hadn't, and he didn't. Later, as an adult, when he went to New York City and Boston for the first time, he saw not only that these fantastical places were indeed real but that they had entire systems of medieval serfs servicing them.

Harvard and MIT might have their share of geniuses, but as far as Ben could tell, Boston was full of dum-dums. New Haven wasn't even a city so much as an overworked teat that Yale sucked dry with insistent regularity. "Walking around those campuses took all the magic outta those places for me. Before I visited, they were these mythical institutions, pumping out the next generation of America's elite. They certainly pump out the next generation of America's elite, but not the way that you think. They're grooming facilities for persons born into a certain caste. The king doesn't dress himself. The king has never dressed himself. The king cannot dress himself."

Other than lording over their army of undereducated blue-collar white kids at the cafeteria, berating the Puerto Rican women who clean their dorms, or screaming at the Black gardener while they're canoodling on the quad, Ben wasn't sure what exactly students at these places did. At U-dub, students worked part-time jobs in the evenings and studied on the weekends. So far as Ben could tell, Ivy League students went to one of the campus bars in the evenings and to the ski lodge on the weekends. As ever, bourgeois ease and comfort exist because of working-class sweat. "Say what you will, but Ivy League life certainly prepares one for a life as the master of a South Carolina plantation in the eighteenth century. Now bow to the people whose lives your labor makes possible."

Ben didn't know all that yet. He hadn't realized that he was at the beginning of a cycle, a cycle that his counterparts at the DPD were at the end of. Those Ivy Leaguers at the DPD had risen to the pinnacle of their ability. They had achieved all that the descendants of descendants of descendants of someone with a creative spark could accomplish. For them, at some point a hard-working ancestor had toiled to put a child through college. That child did, or created something that no one had before. That child's children reaped the benefits of that novel idea. Those people's children were so far removed from that original spark of genius but so bathed in its wealth that they lost the ability to think interesting thoughts and instead focused their attention on class and status. Those people's children became so decadent that they believed in their own superiority, despite their being quite average in most respects. Those people's children, or the ones who come after them, will be so far removed from the original wealth and privilege of their bloodline that they will multiply and disperse, live and learn more modestly. Their lives will become average, and their children will live average lives. Some will even become working-class, and undereducated. Then the machine will be ready for another spark from someone unique, appearing in the hoi polloi of society.

The natural rise and fall of all things, the recycling of human experience, when put into perspective, turns the elite into an average commodity and turns Ben into a unique and scarce resource. Big Ben had pushed the door open for him, and a unique quirk of the mind coupled with a Rainier tall boy worth of tenacity and courage propelled Ben out of his class. He achieved that most illusive of illusive things in American society: social mobility. Banging around somewhere in his head, unbeknownst to him, was an idea no one had ever had, or an adaptation on life that would eventually change the trajectory of his own bloodline. Someday he would have spoiled-rotten mush-brained great-grandchildren that he couldn't stand, and those great-grandchildren most certainly would go to Harvard or Yale—or both if they were as dumb as George W. Bush.

But he didn't know all that yet.

Chapter 9

For Ben, it was the night of his high school graduation. He was invited to a couple of after-graduation parties. He was well-liked at Mount Tahoma High School. The popular kids—jocks, cheerleaders, and the like—all welcomed him. They were popular at a public high school in a beat-up little city. Tonight was their swan song. Tomorrow they'd be nobody. They were actually nobody all along, but high school had cloaked that fact from them. Ben didn't like them, not a one. He didn't hate them either. They were just who they were, and Ben wasn't whatever that was, even if they wanted him to be. He knew the star wrestler, Matt, would go to some vocational school, marry a girl from Tacoma, and have some kids. Matt was Ben's dad, just thirty years later.

After the graduation ceremony, Big Ben, Barbara, Ben, and Ben's little Lisa had dinner at Johnny's Dock. Johnny's is what passed for a nice restaurant in Tacoma. The parties weren't getting started until eight or nine, and he had plenty of time to get to some or even all of them. He didn't. He blew off those graduation parties. Since graduation day was the last time he'd purposely see anyone he went to high school with, he didn't see the point of drawing it out by going to any of their parties.

Graduation family dinner was just like any other fancy family dinner. It was more for Ben's parents than for him. They deserved a nice meal. They'd gotten a kid over the first major hurdle of life. After dinner, Big Ben gave Ben the keys to a beautifully restored 1965 Plymouth Barracuda. It was midnight blue, had Crager five-spoke chrome rims, and that fastback wraparound rear window. Big Ben had been restoring it in his buddy's garage for months. He'd been working on it most evenings and every weekend.

Big Ben had met them at Johnny's, and he'd driven the Barracuda. Barbara and Lisa were already in the Camry when Big Ben leaned into the driver's-side window of the Barracuda, where Ben was running his hand over the freshly Armor All'd dashboard.

"U-dub is in Seattle, kid. Now, if you wind up moving to the dorms up there, you got a way to get back down here to visit us. And trust me when I tell you that you will visit us."

Big Ben motioned like he was breaking something over his knee and pointed at Ben while he spoke.

"Don't get fucked up and drive tonight either, kid. That fuckin' car took months to restore. If you're going to get drunk and smash somethin' up, take that shit box over there your mom calls a car."

"Thanks, pap. I'll behave."

"I love you, kid."

"I know. I'm gonna take off."

Ben had never driven anything but his mom's Camry, his dad's truck, and the driver's ed car. The Barracuda was a stick. His dad's truck was a stick, so he knew how to drive it, but it wasn't second nature yet. He pushed the clutch in. Johnny's parking lot was relatively empty, and the asphalt was wet, so he floored the gas pedal and popped his foot off the clutch. The rear tires spun so hard that the car lost traction and started to skid. He let off the accelerator a little and steered out of the inevitable donut. From that moment on, he pretty well had the hang of the stick.

On his way out of the parking lot, Ben glanced over and saw Big Ben standing next to Barbara's Camry with his arms folded, watching Ben, shaking his head. Ben leaned on the horn as a final adios to his family.

The first place Ben went was the Lucky 7 on Ninth and MLK. It wasn't the best spot to stop. It was right where Mike had been shot. In all honesty, even six years later, it was still mostly an open-air crack market. But they sold beer to teenagers, so it was a necessary first stop. He grabbed a six-pack of Rainier tall boys. He was heading over to Josh's to pick him up and go to a show. Ben wasn't interested in getting wasted. He just wanted to drink a few beers so he could have a buzz at the show. Plus, he knew Josh would have weed. He figured Josh would drink a couple of the Rainiers. That would keep Ben from getting too drunk. The weed would wear off long before he had to drive home, all nice and safe, just like Big Ben said.

The Paradox was in this old single-story building on Puyallup Avenue. Ben wasn't sure what it used to be, but it was so beat down, old, and nasty, he knew it had been something else at some point. Six months earlier, it had been no place, boarded up for who knows how long. All punk venues opened up in some dilapidated purposeless shack. That place fit the bill exactly.

It sat in the shade of the Tacoma Dome, straddled between the dome and the downtown side of Commencement Bay. Ben wasn't sure, but his best guess was that the Paradox building used to be a fish-processing plant or some sort of minimal consumer goods distribution center. Most of the buildings down there had, at some point, been a cog in the Port of Tacoma's massive system of logistics. The port was outsized to say the least. It was one of the defining characteristics of Tacoma, that and all the GIs. Despite being a quarter of Seattle's size, Tacoma's port was nearly as large as the massive Port of Seattle. Sixty years ago, trucks would have brought goods to a building like this one, where they'd be unloaded manually by longshoremen. There they'd sit until another truck came along and picked up this or that to go cross-country to its final destination. There were now much larger distribution centers outside of town and much larger trucks, and, because of automation, a much smaller army of longshoremen. When you added the logging industry into the other distribution chain job losses, it was easy to see how western Washington had become a sort of ground zero for blue-collar plight and socioeconomic depression.

A few of years before that, the Warped Tour had been up at the Tacoma Dome parking lot. Josh and Ben had been skating downtown. They had been kids, really kids, teenagers not even old enough to drive. They barely had money for the bus to get downtown, much less go to the show. Sometimes they'd just skate to downtown, since half of the ride was downhill. Since half the return trip was up the same hill, they always kept bus money for the ride home.

That bus money was all they had on them as they sat outside the Texaco on Pacific Avenue down the road from the dome. This girl with Manic Panic fire-engine red hair was walking toward the gas station parking lot. She was being followed by this jock in a Camaro. He was lobbing lewd comments at her, and it wasn't clear if he wanted to fuck her or kill her. Either way, Ben had picked up a rock and thrown it right at the

Camaro's windshield. It had spider-webbed it beautifully upon impact.

That Brian Bosworth–looking jock had slammed the Camaro into park and gotten out. Josh and Ben started toward the Camaro with their boards raised into bludgeoning position. All skaters know that a skateboard is not just your recreation and mode of transportation but also a deadly weapon. Faced with two feral teenagers and a now emboldened and angry young woman, Camaro man retreated. That young woman was in a band—no one Ben or Josh had ever heard of, but it was on the Warped Tour lineup—and as a thank-you, she gave Josh and Ben free passes.

Ben pulled up to the curb at D Street about a block away from the Paradox. He heard the front passenger-side rim scrape the curb, and he was relieved. Anytime he got something new, he could never relax until it got its first scar. The need to keep possessions pristine was a curse, one that Ben suffered from. That first scratch on a new skateboard deck hurt him emotionally, but it also started a process of acceptance that always resulted in the ability to use the possession in the manner in which it was intended. A board was meant to be ridden. Scratching it on a curb was kind of the point. A car was meant to be driven. Scraping the rims on a curb was inevitable. All was as it was meant to be. Ben exhaled.

High school graduation was a transition time for lots of people. At his school, most of those people were having a last hurrah at some after-graduation party. Josh lived in Lakewood, so they didn't go to the same school. Josh had graduated that day too. Neither of them was missing anyone or anything from high school that night, and nobody from high school was likely missing them.

They drank a few Rainiers and smoked a few bowls before heading into the show. They sat in the Barracuda so long they missed most of the opening bands. "No harm done. No loss there. Most of those openers were kids our age in bands that could barely play, but we made it in for the Psychedelic Razors." They played about ten songs in like eleven minutes. Then they just walked off the stage. Everyone in the crowd was silent. Nobody had seen anything like it before. This wall of noise just came at you and entertained your ears by violently smashing into your eardrums repeatedly. Then it was gone, just like the band, gone. "Well, not really gone; they had bolted to the door at the side of the stage and were loading their gear. They were clearly in a hurry to get the fuck out of there. They didn't even bring any merchandise to sell."

Outside, Ben could see the singer under the streetlight by their van. There wasn't much light in the Paradox. During their set, he could tell that the singer was a girl, but that was about it. Under the streetlight, he could properly see this little female powder keg who had exploded her voice all over a crowd of Tacoma punks.

She was a little Latina girl, maybe twenty-one. Her eyes were blackened all around with makeup that extended to fading vertical points continuing north and south of her eyes. She had on tight black jeans that were peg-stitched up to the knees, a denim vest with crusty punk band patches all over it, and loosely dreaded shoulder-length black hair.

"I knew they had a seven-inch because I saw it at Mother Records, but I didn't get it because I didn't know if they were any good. I figured if I liked them, I'd get it at the show, but they didn't bring any fuckin' records to sell, or anything else like T-shirts either. I asked the singer girl if they had any of the seven-inches."

She just pulled out this little journal and tore a corner off one of the pages. She wrote down a phone number and a name, "Maria." She capitalized the A and drew a circle around it so that it looked like an anarchy symbol. "It was a weird number, though, a 509 area code. I didn't know where 509 was. I thought maybe it was Portland or Idaho, eastern Washington maybe? I was pretty sure they were a Seattle band, so I figured she must have written down an old number, or wrote it down wrong, or maybe she was just giving me a bogus number? Whatever, I don't know. I found that slip of paper with her number on it crammed into one of my record sleeves years later. And it wasn't even in a Psychedelic Razors record—it was some other band's record sleeve. And I never got a copy of that one seven-inch of theirs either."

The little powder keg singer looked at Ben and said, "We ran out of seven-inches. We're printing more. Call me in a few days, and I'll tell you when we're going to have more."

After that, she and the rest of the band jumped into their van so quick it was like they'd been practicing getting away from a bank heist. Then she was gone.

Chapter 10

Maria wasn't from Seattle. To be honest, she didn't know where she was from. One upon a time, her parents were farmworkers. Her father, Juan, was a migrant farmworker. He typically left Washington by the end of August and was back by June. Her father and her mother, Luisa, were married, always had been. Maria had a sister and a brother. Three was the right number of children for a family like theirs, plenty of hands to pitch in and work but not so many that it was a burden to feed them. Plus, there was enough of them to keep one another company.

Maria and her siblings were citizens, as was Luisa. Juan was not a citizen, and due to several illegal entries into the United States, he never would be. In fact, he was permanently barred from citizenship, permanent residence status, or even going on vacation in the states. In the Yakima Valley, if you stayed for the summer, nobody—not the cops, not INS—ever bothered you. You were an integral part of the agricultural economy, which was the lifeblood of eastern Washington. However, if you were illegal and showed up before things started to bloom or stayed until the leaves on the trees started to turn brown, you were in for trouble. Everybody in town knew who was legal and who was illegal, who stayed all year round and who arrived with the sun.

Luisa had been born in the Yakima Valley, born on a kitchen table in the house in which she would eventually raise her own family, if one was to believe the family stories. Her father had been a migrant farmworker, ranch hand, mechanic, jack-of-all-trades. Her mother was a citizen, born to migrant farmworkers. Luisa's parents had come to the Yakima Valley in the fifties for work. Much like Maria's father, Luisa's father spent most of the year traveling for work—and to stay one step ahead of the authorities. In the winter, he'd lay low in Juarez, his city of origin. After their third year in the Yakima Valley, two pivotal things happened to Luisa's parents. First, they secured a bank loan to purchase the house where Maria and her siblings would be raised. Second, Luisa was born.

The house was sacred, as it was social proof—a calling card denoting permanence and belonging. Of course, it had to be purchased in Maria's grandmother's name, as her grandfather was illegal. The simple ranch house had a little farm-style fence that was good for nothing more than marking the property line. It was practically new when Maria's grandparents bought it, not so much by the time Maria and her siblings were growing up in it.

When he was away, her grandfather sent letters and money home at least once a month, every month he was away—until he didn't. This wasn't just a story she'd been told; the letters were in a cabinet in the living room. When Maria was little, she used to look at the postmarked stamps and wonder what her grandfather was doing in Caprock, New Mexico, in November 1957 or in Elgin, Arizona, in February 1961. The letters were sweet. Her grandfather always closed with "Love to you and little Luisa."

Those letters also revealed something important about her grandfather. He would routinely write about what a comfort it was to him that he never had to wonder where his family was and always knew where home was, even if he couldn't be there most of the time. It seemed clear to Maria that her grandfather, from afar, took almost as much pride in having a permanent address in the United States, as he did from having the house itself. While the letters themselves were written with a very relaxed hand, their home address on the envelope was written very clearly, very purposefully, never sloppy. Having that home for his family was of paramount importance to him, even though he could never step foot in it without being effectively outside the law. His greatest comfort was having a nap on his favorite chair, surrounded by his wife and daughter, in a home he could never legally inhabit.

One month, no letter arrived. The last letter in the cabinet is postmarked November 1965. There was no December 1965 letter, and there were no letters from 1966 at all—or any year after that. If her grandfather's pattern over the previous years had held true, he would have been in Juarez in December 1965. Maria's grandmother had sent letters to the couple of addresses she had for her grandfather's family in Juarez, but there was no response. Of course, receiving a response would have been miraculous, as in a city like Juarez, there was little chance that any of her grandfather's family had the same address as they'd had years before.

One way or the other, at least for them, her grandfather's story ended right there. If it had been someone else, any other man, Maria would have figured he'd met another woman, started a new life. That didn't square with the man she'd come to know from his letters. That home, his wife, their daughter, had been a light at the end of a monthslong tunnel that he traveled every year just to get back to them for a few months. During the growing season in Yakima, he worked a minimum of twelve hours most days, but delighted in the couple of hours he was able to spend with them before showering and collapsing into an exhausted sleep coma.

After he was gone, Maria's grandmother worked more and kept up the house payments. When school let out in June, little Luisa picked fruits and vegetables at this farm or that, in order to augment the small amount of income in the house. When Luisa was a teenager, she met Juan. He was in his mid-twenties but had already been permanently barred from reentry into the United States, meaning that he lived much like Maria's grandfather.

Maria was born in 1978, and her siblings arrived in rapid succession after that. When Maria was eleven, her grandmother had a heart attack. She didn't go to the hospital right away because she didn't have any medical insurance and was worried about bringing a financial burden on the family. Apparently, the heart attack was fairly mild, and her grandmother sincerely believed it was just some bug or indigestion. Two days later, an ambulance picked up Maria's grandmother after it was clear she was very ill. She expired on the way to the hospital. She had recently made the final payment on the house, and the deed had come in the mail a few months after that. Maria's grandmother lived a total of eleven months in a house that she, not the bank, owned.

So, to the best of Maria's thinking, she was from Yakima. Her grandmother, grandfather, mother, and father had each surmounted mountain-sized obstacles to ensure that she and her siblings could be from Yakima, in the United States, so that's where she was from.

Being a natural-born US citizen and the descendant of migrant illegals came with certain expectations. Maria had never picked a fruit or vegetable in her life. When Maria was growing up, Luisa was a grocery checker at the Safeway near their house, a union job. Juan sent money home when he was out of town and brought home his paycheck when he was in Yakima. By that time, Juan was a carpenter and handyman. The little ranch house was paid for, and each of the kids had their own room. So little Maria studied. She couldn't be idle, not even if she wanted to be; it wasn't in her genes. Her parents and grandparents had kicked the door open for her, and now she had to walk through it.

After high school, her first stop was Gonzaga University, a few hours east down I-90. College was an esoteric concept to her parents, but without ever stepping foot on a university campus, Juan and Luisa knew they wanted their children to go. To them, it was like the yellow-brick road—and Gonzaga University was the Jesuit Catholic city on a hill. It appeared to be the path to the promised land, even if they lacked a clear picture of what the promised land actually was. But it wasn't for them to find out; it was for them to be the bricks in the wall that supported the next highest brick, and Maria's grandparents had been the bricks supporting Luisa, and so on and so forth. The fact that Maria was studying at a Jesuit Catholic university fulfilled for Juan and Luisa all the aspirations they'd had for themselves as parents.

But what does a little Latina girl from farm country do after college? Her parents and younger siblings, one of which was a sophomore at WSU by that point, thought that a bachelor's degree in English was the only credential necessary to get a six-figure job in the city. That's what Maria thought on her first day of college too. It didn't take long to figure out that all her professors had PhDs, and that everybody with money had a professional degree. Lawyers, architects, doctors, these were the high earners.

College had effectively given her the necessary credentials to get an entry-level job in some anonymous office tower in Seattle. That prestigious honor was augmented by her ability to afford a one-bedroom apartment in a low-rise turn-of-the-century brick apartment building on Capitol Hill called the Gayle.

The move to Seattle was hard. Seattle was actually closer to Yakima than Spokane was, but for some reason Gonzaga didn't seem like it was far away from home. Spokane had a similar feel to Yakima, despite the fact that it was much larger. Spokane was by far the largest city she'd ever lived in up to that point. Before Seattle, she'd only ever lived in two places: Yakima and Spokane.

Seattle may have been closer, but it was on the other side of a mountain range that sprawled upward so high that sometimes when you were near it, you'd have to look straight up to even see where the sky began. The geographic hurdle was still somehow lower than the cultural one. She wasn't conservative politically. She was the singer in a hardcore band, for Christ's sake, but somehow railing against all the Republicans in Yakima and Spokane seemed more comfortable than dealing with the counterculture weirdos in Seattle. She should have fit right in, but she was a small-town punk girl, and everyone she met in Seattle seemed as though they'd grown up there.

The guitarist from her band went to Seattle as well. The bass player and drummer stayed in Spokane and started another forgettable band. Once they were settled, she and Adam—the Psychedelic Razor's guitar player—began their search for a new bass player and drummer. In Seattle in the year 2000, finding a punk-rock drummer couldn't have been easier. They put a handwritten notice on the corkboard at the Vivace café on Broadway. By the next day, they had three would-be drummers. They didn't choose the most talented one, because he was pretty arrogant. They didn't choose the worst guy, either, because he was objectively terrible. Maria was convinced that he had borrowed some drums and, never having played them before, taught himself "Tequila" an hour before the audition. And he couldn't even play *that* properly. For Maria and Adam, at least for the time being, the middle guy would do. A decent bass player was a little harder to locate, but by the end of the week, the Psychedelic Razors were up and running.

For a couple of years, that life suited her. As far as her parents and sibling were concerned, she was a rock star. In reality, she had to beg club owners to let the band play, and she made so little money that all she could afford was a latte at Vivace for breakfast and two cheeseburgers and fries at Dick's for dinner. She always skipped lunch, but somehow she was still broke most of the time.

Over the next few years, the Psychedelic Razors petered out. In the late nineties, the Murder City Devils changed the punk landscape in Seattle, effectively remaking the city's music scene in their own image. Their evolution away from sixty-second songs to something a little more blues and rock and roll severely dampened the aspirations of bands that still prayed at the altar of holy hardcore. The Razors cut a few more seven-inch records, on a few forgettable small record labels. In 2001, the year before they called it quits, they self-released a discography on CD and did a two-month US tour. Maria returned to Seattle with eighty-two dollars—her part of the "profit" from the tour. She'd taken a leave of absence from work, but upon her return, it became quite clear that they didn't require, or desire, her return.

Her life as a musician was beyond over, and she mourned her lost stardom. Not that singers from hardcore bands craved fame, but any notoriety and recognition would now forever elude her. She was late on rent because of the tour. Now that she'd finally settled into the city, she was terrified that her life as a Seattleite was close to being over. She had fucking hated her job, so while she had no idea how she was going to make a living, she cheered the demise of her life as a downtown cubicle drone.

On that Monday, she picked up her tiny and insignificant possessions from her cubicle, as well as her last paycheck. She used the overwhelming majority of her check to get current on her rent. On Tuesday, she walked to the Kinkos on Roy Street and made several copies of a flyer seeking a roommate. She walked to the Vivace and tacked up one of the flyers on the corkboard. When she went up to the counter to order her latte, she spied something new: a sign that read "Help Wanted."

Chapter 11

I t was the year 2000, and at some point in recent years, people coming of age around the beginning of the millennium began being referred to as millennials, or Gen Y. Ben was born in 1981, so as best as he could figure, he was Gen X. But being born at the end of 1981, he had much more in common with older millennials then he did with Gen Xers born in the sixties. Was he the last Gen Xer born, or was he the first millennial ever? Was he welcome in either tribe, or rejected by both? Forever in-between here and there was Ben's lot in life.

The acute aloofness that the world had exhibited toward him was all the more obvious that first quarter at U-dub. U-dub filled a particular niche in American culture. It was effectively an Ivy League university, professionally camouflaged as a public university. It wasn't just that it had a great medical school and a first-class university hospital, or even that it had multiple Nobel laureates on the faculty. It wasn't that it had amazing architecture and stellar science programs. It wasn't that it had a great law school. It wasn't the huge endowment or the active and noteworthy alumni. It wasn't the enormous, well-manicured campus grounds, or the corporately sponsored state-of-the-art facilities all over that well-manicured campus. It wasn't the ridiculously well-funded football program and its fourteen Rose Bowl appearances, or the fact that in a city the size of Seattle, it was the largest employer in the county. It was all those things and a thousand more, in conjunction with one another, that made it a force. U-dub punched well above its weight class.

America needs a handful of universities with the ability to pump out large numbers of skilled professionals whose parents can't afford to send them to Harvard. America needs a class of professionals who have equal skills, if not quite an equal educational pedigree. Somewhere in your city, there's a U-dub civil engineer designing the next generation of your urban infrastructure, or a U-dub medical scientist on the brink of curing some nagging human ailment. America sinks or swims on the work of such people and therefore thrives or withers with the vitality of cutting-edge public universities.

To say Ben felt out of place would be to say that the *Titanic* had encountered some minor difficulty on its maiden voyage. After Mike died, he went from being the invisible only child to the middle child in a family with only two living children. It wasn't that he thought his parents' reaction to Mike's death was wrong. Because it wasn't. They reacted the way anyone would. His mother mourned a lost child and gave birth to a new one. There's no space in that situation for a defiant teenager, none except as the typical pain in the ass that most teenagers are. Ben's dad took a couple of years to mourn and came out the other side fairly well intact. By that time, Ben was effectively grown. While it was nice to have his father back, it didn't change the fact that for years, Ben was the invisible child.

There just weren't many people like him there. He wondered

whether there were people like him anywhere. The odd inner workings of his mind made him question whether he could find even five like-minded individuals on the whole of planet Earth. There weren't that many locals at U-dub. Before coming there, he'd assumed it was all locals. The students who were local all seemed to be from middle-class families, not working poor ones, some even scratching at the basement door of upper middle class. The remainder were international students and kids from rich suburbs situated just outside major urban population centers. One look at the demographics of the student body, and the prevalent Greek system at U-dub all of a sudden made sense. "Think about it. What do spoiled suburban kids like more than a kegger and fuckin' each other's girlfriends? Nothing. That's the point.

"Those places have a way of making you feel outta place in your own home. U-dub is the largest employer in King County, but if you work there—that is, if you work there but aren't faculty—you're the outsider. You could have lived in Puget Sound your whole life, worked at U-dub for decades, but eighteen-year-olds who just moved into their freshman dorm are your societal superiors. You're in their space. They stay for four years yet somehow have greater vested ownership in the place. The outsiders have immediate agency, which the locals are permanently deprived of. I guess the caste system around institutions of higher learning in America extends to places outside the Ivy League. Ha, who fuckin' would have thunk it! But there it is."

Ben was never comfortable in his body back then. Straddling two worlds, he no longer fit cleanly into the old one, and fitting into the new one was still a long way off.

He was the townie, but not even a townie in Seattle. He

worked part-time at Hal of a Sub on Ninth and Pacific in downtown Tacoma. Ben laughed to himself one night as he was making someone an egg salad sub. "Fuck, I'm not even good enough to work at some shithole sandwich place near the university." Most afternoons, he'd head to the sandwich shop to work the four-to-nine shift. Most nights, he'd head home after his shift and study until one or two in the morning. Most mornings, he'd wake up early and drive to Seattle for class.

Because he couldn't be one or the other, eventually he became both without really being either. A person can't straddle two worlds forever. Eventually, a person has to become one or the other, or they have to take the virtues of both and become an entirely new thing. In time, the ability to pierce that bubble of entitlement and speak with credibility to those on high about those down below would become a great asset to him, but that was still a long way off.

During his first year at U-dub, all Ben knew was that his friends at home were beginning to speak a different language than him. They were starting to talk about apprenticeships and vocational training. They were learning how to turn the wrenches that kept civilization civil, and Ben was learning how to write essays about useless academic concepts and theories. Worse still, his friends were making money, and all Ben was doing was incurring student loan debt. The language his fellow students spoke was more foreign than the one his friends at home spoke.

With people at home, it was sad that there was an ever-widening rift between where he and they were, but at least there was a common starting point. With the people in class, there was no foundation. It was moving suddenly into something instead of being edged slowly out of something.

Ben's bewilderment didn't come from a place of animosity either. In fact, to people at home, Ben was a glowing beacon of what was possible despite being from blue-collar nowhere. To his fellow students, the ones who knew where he'd come from, he was the token that illustrated what they perceived to be their own magnanimous nature. That said, until Ben figured out who he was, all the blue-collar pride of compatriots and upper-class guilt of misguided shit-heels couldn't make him feel comfortable in his own skin.

Someday he would figure out that he was the tool that neither side fully possessed, a genuine and unique thing. And it was because of this, and the fact that he was never going to fit easily into either place, that made him valuable. Back then it would have surprised Ben to learn that the people he grew up with were rooting for him because his social mobility gave them a seat at the big table of society. To those upper-class, socially insulated pretenders, he was an enigma. He could fade into their world and move freely about in the one he grew up in. He was a shade apart from both, and neither in nor out of either. Ben was a genuine go-between, and he used his talents to manipulate people in the world he had to exist in, while simultaneously opening doors for people in the world he'd originated in. It wasn't a skill that was teachable, and it wasn't something that could be purchased. It was an uncommon switch that showed up in a unique brain from time to time. It was the spark that brought the campfire to life and provided warmth to its tribe.

There were so many places that Ben was neither in nor out of, that it made more sense for him to make a home in his own mind, to view that home as a third place in between whichever poles were pushing and pulling him this way or that. There was more to it than that, but during his first year at U-dub, that was about all the sense he could make of it.

Usually when he was driving home in the afternoon, he'd talk to himself because he had no one else to talk to. He could tell Big Ben or Josh about what he was learning in class, and they'd listen, but they wouldn't really hear him. What he was learning would never matter to them. It barely mattered to Ben, and he was the one learning it. As far as talking to his fellow students, it was the rare occasion that he could talk to them even if he wanted to.

Leaving Seattle for Tacoma at two in the afternoon meant he'd barely make it back to Tacoma for his four o'clock shift at Hal of a Sub. It wasn't that Tacoma was far away, it wasn't, only about thirty miles; it's just that traffic was that bad. I-5 was the in-between place on those afternoons. Maybe, he thought, I should just live on I-5. "I mean, I must fit in there, because I-5 is nowhere, at least that in-between part of it was. Sometimes I think there should be a little hammock that exists slightly out of this dimension, just a little room that I can slide into where no one else can go except me. If I don't fit cleanly into this world, it's only fair that the universe has a little pocket dimension where only I can go."

There was no pocket dimension, but there was that in-between place in Ben's mind that he was, at that time, just beginning to adapt to living in. He didn't need much human interaction, so he just spent more and more time in there. He'd invented that place a long time ago. Really, he didn't invent it at all. It was just there, always. There wasn't a time he could remember when it wasn't there, but he'd furnished it after he discovered it, that much was true. He'd always needed it, because he'd always found a way to push himself to the periphery of any situation.

Skateboards and punk bands had pushed him to the periphery in high school. If he'd played football and listened to Korn, he'd have been right in the middle of the social scene. He'd never tried, or even desired to be in the middle of anything, but being completely pushed outside of everything, due to his misfit nature, was painful. He never knew why he did it, nor did he have any control over it, but it was a fact.

Ben's rejection of the Catholic Church as a preadolescent, for instance, left him out on an island, so to speak. Whatever the circumstance, he'd always pushed himself into the role of lone dissenting voice in a crowd of cheering group thinkers. And the outcome always remained predictably constant. So he always wound up back in that isolated place in his own mind. Sometimes Ben tried to imagine being within the group, but his mode of being was too dissimilar. He lacked the cognitive tools to even believably imagine himself in the group, so instead, he just left it alone.

As much as Ben could find a home for himself in a mental space where no one else was present or welcome, he still had to live in the actual physical world. When he was on I-5, he'd eventually wind up at Hal of a Sub, U-dub, or home. These places existed in the actual three-dimensional world. Home and Hal of a Sub was Tacoma; U-dub was Seattle. Eventually Seattle became home, at least to the extent that any place in the physical world could be home to Ben, but that was later. During his first year at U-dub, and every year prior to that, Tacoma was home. That is, Tacoma was the place in the actual world where his bed was. Even for several years after he'd moved to Seattle, Tacoma was his only physical home. "There was no in-between place in the physical world for a person stretched between Seattle and Tacoma. Maybe Federal Way, but fuck that place, right! Most of the time, home was the place in my mind where no one else was allowed. I still hope that someday I'll manage to wish my pocket dimension into being. Until then, I'm stuck here on the muddy ball with everyone else."

There were so many gaps between the two cities that no effort could be made to bridge them. The two cities were unhinged but somehow still stuck together. It was an excruciating symbiosis. To Seattle, Tacoma was like having a leg that often refused to cooperate and move in conjunction with the rest of the body. To Tacoma, Seattle was a nursery school full of whining toddlers who needed rescue from a burning building. For Seattle, it couldn't be rid of Tacoma, because even a leg that at times refused to cooperate was still better than no leg at all. For Tacoma, leaving whining toddlers to their own devices in a burning structure was unconscionable, even if you wanted to smack the shit out of every last one of those bratty little snot machines.

During his freshman year, Ben took a girl home for Thanksgiving dinner. Her name was Jennie. "Every other girl on planet Earth is named Jennifer, so kudos to her for mixing it up with her novel adaptation on an otherwise played-out name." Jennie was clearly enamored of the unique working-class perspective Ben offered in their political science course. It was the general freshman poli-sci course that everyone takes for an easy grade, and the curriculum was as broad as an ocean and as deep as a mud puddle. Jennie was from Orange County—the one in California, not Florida. "Yeah, because fuck Florida." Jennie hadn't been to Tacoma before Thanksgiving at his parents' house, and she asked Ben to compare the two cities.

"They can't be compared," he told her. "They're Athens and Sparta. Seattle is more like Portland or Vancouver BC, than it is like Tacoma. You compare Athens to, say, Rome or Carthage, not Sparta. Seattle and Tacoma are parts of one whole.

"But if you were comparing them, there's no contest, not in the context of dominance anyway. Every Tacomaite (it's Tacomaite, not Tacoman) is worth four and a half Seattleites in a rumble. If there's a brawl between Tacoma and Seattle, Tacoma beats Seattle unconscious in under a minute. If there's a knife fight between Tacoma and Seattle, Tacoma disembowels Seattle before Seattle unsheathes its knife. If there's a gun fight between Tacoma and Seattle, Seattle, for purposes of staying politically correct, will refuse to bring a gun at all. Seattle is Athens. Athens has beauty, culture, and opportunity. Tacoma is Sparta. Sparta has bleakness, cruelty, and adversity.

"Tacoma exists to protect the gleaming glass towers of the city on the hill. Seattle exists to project light in all directions from atop the highest glass tower. Tacoma and Seattle are a medieval painting of an aristocrat holding a sword in one hand and a leatherbound treatise in the other, one man with two hands. The pen and the sword. That's all they are."

Chapter 12

Her work ID card read Maria Deloera. She hated the photo. Her eyes were half-closed, probably because she wasn't ready for the guy to snap the photo. Probably, but also probably because she was only slightly less baked that first day at the city attorney's office than she was this morning. She needed it that day, and the half-asleep ID photo was the ongoing legacy of that particular foggy morning. Looking at it was a constant annoyance, but the fact that she needed it to access the office necessitated wearing it on a lanyard around her neck. Looking at it was annoying, having everyone she worked with see it all the time was embarrassing. Apparently, they don't do retakes in Chief Seattle's tribe.

She'd been at the city attorney's office for almost five years when Pete became the city attorney. It was all she'd ever done as an attorney. After leaving that cubicle drone job in 2002, she found a roommate, got a part-time job at Vivace, and went to law school as Seattle University at night. The pay was pretty good for a government job, and the cliché and obvious but still accurate thing to say was that it had great benefits. It did. Her BMW was about two years old, silver, 528xi, whatever the hell that meant. She'd gotten it new. The first couple of years there, she'd refused to get a new car. She wasn't sure she was going to stay at the city attorney's office. More to the point, she wasn't sure she was going to be able to stay.

Most of the prosecutors quit within a few months. Many of those that remained got railroaded out within a year or two by leadership through a process of toothless progressive discipline that tended to leave resignation as very desirable option. Those who couldn't cut it in a trial unit, but refused to leave, were rotated to some cake unit assignment far away from the front lines, specialty courts and the like. The handful who could cut it in a trial unit, and who still wanted to stay after realizing what the job was, lost their courage and became house cats. It was a bargain with the devil, overmatching funds to a pension, little to no copays for medical visits and procedures, flexible hours, and enough money to live on. The trade-off was that your workload kept you beholden to your computer at work, and the constant trial preparation and accompanying caseload ensured that you never went to the doctor during work hours without paying for it by working late into the evening. Maria hadn't even been to the dentist in two years. It was easier to floss really well in the morning and hope your teeth were fine than it was to take off a couple of hours in the afternoon to go to a dentist's appointment.

Every time she considered the ludicrous nature of the problem, she would wonder what to do about it. There was no solution, though. While she loathed working for the city, she knew working for a downtown law firm would be worse. The fact that her medical benefits were so great that she could get all the surgeries she wanted seemed like an upside-down rationalization to stay in a job that was objectively terrible. The city allowed employees to roll over as much sick time as they wanted. That made sense to Maria, since she was always so underwater with work that she never used any sick time. Maria had almost eight weeks accrued. On the rare occasion she took a sick day, she typically ended up working at home anyway.

"Ha, if I ever get sick enough to take advantage of my Cadillac benefits, all I have to do is use some of the hundreds of hours of sick time I've accrued and work until eleven at night while I recover from surgery. What a bargain!"

She was thinking out loud.

Actually, she was talking to herself, but she didn't care to frame it like that. Thinking out loud sounded better. She was a trial prosecutor, a storyteller, and stories were all about the framing.

A couple of years ago she stopped wrestling with reality. She stopped caring about whether she would win or lose this trial or that. She stopped worrying about whether she would be gently persuaded to resign by her superiors. Once she settled into the job and stopped giving a fuck about the outcomes of her behavior, she finally fit in. She gave a fuck, but more so about the battered women she saw every day, never about the office, the court, or white-bread slimeball defense attorneys. Apathy, security, and monotony were the pillars holding up government jobs, and the city attorney's office was a prime example.

The BMW was nice, only a couple of years old. The apartment was nice, only a little too close to a very loud gay bar on Capitol Hill. The clothes were nice, only slightly less expensive than the very expensive ones. Someone had once told her that more education equals more freedom, a professional degree ensures security, and lawyers are rich. In fact, this was all bullshit. Most lawyers aren't rich. Because they worked so many hours, Maria doubted that many of them made much more than minimum wage. A professional degree only secures a different kind of security—the ability to be middle class in the big city instead of the sticks. More education never equaled more freedom. Student loan debt ensured that most people with multiple years of higher education were more hemmed into servitude than her parents and grandparents ever were.

When her '81 Corolla finally died, she knew she wasn't going anywhere. She was trapped in a professional cell of her own making, shackled by golden handcuffs. Her devil's bargain was complete. She wore the golden handcuffs. To celebrate this acceptance of ultimate failure, she got a brand-new BMW. She'd leased it, which seemed like a glorified version of renting to own your furniture. Immediately an image from last Thanksgiving popped into her head of her mom frantically scrubbing red wine out of a couch cushion. Maria had gotten a little tipsy, and her wine splashed onto the couch. Through her mother's eyes, it happened in slow motion. Maria couldn't help but laugh.

It wasn't humorous; it was ludicrous, like most things. Maria's mom had been paying for that couch since Maria was in high school, and she still didn't own it. Maria hated that couch and considered hauling it out to the yard and lighting it on fire. Freeing her mother from that couch would do her good, Maria smugly thought to herself. Right about then, she knocked over her pipe. Ash and hot coals fell onto the leather passenger seat. She frantically tried to stamp it out with the palm of her hand. She then scrubbed at it with a Wet-Nap from the pack she kept in her purse.

"At least my stained rented pile of shit has a sharp silver paint job and leather seats. Maybe I can haul it out to the yard and set it on fire. But I don't have a yard because I live in an apartment in the city. Oh well."

She was thinking out loud again, not talking to herself, thinking out loud.

Right about then, that new white boy from the office appeared, wearing his cleanly pressed white-boy suit, and not shockingly a white shirt. She was used to white boys. Her band had been full of white boys. Seattle was full of white boys. College and law school had definitely been full of white boys. The DPD was full of Ivy League white boys, the second worst kind of white boy next to the frat bro white boy. The city attorney's office was full of white boys too, like her supervisor, Alan Thorpe. Now the city attorney's office had another white boy, which in her opinion meant the city attorney's office wasn't just full of white boys but overfull.

He walked up to the BMW with that typical white-boy swagger. He knocked on her window. She rolled it down, and a cloud of pot smoke hit him square in the face.

"Did you bring enough for the whole class?"

He paused for a minute, listening. "Hey, is that Jawbreaker?"

"All right, maybe you're okay—for a white boy," she said.

Chapter 13

A couple of months later, Ben was sitting at the counsel table in Courtroom 1002 at SMC. Because the city attorney's office didn't do any of the felony prosecutions, SMC was effectively the perpetual farm team, triple-A ball exclusively. The only courtrooms at SMC with any natural light were the ones on the end of the building. Courtroom 1002 was sandwiched in the middle and thus was one of the courtrooms with no windows. These courtrooms seemed extra dark too. It was as if they artificially lowered the lights to make the courtrooms seem more sinister. Ben felt like he was sitting in a courtroom in one of the Christopher Nolan *Batman* movies.

He wondered why the aesthetic of every courtroom was wall-to-wall paneled wood. The SMC courtrooms were more "American gothic" in their appeal, whereas down the road at King County Superior Court, the courtrooms had more of a "frontier justice" mood to them. "Just once, I'd like to see a mod style courtroom. The judge's chair could be one of those swiveling ball chairs with lime-green cushions. The counsel tables could be walnut with decorative horizontal slats, and they could hang a print of Andy Warhol's Elizabeth Taylor portrait. The defense could show up to court on Vespas, and the prosecutors on Triumphs. What a world that could be, mods and rockers duking it out in the wettest of Pete Townsend's wet dreams."

As TDA supervisor for SMC, Tim was TDA's great white hope that day. Ben figured Tim stuck around SMC, instead of rotating to a superior court assignment, because he was a bully and got off on beating up the new city prosecutors. In superior court, the defense didn't have the same unfair advantage. The jury pools came from the whole of King County and, as such, were more conservative and therefore friendlier to the government. Over there, the judges were professionals who were more interested in making good law than they were in carrying this or that side's water. Those superior court judges took their responsibilities seriously. At SMC, prison abolitionists stood at the door and handed jury nullification pamphlets to every potential juror who arrived. Most of the judges were actively out to get the prosecutors. And the jury pool was composed of rich, educated Seattleites carrying around about three tons of white guilt apiece. They were apathetic toward the government at best, and openly hostile at worst. And of course, the DPD attorneys were well armed and prepared to take down any city prosecutor that survived all those obstacles. SMC was kangaroo court, and Tim was the silverback gorilla and self-appointed guardian of the accused in Seattle.

Tim credited himself as being quite clever. He called the city prosecutors G-men, and he called the new prosecutors junior G-men. He was big, too, like about six four, not really built but big. He'd adopted the public defender uniform—that is, tweed sports jacket, gingham-patterned button-down shirt, denim slacks, cheap polyester tie, and brown Dockers brand oxfords. This universally accepted public defender uniform is professional camouflage nearly as convincing as Ben's own, but only to the untrained eye.

"Tim went to Harvard Law School. Dressing like a community college English professor was only level one of his deception." The shit-eating grin he wore only thinly veiled the silver spoon in his mouth. Unfortunately for everyone, from time-to-time Tim saw fit to open his mouth and speak. Fortunately for everyone, when he did, they got a peek at that baked-in rich boy entitlement. As convincing as his uniform could be, there was no professional camouflage for his vernacular, and that day, when he stood up to do his voir dire, everyone in the jury venire started seething with resentment. It was certainly the case that people in Seattle almost always acquitted defendants of misdemeanor crimes, mainly because that was part and parcel of the Seattle DNA, but that didn't mean they liked being talked down to by grotesquely tall wads of Ivy League–brand white bread dough.

At the morning recess, Ben was standing at the urinal unloading the half a pot of coffee he'd drank that morning. Tim walked up to the urinal next to him. Ben wasn't short. In fact, he was somewhat tall, but he immediately felt Tim looming over him, using his odd height to try to intimidate him. Ben always preferred fighting guys who were taller than him. "It's because their balls are right at perfect gut-punch height. Most people will cover their face when they're fighting, some will cover their stomachs, but nobody cups their balls to protect them. If their balls are at punching height, I punch 'em in the balls. Tall guys should protect their balls, not their heads. Who's going to punch some eight-foot-tall guy in the face. Use your brains tall guys. Seriously."

"What do you think you're going to do in there, junior G-man? I don't know why you prosecutors even bother showing up to trials here. You never win. You're certainly not going to win this one."

"I don't have to win, Tim. All I have to do is give you a bloody nose. Once people see you bleed, your aura of invincibility fades away."

Ben turned toward Tim, cock out, midstream. Piss shot onto Tim's pantleg and splashed up from the tile floor where it cascaded over those ugly-ass oxfords that encapsulated Tim's entitled little feet.

"Are you fucking crazy? What the fuck's the matter with you!"

"What the fuck's the matter with you, Harvard? You're the one with piss all over your shoes!"

Ben glanced up at Tim's frightened eyes. Right then, Tim could have been ten feet tall and wide as a refrigerator and it wouldn't have mattered. Ben knew something that most people didn't. Dominance doesn't belong to the loudest ape. It belongs to the ape with the fortitude to piss on the loudest ape.

Tim didn't hang around to wash his hands. He didn't even bother to wipe off his shoes with a paper towel. He backed up and nearly fell over the garbage can by the door. Ben never flushed public urinals, and he never washed his hands after he pissed. "Why fuckin' bother? All I ever touch in there is my own cock, and I like the way it smells on my hands. It's the aromatic scent of me. I'd brew it into a tea if I could." After Ben zipped up, he grabbed a paper towel out of the wall dispenser, opened the door with it, and pitched the paper towel onto the restroom floor. Just because he didn't wash his hands didn't mean he liked touching filthy door handles.

Ben had a rapport with people, and even though he'd never done a voir dire before, he was charming and likable. Everybody knew that jurors made up their mind during jury selection. The only point of the trial was to give jurors something that they could use to justify their predetermined outcome. It was a popularity contest that defense attorneys didn't even have to be popular to win. They just had to be on the politically popular side of the ideological spectrum. In fact, they could be patently unlikable and still win the trial, and they normally did.

The prosecutor has to be likable as a person to sway the jury during jury selection because the prosecutor is advocating for the politically unpopular position. That is, conviction. The defense attorney, even pompous ones like Tim, were advocating for the prevailing politically popular position. That is, acquit no matter what.

Ben didn't win that trial, but he didn't lose it either. It was a hung jury, but a hung jury on a misdemeanor assault in SMC was a victory of sorts for a prosecutor. For the first time in his life, Ben recognized how being in between worlds could be useful.

A jury venire is a cross section of the population. How does one speak to the socioeconomically unfortunate in the venire without pissing off the rich fuckers, and vice versa? Most people, including most trial lawyers, never figure it out. Tim certainly never did. He just went on winning cases by parroting what most Seattleites wanted to hear. He probably even thought he was likable, since he kept winning. He likely never understood that he won because he was preaching to the choir. That day, Ben figured something out, one little piece of the puzzle that would one day expand into a clear picture of his existence and purpose. He figured out that communicating with people wasn't something that you could learn how to do. If it was, Tim would have mastered it long ago. No, communicating with people was a gift, definitely something that a person could get better at, but a gift you were born with nonetheless.

Back then, there was a ritual at SMC. The newer attorneys at the various public defender divisions in Seattle would come down to SMC anytime there was a trial. They'd come to gawk at the prosecutor the way people gawk at the animals in a zoo. They'd come to take notes. Most importantly, they'd come to watch the city prosecutors eat a slice of humble pie after being trounced by Tim. Typically, the writing was on the wall by the time the prosecutor called their first witness. But that trial had a different tone. The public defenders in the gallery could see it as well. There was a scent in the air. It was fear and desperation, and perhaps a little urine as well. Nobody could remember the last time that a public defender in trial at SMC had seemed unsure about the outcome.

The defense would lose trials from time to time, but those were always aberrations. The occasional loss could always be chalked up to something like overwhelming evidence that even a Seattle jury couldn't ignore. The trial that week was different. It was different because a prosecutor had figured out a way to break through the noise. Ben was starting to figure out the code he had to break in order to win. Ben was able to convince some members of a Seattle jury that they should care that somebody got punched by some random stranger. Defense didn't sweat much about losing a couple of trials where overwhelming evidence made guilt irrefutable, but a prosecutor who could sway opinion with nothing more than a charming demeanor and persuasive rational inferences was a serious problem for them.

A hung jury wasn't an acquittal, but usually it was just as good as one, since the city rarely retried the defendant after a hung jury. Usually, it was cause for an end-of-week happy hour where the defense attorneys could slap each other on the back about how righteously great they all were.

That week, a few wondered how the victim who got punched felt. A few wondered why Tim wasn't his normal boisterous self. More than a few wondered how an upstart provincial townie had taken the reigning champion of SMC twelve rounds. The remainder wondered if they were witnessing the beginning of the end of a golden age for public defenders in Seattle. They had their happy hour that week, but it was a fairly morose affair.

Erin O'Connell was there that evening. Erin had been in the courtroom gallery for most of the week, not that anyone had taken any notice. But at that Friday evening happy hour, a couple of her colleagues noticed that Erin seemed cheerier than usual, certainly cheerier than the rest of them. Three or four of them even thought that Erin seemed downright giddy. None of them guessed why. She didn't say it out loud. She barely even allowed herself to think it, but to her, that Friday had been the best day at work that she could remember having in years.

Chapter 14

As one might expect, in any given life, many eventless months will come and go. In Ben's 2010, this had certainly become the pattern. He settled into the job, and even learned how to be fairly good at it. Most of it was negotiating plea deals and going to the multitude of pretrial hearings that is an integral part of being a prosecutor in a busy city attorney's office. By November, none of the DPD attorneys had challenged Ben to a metaphorical or actual pissing contest, and Tim, who had been scarce since their trial, had not challenged Ben to a rematch.

It made no difference to Ben. He knew Tim wouldn't do anything. "What on earth could he possibly do? Is he gonna call the Seattle Police Department's non-emergency line and say, 'I'm a public defender, and this prosecutor peed on my shoes several months ago'?" No, Tim couldn't do that. He may have warned a few of his confederates to steer clear of Ben, but broadcasting the incident to a wide audience would only serve to make him look flaccid. Besides, any cop taking that report would piss themselves laughing while writing it. Also, as a criminal defense attorney, Tim knew it was an unprovable case.

In an odd way, Ben had hoped Tim would do something.

Technically, peeing on Tim's shoes was a misdemeanor assault. Ben was delighted by the idea that if Tim had wanted to report it, he'd have been reliant on a Seattle cop to take the report, and reliant on a prosecutor from Ben's office to prosecute the case. Tim spent his working life explaining away similar transgressions on the part of his clients as inconsequential, not a public safety concern, and not worthy of wasting the criminal justice system's time. Ben wondered how inconsequential such events seemed to Tim after he had to throw out his pee-soaked shoes.

Similarly, it appeared that the male DPD attorneys had some safety concerns, because not one of them would step into the restroom when Ben was around. Every area of the courthouse had cameras on it, but the restrooms were black boxes. Everybody knew people went in there to pee, but nobody outside could ever know for sure where the pee went. Ben could actually see some of the male DPD attorneys squirm during recesses, trying to hold back the contents of their coffee-saturated bladders when Ben was around.

Of some note, Ben had been fucking Erin O'Connell for about six months. To Ben, she was an interesting woman. Erin had blond hair and big breasts, but she pinned her hair into a bun and kept her breasts hidden under cleverly tailored blazers. She also wore glasses, glasses that Ben was pretty sure she didn't really need. She always wore makeup, but it was the kind of makeup designed to make a person's face look plainer, no dark lipliner or loud eye makeup.

Sometime in early June—Ben couldn't really remember the specific date—Erin cornered him in the courthouse elevator. It was the first time he'd noticed her breasts, likely because it was the first time he'd ever seen her with the top two buttons of her white button-down shirt undone. It was Friday, and she seemed sort of sloppy drunk, so Ben assumed that the DPD happy hour had started a little early for Erin. When the elevator got to the lobby, Erin sauntered out, expecting Ben to be following behind. When she turned to see if Ben was looking at her, he wasn't. He hadn't gotten out of the elevator. Instead, he hit the button for the tenth floor. Through the closing doors, Ben said, "I forgot my phone upstairs. Later."

When that Monday rolled around, Erin became more deliberate. Ben was finishing his morning pretrial calendar, and Erin was lying in wait in the hallway outside Courtroom 1103.

"Let's go get some lunch," she said.

"I never eat lunch," Ben replied.

"Then watch me eat. Come on, I'm hungry."

They didn't actually get lunch that day. Erin was attractive, but good Irish Catholic Republican militants don't fuck evil Protestant loyalist militants who lived across the bog. She was looking at him and preening again. Ben figured the quickest way to kill whatever this was in its cradle was to say something inappropriate and offensive.

"I'm not wasting my afternoon on lunch. If you want to waste my afternoon, it's gonna be at my place."

Erin looked up at him with her big doe eyes and spoke quietly, her full, pouty lips forming the words. "I'll drive."

That had been a good afternoon, but she'd been sleeping over a lot since then. It wasn't that Ben didn't like girls, and it wasn't that Erin wasn't attractive. It was just that Ben mostly liked being on his own, and someone being around all the time seriously cut into the time he liked to spend playing *Halo*. He also didn't like sharing his bed, but she kept staying so late after they had sex, she'd just sort of invite herself to stay the night. Ben spent a lot of nights that summer sleeping on his couch, because, most nights, he'd wait for her to fall asleep in his bed, and then he'd move to the living room and play *Halo* until three in the morning. Things kept being left at his place as well. "Said another way, Erin kept bringing girl crap over to my apartment and leaving it all over the fuckin' place."

By November, Erin was under the impression that they were in an exclusive relationship. It was mostly exclusive, but that had more to do with the fact that Ben didn't like wasting his free time conning women into sleeping with him. He preferred call girls, and the Internet had streamlined transactional sex into one-stop shopping. He'd only had a few over to his place since June, mostly on account of Erin always being underfoot. In any case, Erin was mostly right about the exclusivity of their relationship. In other words, Ben wasn't dating anyone else. "Call girls yankin' your crank for cash doesn't really count, you know."

It was November, and Ben loved Thanksgiving. The Sunday before, he was sitting in his living room watching a PBS documentary about the Troubles. He wanted to nap in his bed, but Erin was in there reading a book. They were talking about Derry on the documentary. The Brits renamed it Londonderry way back when.

"Those fuckin' WASP loyalist motherfuckers got some fuckin' nerve. They think they own every-fuckin'-thing."

"I can't hear you, babe. What'd you say?"

Ben glanced down the hall. From his couch, he could see she'd propped herself up on his pillows into a sitting position to read. There she was, like always, occupying his room like she owned it.

"This fuckin' WASP loyalist motherfucker got some fuckin'

nerve. She thinks she owns every-fuckin'-thing."

"Babe, come in here and tell me. I can't hear you all the way in there."

Ben wasn't talking to her, even if he was talking about her.

"Never-fuckin'-mind," he shouted down the hall at her.

Big Ben called on the phone, and Ben talked to his dad for about fifteen minutes about the plan for Thanksgiving.

After Ben hung up, Erin came out to the living room and said, "What time are you leaving on Thursday?"

Ben was actually thinking of heading to Tacoma Wednesday after work, but instead he told Erin, "I don't know. Probably after I get up on Thursday. What are you doing on Thanksgiving?"

"Well, my family is in Massachusetts, and I have too much work to just up and leave over the holiday weekend."

Ben pretended to think out loud. "Hmm. There're so many people from your office from out of state, I'm sure they're having some sort of get-together. They probably all buy a bunch of liquor and get wasted at somebody's place. That would probably be fun. Maybe?"

"Is that something you'd want to go to?"

"What? No! Why would I spend my Thanksgiving with those fuckin' assholes? Besides, you just heard me talking to my dad about going to my parents' house."

"So, did you want me to stay over here Wednesday night and bring some extra clothes with me?

"You mean like a coat? Is it supposed to be cold on Thursday? I don't fuckin' know. It's never that cold around here, so I never really wear a coat."

"The extra clothes would be so that I have something to wear to Thanksgiving dinner."

"If you want to bring extra clothes with you, that's your business. You don't really ever ask if you can stay over any other time, and half of your wardrobe is already strangling my poor closet, so I'm not sure why you're asking now."

"I don't know, Ben. I guess that if I'm going to meet your family, it might be nice to have something clean to wear."

"What?"

The thought that she was angling for an invitation had genuinely not occurred to Ben.

"So, you want to go to Tacoma with me?"

"Yeah! Dummy! Where else would I be on Thanksgiving?"

"Maybe, like, with your friends at work, or your family in Massachusetts."

"Do you want to come to Massachusetts with me?"

"Fuck no! That sounds fuckin' terrible."

"What's that supposed to mean?"

"Don't you think that would be a little awkward, me meeting your family?"

"Why?"

"Because my dad is an electrician. Because my dead brother was a crack addict. Because I grew up in the most stereotypical white-trash, working-poor neighborhood imaginable. Because I went to a state school. What do you think, me and your dad are going to sit and watch the Apple Cup? Get fuckin' real! Grow up! Grow a fuckin' brain! Why would your parents want to meet me?"

"Maybe because I've been telling them about you for months."

"Why would you fuckin' do that?"

"Because I want them to know that I'm in a meaningful, committed relationship."

"But you're not!"

"Then what are we doing here?"

"I have no idea what we're doing here, but just because you're always hanging around doesn't make this a relationship."

"This isn't a relationship. So I'm supposed to believe that your parents don't want to meet the woman you practically live with?"

"I doubt it!"

"Why?"

"There are a lot of people my parents don't know exist who they wouldn't necessarily want to meet."

"They don't know you have a girlfriend?"

"Nope. Because I don't have a girlfriend. And to be honest, even if you were my girlfriend, I doubt I would call them up and tell them about you."

"Wait, what? Why?"

"I don't know. I just don't do that. What do you think people like my parents would have to say to someone like you?"

"What's that supposed to mean?"

"We fuckin' hate people like you. We tack pictures of people like you up on dartboards at the corner bar. My ancestors burned effigies of people like you in the town square. I don't tell my friends about you either."

"What! What about your friend Jason at work?"

"I was talking about my other friends, but no, I definitely don't tell people at work about you either. Why would I do that?"

"Why not, we all work together."

"No we don't, people at my office hate you more than my parent's would. Do you really think I'm going to tell an office full of union member municipal prosecutors about the Ivy League public defender I'm bangin'? I think there's actually a dartboard at my office with Tim's face tacked to it. I mean, why would you tell people at your office that you're fuckin' me?"

"I have. I've told them all, lots of times. I have a picture of you and me on my desk."

"Really? When did you and I take a picture together?"

"You're a fucking prick! And it's a selfie I took of us at the Dick's on Capitol Hill."

"Yeah, I remember the cheeseburgers that night. Dick's is pretty good, especially after a few beers. It's the milkshakes too, you know."

"Prick! Prick, prick, prick!"

"All right, I'm a prick. So, I'm gonna take off."

"This is your apartment."

"Yeah, but it's been a while since it really felt like my apartment. I've actually been spending a lot of time just sort of hanging out in my Barracuda lately."

"You sit in your car?"

"Yeah, you know, the app store is starting to get some pretty good games for your phone, so I've been doing that a lot. You can kind of sit anywhere and play games as long as your battery holds out, and I got a cord that charges my iPhone off the cigarette lighter. I got a pillow and a sleeping bag down there too, CDs to listen to as well. It's pretty cozy. I put a sixer of Rainier tall boys in a cooler in the trunk, and there's some chips in the back seat."

Erin started pacing back and forth on the living room rug, hand on forehead, talking to herself. "I cannot believe this! It's like we're from different planets. This isn't how people are supposed to act. This isn't how normal people act. What is the matter with this guy?"

"So, like I said, I'm gonna to take off."

"I'm going to your parents' house on Thanksgiving."

"Don't you think that would be a little awkward?"

"I can put up with a little awkwardness. Don't worry about me."

"I'm not. I meant it would be a little awkward for the rest of us."

"I'm coming to Thanksgiving with you!"

"So, I'm gonna to take off now, alright."

"I'm coming to Thanksgiving."

Ben wanted the last word, but not as bad as Erin did, so he bit his tongue as he moved toward the door.

Chapter 15

Ben slept in the Barracuda that night. When he went up to his place in the morning, Erin was gone, so he grabbed a shower and put on his clean suit and shirt. He got his buddy Jason to cover his pretrials Monday afternoon. He had no appearances in court on Tuesday or Wednesday. He was planning on leaving straight from work on Wednesday for his parents' place. Up in SMT, he felt fairly well insulated from the outside. You couldn't get onto the fifty-third floor without a badge, so he was pretty sure he wasn't going to run into Erin. He'd let his cell phone battery go dead, so he had plausible deniability about not returning her calls and texts. "I can't very well answer a phone when I lost it and the battery's gone dead, you know."

Ben liked Erin. He actually really liked her. "Outta all those preachy Ivy League carpetbaggin' pieces of shit over there at the DPD, she was the best of them. I always thought she must have been switched at birth, because not one of those self-righteous windbags ever picked up on how fucked up them being here was.

"The DPD never hired people from around here. I went to school with tons of people from Seattle who wanted to be public defenders. Not me, I never fuckin' wanted to work there, but some of the people I went to school with did. The DPD wouldn't even interview them most of the time. Refusing to hire people from around here and then going out and hiring rich white kids from the other side of the country was a slap in the face to the community. Worst of all, those rich kids didn't even need the paycheck. The DPD literally paid rich kids money they didn't need while denying lawyers from the community, who did need the income, any opportunity to represent criminal defendants."

Erin was the only one of them who ever recognized that she was carrying around five generations of blue-blooded white guilt. Pushing her way into a job that was better suited to people from the socioeconomically disadvantaged communities that most criminal defendants came from wasn't to help them. It was to help herself. It was do-gooderism born of guilt. The indigent and accused of Seattle didn't need Erin's confession or penance. Erin needed it. She got it by stealing a job in a place she wasn't wanted, representing people who despised her. The world didn't need her penance either. As with most things in life, what appeared to be altruistic on the surface was nothing more than a paltry attempt to wash clean a guilty conscience. Erin recognized that the best thing she could have done for the downtrodden was to simply stay in her lane. Attempting to do social mobility in reverse just continued to disadvantage and displace those below her, and in the most ironic way imaginable, she'd continued to perpetuate the cycle of domination that her lineage had been guilty of all these generations.

Ben liked Erin because she was self-aware. He liked that she had the courage to stare at the boogeyman of her existence and accept the ludicrous irony of it all. She was the best version of what she could be. Her ability to focus on one singular point on the horizon and move toward it helped her to become the only self-aware DPD do-gooder Ben had ever met.

At that very moment, it was precisely that singular focus that was driving Erin to locate and trap Ben on that Wednesday afternoon. Erin was stubborn but focused. Ben was sloppy but clever. Erin also thought Ben was charming in a neo-roguish sort of way. His cell kept going straight to voicemail. She'd stopped by his apartment more than once in the early part of the week, but Ben was good at slipping by her. She'd be watching his apartment building's secure front door, waiting for her chance to confront him. Then she'd look up at his living room window, and he'd be standing there.

That ghastly muscle car he drove would always magically appear, parked on Harrison Street where he always parked. She couldn't stand that thing. Whenever she was sitting in it, all she could hear was that loud fume-spewing motor, worn-out springs squeaking in the seat, and that music. It smelled like spent gasoline inside. But the music, she thought, the music was always up way too loud, just racket, not really music at all. Punk rock, she rolled her eyes even though no one was there to appreciate it, whatever that meant. She was thinking about the first time he drove her home. That idiot never wore his seatbelt either, she thought, even on the interstate. Erin never felt safe in that steel trap, even with her seatbelt on. It always jerked forward when Ben shifted it into a higher gear. It was built when cars were essentially just rolling coffins. Be that as it may, she still managed to somehow not to hear it creep up and park on Harrison. She started wondering if Ben had installed some secret silent mode in his car.

On Monday evening, she buzzed his apartment. No answer.

While she was standing there, she started to realize that he never answered his buzzer. She was beginning to think it didn't even work. That would figure. That building was the sort of building that nobody ever bothered to fix up. She walked around the building to discover that he'd turned out the living room light even though she'd seen it on a few minutes before. On Tuesday evening, she parked right in front of his apartment building's secure front door. She figured there was no way for him to slip past her if she was six feet away from the door, but he did. She saw that car of his, saw the living room light, and buzzed. No answer.

"She didn't know that I had found the super's key ring a few months back. I called him up and gave him the key ring back, but not before I ran over to the QFC and copied a few of the more important keys on that ring. Paramount among them, the key to the service entrance around back. Also, I'd snipped the line to the door buzzer in my apartment when I moved in. I hate that fuckin' thing. Neighbors buzz you when they forgot their keys. Random weirdos buzz all the apartments for shits and giggles. Angry ex-girlfriends are an omnipresent hazard, so you don't want to give them another way to get ahold of you. Why would anyone want people on the street to have a direct line to your inner sanctum! If you want to get ahold of me, just yell up to my apartment window like a normal person."

By Wednesday, Erin wasn't fucking around anymore. She left work an hour early, drove her black Mercedes into the SMT parking lot, backed into the stall next to Ben's car, and waited. The way she'd backed in was driver's side to driver's side. She was so close that there was no way to open the driver's-side doors of either vehicle.

Ben really was clever, but he was sloppy. Most of his slickest moves were actually just on-the-fly innovations. He moved through life quickly, and he missed a lot of details. His written work, while well thought out, could be riddled with typos and obvious errors. His failure to anticipate fairly expected tactics by opposing lawyers left him scrambling on the record more than once.

Ben's brain didn't work correctly until he was threatened in some way, but once threatened, the most genius work-arounds presented themselves to him. This phenomenon garnered him a reputation at work. People always thought his folksy vernacular was just a put-on. They thought his supposed blind spots—missing obvious legal maneuverings from opposing attorneys—was just him baiting a trap that he would spring at the right moment. Nobody thought that someone could be so absent minded when given all the time in the world to prepare, but so brilliant when cornered.

Ben did plan, and he hated that he seemed cursed to miss fairly blatant obstacles sitting in plain sight. But he loved the fact that he was able to pivot in real time. Many times, in the coming years he'd be performing a direct examination during trial and he'd hear a witness say something a certain way, something he wasn't expecting, and he'd look over and see that the jury had heard it the same way. He'd literally depart from his written questions altogether and follow the line of questioning to wherever it led. Often, he'd start a closing argument, referring to his notes, then pivot mid-sentence and take the whole thing in another direction.

Ben had a read on people that never failed him, and a situational awareness that gave him a five-second head start on everyone else. He'd swerve to avoid a car crash that nobody knew was imminent. He'd move out of the way of objects coming at him that weren't even in transit yet. He'd spot the overarching weak point in someone's argument before they finished their first point.

"Planning is important. I wish I was better at it, but I'm sort of shit at it if I'm being honest. Pivoting is more important. No matter how good your plan is, you're going to have to pivot. No matter how shit your plan is, you're going to have to pivot. If you're thrown unexpectedly into a situation that nobody could have reasonably planned for, you're going to have to pivot. A smart man once wrote, 'The best laid schemes o' Mice an' Men Gang aft agley.' More recently, an even smarter man said, 'Everybody has a plan until they get punched in the face.' My brain operates in two-wheel drive most of the time, and two-wheel drive is more than sufficient for most occasions. Jeopardy always flipped the four-wheel drive switch in my brain. It hooked the bumper winch to the tree stump and pulled until the fuckin' thing popped outta the ground."

That Wednesday afternoon, Ben had missed a pretty obvious sign like usual. He'd been dodging Erin for almost three days. He'd seen her car at his apartment building both Monday and Tuesday after work. Both evenings, he was able to park without her noticing pretty easily. Both evenings, he pretty easily slipped in through the service entrance around back. His phone was dead in his bag, and the door buzzer had been dead since he killed it on move-in day. He didn't go straight to bed either night, but he killed the lights almost immediately.

Ben doubted that Erin would be skulking around his building for a third day in a row, so he started thinking again about packing a bag and heading to his parents' house that night. His floor at work was key-card access only, so he knew she wouldn't be surprising him there either, but he didn't think about the SMT parking lot.

Ben left the office that afternoon, descending the great vein of the gigantic penis. When he reached the lobby, the little tacky lobby, Ben gave it a once-over. If Erin was going to be somewhere, the little tacky lobby, he thought, would likely be the place. He made his way through the other lobby, the big tacky lobby, to the bank of elevators that went to the parking structure. Maria Deloera from his office was standing there, waiting.

It was always awkward, Ben thought. "It must be, isn't it awkward for everyone?" Ben could connect with people without effort. He couldn't understand how, because he genuinely found most human interactions to be uncomfortable and unwanted. He chalked it up to his brain's four-wheel drive. "Awkward small talk with a coworker is all about posturing. It's strategy. It's adversarial. Every human interaction is essentially conflict. Sometimes it's good-natured debate, but it's always a metaphorical brawl for dominance. Who moves first? Is making the first move cool, or is it desperate? Is waiting silently stoic, or is it creepy?" Maria broke the awkward silence.

"Plans for Thanksgiving?"

"Just gonna go down to my parents' place in Tacoma. You?"

"Yeah, family stuff, you know how it is."

The elevator arrived. Ben hit P2. Maria hit P3. It was one of those little steel coffin elevators, not like the nice ones you see in beautiful buildings. Ben and Maria were used to being shoved into these little steel coffins with other people. The elevators at SMC were very similar. They weren't used to being shoved into these little steel coffins with each other. In fact, other than that time Ben saw her getting baked in the parking garage, and the gossip scoop on Ben's first day (the extent of Maria's efforts at peer mentoring), they hadn't interacted much at all.

The coffin lid slid open on P2. Ben started walking.

"See you after the holiday," he said.

"See ya," she replied.

He didn't make it very far. He'd taken only two steps out of the elevator before the four-wheel drive kicked in. There weren't many cars left on P2 the afternoon before Thanksgiving. Ben could see the unmistakable front end of the Barracuda from his vantage point, but the rest of his car was being blocked by another. It was black and shiny, cold and hard. It was like Darth Vader popping unexpectedly out of the jungle on Dagoba. That steel hood ornament, the three-pointed star of the Mercedes-Benz company unmistakable.

Ben locked eyes with Erin. She was wearing a high-buttoned black blazer with a starched white button-down shirt. Her blond hair was up in a twisty bun. She looked like a Gestapo officer, and Ben started hearing German shepherds barking in the background. He saw her leaping from the driver's seat, shouting orders in deliberately abrupt German syllables. She was pointing a Walther at him, a P38, a Luger maybe, he couldn't tell for sure.

It wasn't a hallucination because it only happened in his head, not in his eyes. It always happened like that. It took half a second for his brain to characterize an event as dangerous, and to do so in overly theatrical detail. Erin really did leap out of her car, but for some reason unbeknownst to Ben, she climbed over center console and popped out the passenger side. Ben's four-wheel drive brain buckled Ben's knees without asking him for permission to do so. Now he was three feet tall. That got him below the eyeline of the cars, but he knew that wouldn't confuse Erin for long. Ben didn't underestimate Erin. He assumed her huntress instincts were likely as keen as his prey instincts were. For a second, the sharp pain that stabs through the heart when a person is startled kept his from beating at all. That was a second ago. Now it throbbed against the inside of his rib cage. "Beads of sweat form on your brow in less than a second. How is that even possible? No time for that." His field of vision narrowed, but what he could see, he saw in great detail.

He heard the elevator door start to close behind him. The little steel coffin had become a lifeboat. He spun 180 degrees and duckwalked in his Prada's to the elevator door while Erin goose-stepped toward him in her jackboots. He'd taken two steps out of the elevator, but now with the duckwalking, it took him five steps to get back; meanwhile, Erin's blitzkrieg death march eroded the space between them with frightening speed.

The elevator door was one of those shitty ones that opened and closed from one side instead of two doors opening in the center, so Ben had to dive for the still open right side and slither through like a snake. He was in the lifeboat. Unfortunately, in order to keep elevator doors from crushing people, there's a sensor that opens the door again when someone squirms through, as Ben had just done.

Ben scrambled to his feet. Maria was staring at him with puzzled amusement. In fact, she looked as if it was the funniest thing she'd seen all week.

Gestapo Erin was bearing down on them.

"Push the button! Push the fuckin' button!" Ben muttered to Maria through clenched teeth.

Maria was openly laughing by that point.

As the elevator door closed, Ben looked at Erin and said, "See you Friday, babe."

Clearly Maria wasn't sure what the etiquette was in this sort of situation, so she just kept giggling and directed a fingers-waggling wave toward Erin as the little steel coffin's door finally, and mercifully, sealed her and Ben inside.

Ten seconds after the elevator door had opened to reveal the situation he'd failed to plan for, Ben was safely traveling to P3 with Maria. He was safe for the moment, but he wouldn't be safe for long. Erin could see where the elevator was traveling, and it wouldn't take her long to make her way to the stairs. She was an extremely smart and motivated girl. From there, she'd be on top of him again in less than a minute. She was fast too, probably from all the tennis, and with how slow the elevators were at SMT, he genuinely feared she'd be waiting outside the elevator when it arrived on P3.

"What the fuck was that all about, white boy?"

"Nothing. What? Why? Why do you ask? My car isn't up there. It must be down here."

"And the ducking and diving into the elevator?"

"You know how long it takes for the elevator to come back once the door closes. Who needs that? You gotta seize the day. Carpe diem and all that, you know."

"And what about Erin O'Connell, looking like the Terminator, closing in on you like you're Sarah Connor?"

"Hey, man, whatever. That's how I roll. She can get the next elevator. We don't need to wait around for her. I hate when people are like 'Hold it for me, please!' and they're like way across the other side of the parking lot. Man, you're either here when the door closes, or you're not. I'm not sittin' waitin' on that nonsense. And I really got more of a Nazi vibe from her than Terminator."

The door opened on P3. Ben peeked around quickly. Erin wasn't there. Yet.

"Where's your car, white boy?"

"I must have, like, taken the bus or something. Fuck me. I mean, I'd forget my head if it wasn't attached, you know, Hey, whatever. You feel like dropping me off somewhere? Anywhere?"

"Yeah, okay."

They were walking in tandem past the empty parking stalls on P3.

"Where do you live?"

"Capitol Hill."

The telltale chirp of a key fob opening her BMW's doors echoed across the steel and concrete of the empty parking structure.

"Get in."

A second after sitting down in Maria's BMW, Ben realized why Erin hadn't intercepted him on foot. He watched her black Gestapo car pull around the P3 ramp.

"Would it be weird if I sat in the back seat?"

"Yes. Yes, it would. That would be really weird."

"Then I assume lying down on your back seat would also be weird."

"Yes. Yes, it would, but go ahead and do it anyway."

Maria started driving toward the exit ramp. Erin was driving toward Maria's car. Erin stopped and rolled down her window like she wanted to chat. Maria didn't slow down. She just looked at Erin and did her fingers-waggling wave again.

Once they were on Sixth Avenue, Maria got her pipe out of the ashtray. It had a sticky green bud with crystals and orange hair all over it.

"It's all clear if you want to sit up front."

Ben climbed over the seat at the Sixth and Cherry stoplight.

"You want to get baked? Don't look at me all judgmental. I only get baked so I can get through the workday."

"No judgment from me, but you're not at work."

"I plan to work on a motion tonight, so technically my workday is still going."

"You want to go get a Rainier at Linda's Tavern instead?"

"Yes. Yes, I would. I could do a Rainier."

Chapter 16

Up at Linda's, instead of a Rainier, they had a few pitchers of Rainier. They smoked a few more bowls too. It wasn't late, but Ben figured heading down to his parents' place that night wasn't going to happen. Ben was pretty wasted. He'd drank more than Maria. Maria was pretty tipsy but more or less in good shape, considering.

"White boy. You want me to take you back to your car?"

"Yeah, I guess."

Ben stumbled out of Linda's. Maria walked, mostly. Maria drove him down to the SMT parking garage. It was only about a three-minute drive. As they pulled into P2, Ben almost expected to see Erin's Mercedes sitting there. It wasn't. He saw the Barracuda sitting alone, the last kid at school, stuck in detention. Ben knew how his car felt. "Yeah, I been there, done that."

"Are you good to drive, white boy?"

"Probably."

"You need a bump?"

She pulled out a little brown-glass coke vial. She unscrewed the top. The lid had a teeny-tiny spoon attached to it.

"Don't look at me all judgmental. I only take a little bump when I'm too drunk to drive home."

"Bring it on."

She scooped up a heaping spoonful, but considering how small the spoon was, it was still barely anything.

"One for the left nostril."

She scooped up a second spoonful.

"And one for the right. That'll get you back to Capitol Hill."

Ben did get back to the neighborhood in one piece, but when he got to his apartment building, he saw Erin's Mercedes. She wasn't in it, but there it was. She wasn't waiting by the front door or over at the teriyaki place around the corner. He was pretty wasted still, and it took a couple of minutes of fiddling before he could get his copied service-entrance key into the lock. "The fuckin' lock kept floating around. And when it would finally stop floating, the key would start floating around. It was like docking two ships moving around each other in outer space." Once he got in, he peeked into the elevator lobby. He didn't want to take the stairs, and he figured if Erin wasn't in the lobby, he was probably good to take the elevator.

The elevator dinged and the door opened. He forgot where he was right at that moment. To Ben, it felt as if he were missing a chunk of time, as he couldn't remember what had happened since he walked by the teriyaki place on Broadway. He quickly gathered that he was in his apartment building, in the elevator, and it had just opened onto his floor. His apartment was around the corner from the elevator bank. He started walking but stopped suddenly. He heard a voice, a conversation, or one side of a phone conversation. He didn't know what it was about, or who the person on the other end of the phone was, but he knew the voice of the person in the hall.

Somehow or other, Erin had managed to get into his building. "Seriously, though, how hard could it be for a pretty blond girl to get someone to let her into an apartment lobby on a cold fall evening?" Ben peeked around the corner and could see her standing near the hall fire escape window by his apartment door. He'd made sure to never let Erin get a copy of his apartment key, and now that foresight had paid off. It took a minute to remember why he was being so cloak and dagger about coming home. But once her saw her, he knew. Luckily her back was turned to him. She should have heard the elevator ding, he thought. Apparently, she didn't. He didn't take the elevator back down. "She didn't hear it ding that first time, but she would probably hear it when the doors opened again." Ben beat a hasty retreat to the stairway door.

Down at the Barracuda, he experienced the floating lock and key syndrome again. It took a minute or two, but he finally managed to get into his car. Weeks later, Ben would wonder how all those little telltale scratches around the driver's side door lock got there. The ignition was a little easier to peg. They aren't flush with the surface like a door lock, and the raised part is like a little cradle to help you get the key in. Ben figured they must make the ignition like that so you can get your car started when you're drunk. It appeared, he thought, to be modeled after a cock and pussy. "It's considerate, because if it's cold outside you can get your car started and get the heat going. A drunk person could freeze in the winter if they couldn't get their car started." Considering how easy they'd made it to start the car, he wondered why they'd made the car's door locks so hard to operate when you're drunk.

Ben was mostly satisfied with that as an explanation. He was still dissatisfied with the car door lock but appreciated the ignition. Then his car door lock made him remember trying to get into his apartment building that night, and he was immediately disappointed by the makers of residential door locks. "It's like they don't even care if drunks freeze to death on their own doorsteps, within a few feet of a warm bed. It's very disappointing to me."

It was cold that night before Thanksgiving, unusually so. It was rarely too cold in Seattle, but that night it was. Ben tried to fall asleep in the back seat of the Barracuda, but he couldn't. After about an hour, he climbed into the driver's seat. He was still seeing double, and the coke had long since worn off, but he figured he had one other option. From where he was sitting, his double vision caused him to see two of Erin's Mercedes. Going to his place was off the table. Going to his parents' house was too far even for him to risk in his state. But Maria had told him over Rainiers at Linda's that she lived at the Gayle.

Ben knew where it was because he'd been there before. His brother's best friend Jack had lived there for a while. It was a year or two after Mike died. Ben had caught the bus to Seattle to go skate up on Capitol Hill. He was by himself. He used to skate all day long on Saturdays and Sundays by himself. That morning, he couldn't sleep. He tried to sleep in, but by ten o'clock he'd given up and rolled out of bed. He ate some raisin bran, packed a peanut butter and jelly sandwich into his backpack, and headed out to catch the bus to downtown Seattle.

"That major-label Jawbreaker record had just come out. The one that Maria was listening to that day in the parking garage. So that was like nineteen ninety-five, then? Yeah, something like that, because I was fourteen. I was listening to it when I was walking by the WaMu bank branch there. All the cool kids who were older than me hated it. 'They sold out' is all I heard that whole summer. Fuck those cool kids anyway. Yeah,

Jawbreaker fuckin' sold out. Who cares. That record was great. It's like you can only be punk if you wash dishes in some greasy spoon during the day and then entertain the scene's elite by playing music for them at night. Because God forbid anyone is ever able to support themselves by doing the very thing that everyone loves them for. Anyway, I saw Jack working at the Vivace on Broadway."

Jack was getting off work, or maybe he just took off after his break or perhaps even spontaneously quit, Ben wasn't quite sure. What Ben was quite sure about was that when he got up to take a piss at Jack's apartment at the Gayle, Jack swiped the Walkman with that Jawbreaker *Dear You* cassette in it out of Ben's backpack. "Jack was like, 'Hey, man, I got to go meet someone. Tell your parents I said hey.'" Ben didn't really care. To be honest, Ben was surprised Jack didn't fully rob him. Based on the place where Mike had been living when he died, Ben had expected Jack to bring him to a similar crack den. He hadn't, though. The building was actually nice. He could tell that Jack was in pretty bad shape. Ben couldn't figure out how Jack had managed to rent the place at all.

Ben never saw Jack after that. He wanted to believe that Jack was alive, but the fact that he never saw him around made Ben think otherwise. The fact that nobody had ever called to let him know where Jack's funeral would be, gave Ben some hope that Jack was alive. As far as the Walkman goes, "People got to do what they got to do to get by. I didn't really give a shit about the Walkman. I hope he sold it for a fix or whatever he needed that day. I was pretty sore about the Jawbreaker cassette, but I got a new copy a couple of months later. Hey, Jack, if you've still got that cassette, go ahead and keep it. If you're still kicking around the planet somewhere, give me a call."

The Gayle was the destination. It was only a few blocks away, and Maria lived there. Ben closed his left eye to make the double vision stop and put the Barracuda in reverse without looking behind him. He backed into three newspaper boxes, toppling them over and sending them skidding a few feet down the sidewalk. He got out to have a look. The *Seattle Times*, *Seattle Weekly*, and the *Stranger*. "Bastards." Ben stood there, inspecting the damage to his bumper. He took a *Stranger* and a *Seattle Weekly*. They were free. He tugged on the *Seattle Times* box, but it was locked. They charged for the *Seattle Times*, and the impact had not popped the little lock that kept the box closed. Ben took his newspapers, got in the Barracuda, closed his left eye, and roared off toward the Gayle.

Chapter 17

L uckily for Jack, the Gayle was only a short ride from his apartment building. Luckily for Jack, Maria's buzzer both worked and was clearly marked with her name. Luckily for Jack, Maria took in strays.

Jack hit the buzzer.

"What?" was her response.

"Is there any way I could sleep on your couch?"

"White boy?"

"Uh-huh."

"Seriously? Is she at your apartment too?"

"I mean . . ."

The telltale click-clack of the secure door unlocking interrupted what was sure to be haphazardly prepared response by Ben. The speaker popped back on.

"Number 102. Don't try no BS up in here. You sleep on the couch, that's it."

"For sure." The fact that he was talking into the speaker now without hitting the call button didn't occur to him until it did.

"Oh, yeah, the fuckin' button thing . . . so I'm just talking to dead air. And now I'm doing it even more. And now I'm just one of those people who roam around Capitol Hill and talk to themselves. Okay, now I'm going to stop talking out loud and go back to just thinking shit instead of saying it."

The click-clack of the door stopped, but Ben had been too involved with his one-sided conversation with himself to grab the door handle and open it. He hit the call button again.

"So, like, I just didn't get the thing in time or whatever."

Maria's voice, distorted by the cheap little door speaker, replied.

"Oh my God, you really are just a helpless little man-baby, aren't you."

"I mean . . ."

"That wasn't a question. You better get the door this time, or you're sleeping in your car, buddy."

Click-clack, click-clack, then the door the buzzer sounded.

"I got you now, fucker."

Ben talking out loud to no one again. That time he did get the door open before the click-clack and buzzing stopped. He was very proud of himself, too proud considering what a simple task pulling on a door was.

Ben began walking through the lobby, where those wall-mounted little mailboxes were. All at once he realized that he had no idea which apartment he was supposed to be going to. It had been easy to locate on the speaker box because her name was next to the call button. He couldn't remember if the call buttons had apartment numbers next to the names, but he didn't want to go back to the secure door. He had a genuine fear that if he went back and held the door open while getting a look at the call box, he'd be locked out and really have to sleep in his car. His next best idea was to try to peek through the door's windowpane and read the apartment numbers off the call box without actually opening the door. "Did she say what apartment she lived in? I'm so fucked up that I honestly don't remember."

After that night, and for the rest of the time Maria lived in that building, Ben never trusted that secure door. He never once walked up to it without his heart skipping a beat, and he never heard it slam behind him without him believing it had just locked him out on the front stoop in the cold. The door had traumatized him into future obedience the way a child is conditioned not to touch a hot stove.

That night, Ben's bewilderment continued for two or three minutes. It was late enough that he would feel bad just knocking on random people's doors, but he was beginning to think that was the only way he'd ever determine which unit Maria lived in. He didn't even know if she was on the first floor or some higher floor. He had walked all the way down the first-floor hall, past each and every anonymous apartment door. The only door left was adorned with one of those bright green exit signs above it. Ben didn't know which door to knock on, but he was pretty sure that the exit door wasn't the way to go.

Nevertheless, he stood and looked at that exit door for another thirty or forty seconds. It was a good focal point in what had become a sea of uncertainty. He didn't want to go out the exit door, but he knew he could. Unlike the anonymous apartment doors, the exit door was one he could open and go through without knocking. He wouldn't have to wake anybody up to go through it. He even found himself speculating that there might be a cozy little stairway on the other side where he could sleep. Turning around to face the secure front door again seemed unthinkable. That hallway was a gauntlet of club-wielding anonymous apartment doors, but the secure front door was the terrifying brick both at the head and at the end of that gauntlet.

For a few seconds, Ben considered just staying where he was. Standing there, his nose no more than three inches from the hundred-year-old lead paint on that exit door, wasn't scary at all. It made sense. If he never moved, he'd never have to be scared of Maria's apartment building. If Ben's knees hadn't hurt so badly, he could have stayed like that for an hour or two. But they did, and he couldn't.

So he turned around. Up until that moment, all the things that had scared him that evening—Erin's Terminator-like persistence and Maria's apartment building—all of a sudden became less scary. Now it was the thing at the end of the hall that was the scariest of all. Maria Deloera, ready for bed in an oversized T-shirt, was terrifying because she made him feel an emotion that he never allowed himself to indulge in: desire.

Chapter 18

Maria stood in her hallway, annoyed. This guy, she thought, needed me to rescue him from having to see his girlfriend, some defense attorney, no less. Then he comes here and asks me if he can stay over. Now he's just staring blankly at the door to the back stairway. She wanted to yell "Oi, dipshit, what the fuck are you doing?" Instead, she just watched him, wondering how long he was going to stare like that. After a minute, she was so fascinated by what was happening, she wasn't even annoyed anymore.

He was just standing there, motionless. She thought he looked like a robot that someone had switched off and pushed into a corner. Maria didn't know if he was lost or was just trying to decide if he should leave. Either was fine with her. She thought he was cute, but nothing was going to happen. Nothing. If he was there because he thought something was going to happen, he really should just go. Seriously, she thought, if she'd wanted something to happen, she would have put on something better than her ex-boyfriend's stretched-out Black Flag T-shirt. She continued to watch him, and then he suddenly turned around. He stood there staring for a few beats before he spoke.

"Oh, your place is back that way."

"Yeah. It's the first apartment on the right when you walk through the front door, number 102. You didn't see the unit number on the call box? And I told you which apartment."

"I was scared of the click-clack and buzzing, so I didn't go back over there."

"What? Did you go back to Linda's and buy acid from that guy who hangs out in the corner booth?"

"Um, I don't know what we're talking about any more."

"Me either. Do you want to sleep?"

"Yeah."

"Come on."

Maria's couch was comfy. She brought out a fuzzy blanket and squishy pillow. The pillow was too squishy, and Ben put his head down on one of the firmer couch pillows instead. The squishy pillow seemed like the sort of pillow a girl might put between her legs when she was sleeping. After Maria went into the bathroom, Ben immediately buried his face in it to see if he could catch a whiff of her pussy on it. When she came out of the bathroom, she gave him a cheap toothbrush still in its packaging. "Don't use my toothbrush! Use this."

Ben took the new toothbrush into Maria's bathroom. He unwrapped it, put some toothpaste on it, and ran it under the faucet. He didn't feel like brushing his teeth, but he did suck on Maria's toothbrush while he was pissing. He wanted to see how her mouth tasted. When he first entered the bathroom, he looked for a hamper. He was actually glad he didn't find one because he would have started playing with her dirty underwear immediately. There was no lock on her bathroom, and he imagined that her walking in while he had four or five of her thongs laid out on the bath mat could get weird.

When he came out of the bathroom, Maria was already in

bed. Her bedroom light was out, and she told him to turn out the living room light and go to sleep. So that's what he did.

Chapter 19

Ben didn't sleep through the night. Nobody sleeps through the night. At least, Ben had never known anyone who slept through the night. Ben woke up every couple of hours. He never really had to pee, but since he was awake, he always got up and went anyway. When he woke up, his throat was always dry, so he'd get a drink from the bathroom faucet. He heard Maria get up once and use the bathroom too. Then she went right back to her bedroom and was quiet again. He was up around seven, the third time since he'd fallen asleep. Daylight was just starting to creep into the apartment, but just a little. After all, this was still Seattle, and even plain old morning daylight is mostly cloaked by an unending blanket of clouds. He was definitely a little hung over, so he dozed off again.

He woke up again around nine. Maria was up. The stretched-out T-shirt and bare legs had been replaced by a black spaghetti-strap top and faded Levis. She had on some sort of designer black boots, the kind with wedged heels.

"You awake, white boy? You want to get some coffee?"

"Yeah, all right."

"Where you going today? What did you say yesterday, your parents' house?

"Yeah, my parents' place in Tacoma. You?"

"The original plan was to leave last night after work and drive home to Yakima, but Snoqualmie Pass was pretty bad last night. I thought it might be a little better this morning, but it still looks pretty snowed in from the weather reports."

"What else goes out there? White Pass?"

"Oh, you'd like it if I had to take White Pass, wouldn't you, white boy. How come it's White Pass anyway? Why can't it be Brown Pass, or better yet Latina Pass? There are certainly enough of us on the other side of the mountains to warrant naming a couple of things after us."

This was exactly the sort of question Ben was uncomfortable answering. After all, despite being born in Seattle, he was acutely aware that he was essentially squatting on ill-gotten land. Naming the city after the chief of the Duwamish and Suquamish always seemed more like a slap in the face to Native Americans from his ancestors than an accolade. He started to speak what would certainly be a jumbled mess of a response, but all that came out was "Um."

Maria was just fucking with him, and when she saw Ben trying to formulate a politically correct response in his culturally ignorant little brain, she stepped in and saved him from saying something stupid.

"But no, seriously, White Pass isn't any better. Even if they say it's passable with chains, that just means that you're going to be stuck in the middle of the pass in a five-mile-long line of cars sitting in one place for seven or eight hours. I actually spent a whole Christmas day sitting in my car on White Pass a couple of years ago. The risk of getting stuck in the mountains in your car just isn't worth it."

"Come to Tacoma with me."

"Thanksgiving with the white boy's family?"

"You're from eastern Washington. You can watch the Apple Cup with my dad."

"Hey, smart guy, the Apple Cup is next Saturday, not today."

"Whatever. What the fuck do I know about football? I fuckin' hate football. But my dad loves it. There're always football games on when I go down there on Thanksgiving. So watch some other game with him."

"And what do you do while the football game is on?'

"I just hang around in the kitchen and do shots of Jameson with my mom. And I eat a bunch of the food while she's still getting it ready. Then I feel bad that nobody is helping her, so I volunteer to help, and then she kicks me out of the kitchen for eating all the stuffing while I'm fluffing it. You'll have a good time. I promise."

"Does your dad have any beer?"

"He's got a refrigerator full of Rainier, just like I do at my place."

"Calm down, white boy. We're not going to your place."

"Yeah, not today, but probably some other time."

"Sure we are," she said with obvious sarcasm. "All right, we're off to North Tacoma."

"Sorry, but we're going to South Tacoma."

"Ew, seriously? That's too bad. I've heard North Tacoma is nice. All right, let's go before I change my mind. We have to go get a latte at Vivace first."

"For sure."

Maria and Ben walked out to the Barracuda. Ben walked around back to see the damage the newspaper boxes had done to his bumper. He wasn't happy with what he saw, but he had braced himself for much worse. The Barracuda was old, so it had a chrome-steel bumper, not like newer cars, where the bumper is painted and effectively just part of the frame. The Barracuda's bumper was definitely tweaked from the newspaper box collision the night before, but it wasn't tragic. Ben figured nobody would even really notice it. Right then, Maria walked around the rear of the car on her way to the passenger side.

"Wow, what happened to your bumper? That's super fucked up. Too bad. It's a great car otherwise."

"Yeah. You know, I cannot stand those fuckheads at the *Seattle Times*, the *Stranger*, and *Seattle Weekly*.

"What?"

"Nothing. I just got a score to settle with those fuckers."

"All right. Let's get some coffee, seriously."

Tacoma's city flag should be a graffitied Abrams tank shooting an Olde English 800 forty-ounce bottle at an old brick factory's smokestack. In reality, the actual Tacoma flag was warm and a little disarming. Maybe that was the point: to charmingly disarm people casually passing through the city so that the locals can shanghai and rob them.

South Tacoma was the most Tacoma part of Tacoma. It was the crossroads of the city. In equal parts, the violent gang war of the eastside spilled into a south end that was still partially engulfed by the remnants of the Hilltop neighborhood's 1980s crack epidemic and abutted a west end that fancied itself too fancy for the rest of Tacoma. The only parts of the city that South Tacoma didn't touch was North Tacoma and Northeast Tacoma. North Tacoma was where the bourgie fuckers were, so fuck them anyway. Northeast Tacoma was all the way on the other side of the tide flats. So seriously, that isn't even really Tacoma at all. It was sort of how West Seattle wasn't really

Seattle, just that place on the other side of the port.

Driving through South Tacoma, Pacific Avenue divided the Puyallup reservation and the Latino part of town on the east from the Korean part of town on the west. As you continued south, various Korean neighborhoods faded into various Black neighborhoods and eventually became poor white neighborhoods. Those poor neighborhoods near the south corner, the places where GIs from JBLM who didn't want to live on base or in Lakewood settled, that was where Ben called home.

By noon it was raining. It was always raining, especially between October and May. "Jack and Mike always called those months the dark wet." By Thanksgiving 2010, the dark wet was in full swing.

The Northwest was generally gray and wet most of the year in most places. Tacoma, and more specifically South Tacoma, was grayer and wetter than everywhere else in the Northwest, at least it seemed so to Ben. "It was accurate to say a dark cloud hung over the Pacific Northwest, and an even darker cloud hung over my house."

Maria and Ben pulled up to Ben's parents' house, which was painted gray. The loose pebbles that peeled off the city's cheap gravel-over-tar street were gray. The neighbor's chain-link fence was gray. Even the grass in front of his parents' house appeared to be gray. Big Ben, Ben's mom Barbara, and his little sister Lisa came out to the front porch when they heard Ben's car pull up. Ben wondered if his family was ill, because they all looked somehow gray. Ben's eyes drifted from his family, across the lawn, and to the dirt where a sidewalk should be. Apparently, the city had determined that this street didn't warrant a luxury accommodation like a sidewalk, but if it had, that sidewalk would have been gray.

Even after several years, Maria still wasn't completely accustomed to western Washington. East of the mountains, there was life: flowers and orchards and fields of grass alive with vibrant colors.

She said, "Am I wearing monochrome glasses? How come there are no flowers here? You know all those depressing muted filters you can use on photos now? I'm beginning to think western Washington is where those came from. Every day around here just seems like a slight variation on some drab gray photo filter. Light gray is November. Gray is December. Dark gray is January. Darker gray is February, brownish gray is March. Et cetera. Et cetera. Et cetera."

"What about the spring and summer months?"

"What did I just say white boy? Et cetera. Et cetera. Et cetera. I'm surprised you aren't gray, but then again, your tone of white could be a washed-out gray. It really never is the right color around here. I never really put my finger on it until we turned down this street."

Maria stepped out of the Barracuda and somehow immediately splashed her own vibrant color all over the canvas of that Thanksgiving. Ben was only half joking about Maria watching football with Big Ben, but she really did sit in the living room for two hours watching football with him. The two of them drank so many Rainiers that Ben had to go down to the ampm to get another half rack. The ampm was right down the road, but driving there was still pretty sketchy, since he'd been pounding shots of Jameson with his little sister and mom in the kitchen.

After dinner, Big Ben took Ben and Maria to the garage to show them the 1968 Mustang Fastback he was restoring. The 390-ci V8 was sitting on a work bench next to the cherry picker Big Ben had used to hoist it out of the engine compartment. The freshly rebuilt motor had the chrome Edelbrock valve covers and air cleaner. There were new five-spoke Crager rims and BFGoodrich radials. There was sanded Bondo where Big Ben had done his own bodywork and gray primer all over the body of that Mustang.

Big Ben said, "The motor's ready to go back in. I can't do the paint job myself, but I got a buddy at Sauro's Body Shop who is going to do a high-end black with white racing stripes. How's the Barracuda holding up?"

"Pretty good. I tweaked the bumper a little the other day."

"Pull it around to the garage. If it's just a little bent, I can pop that back into shape."

Maria went back into the house. It was almost time for pumpkin pie, and Ben's mom roped Maria into doing a couple more shots of Jameson with her.

It had been at least six months since Ben had been home. Lisa was already sixteen. It seemed like every time he saw her, she was a different person. Not really a different person, but people change so much at that age, if you don't see them every day it seems like they've morphed into an adult overnight. She looked like an adult woman—a young woman, but still mostly like an adult. People that age often look like adults, but a brief conversation is all that's needed to uncover that you are indeed speaking to a child. It even happened at work. The Rule 9 interns were actually adults, but they were mostly still in their early twenties. Ben was turning twenty-nine in a couple of weeks, and it always blew him away at how different a person he already was from these interns, who were only a few years younger than he was. Lisa was old enough to drive. Soon she'd be old enough to go to college and buy beer.

At sixteen, she was apparently old enough to get stoned,

because she grabbed Ben and Maria and took them out to the side of the house and got them baked. The age of strong weed was upon Washington State. In not much more than a year, it would be legal. The potency of what Lisa had was nothing like anything Ben had smoked before. Afterward, Ben went up to his old room and fell asleep for an hour while Barbara, Lisa, and Big Ben entertained Maria. Fortunately, or unfortunately for her, the way Ben's family entertained typically involved more shots of Jameson. Since it was Thanksgiving, everyone also ate more pumpkin pie and ice cream.

Ben could have slept another hour or two, but he woke up to the sound of retching coming from the upstairs bathroom next to Ben's and Lisa's bedrooms. When he knocked, he was surprised to hear Maria respond.

"I'm okay. I'll be out in a minute."

She thought it was Lisa or Barbara checking on her.

"It's Ben. Are you really okay?"

Maria opened the bathroom door. She was sitting on the floor.

"Your family is out of control."

"Outta control, no way. They're fuckin' boiler plate for around here, garden variety white trash."

"They sure know how to entertain company."

"I said you'd have fun, didn't I?"

"Yep, good time."

Maria put her hand out.

"Help me up. These jeans are too tight now. I ate too much."

"Ate?"

"Ate too much, drank too much, smoked too much. Where did your sister get that weed?"

Ben pulled Maria up to her feet. They were face to face, only an inch or two apart.

"What happens now?" Maria said.

"Behind you. That green toothbrush, it's mine. You can use it."

"Ha ha, because of last night."

"Yeah, that, but seriously, you should brush your teeth."

"Yeah, I'm going to do that right now."

Oddly enough, nothing was embarrassing or weird for either of them. Maria just spun around, turned on the faucet, puked a bit in the sink, and picked up Ben's toothbrush. She started brushing with the sort of vigor you'd expect from someone with a mouthful of regurgitated whiskey and pumpkin pie. Ben let her finish before he reminded her that the toothpaste was in the medicine cabinet. Maria smacked herself on the forehead with her open palm like she was some sort of slapstick vaudeville drunkard. Then she brushed for real.

They walked downstairs together. Ben had his arm around her shoulder, more to steady Maria than anything, but his family took this as an overt show of mutual affection. Ben had never said he was with Maria. Maria had never said they were a couple. But neither of them had ever said they weren't together.

Barbara was pretty sloshed herself. She started gushing, "You two are so goddamn adorable. Let me get a picture. Hang on, hang on, hang on."

It took Barbara at least five minutes to find her camera in the hall closet. It took five more for her to figure out if there was film in it. She ultimately got her picture, but she was so wasted that she snapped it crooked and off-center. To this day, that trainwreck of a photo resides in one of Barbara's family photo albums.

Ben loaded Maria into the passenger side of the Barracuda like a sack of groceries. Ben never wore a seat belt, but he strapped Maria into hers just the same. He yanked the shoulder harness extra tight on her. It was still raining, but it was just that late evening sprinkling that happened every night around bedtime, not the ice-cold darts of marble-sized water that fell before dinnertime. All in all, the drive back to Seattle was uneventful. Maria was out cold in the passenger's seat by the time they crossed into King County. She stayed that way until Ben pulled up to the Gayle to drop her off.

He nudged her.

"You're home."

The way she'd passed out, she was lurched forward but being held up by the extra-snug seat belt. It was, in a word, hilarious.

"Maria, you gotta get up. We're at your place."

Nothing.

He turned on that Jawbreaker CD, the major label one.

Nothing.

He turned it up louder, and Maria gasped herself awake.

"You're home."

She looked at him. She didn't say anything. For a minute, Ben wondered if she was just too wasted to talk. She had that blank stare that intoxicated people get.

He didn't say anything.

Then she leaned in, either because she was falling toward him or because she was trying to kiss him. He couldn't tell which. Either way, Ben had snugged the seat belt up so much when he loaded her into the car that she was effectively pinned to the back of the seat.

The Barracuda had leather bucket seats, so Ben couldn't scoot over to the passenger's side where Maria was sitting.

Instead, he clicked the button on the seat-belt harness, causing her to fall across the center console and into him. He pulled her in closer and reached out with his left hand and put it on her right thigh.

"Aren't you going out with Erin O'Connell?"

"Sort of. Maybe. Does it matter?"

Ben kissed her.

"Did you really pee on Tim's shoes?"

"Does that seem like something that I, a respectable licensed attorney, a prosecutor for the city of Seattle would do?"

Lawyers always answer questions with questions.

"So that's a yes?"

It had been bugging Ben since his first day at the city attorney's office. He knew he'd seen Maria before.

"Didn't you used to be in a hardcore band?"

"Does being in a hardcore band seem like something that I, a respectable licensed attorney, a prosecutor for the city of Seattle would do?"

She kissed him and then abruptly stopped. Maria got out of the Barracuda and started toward her building's stoop. Ben pushed in the clutch, ready to put the Barracuda into first gear. Maria turned around, bent over, and leaned into the Barracuda through the rolled-down passenger-side window.

"You coming in or what?"

II

Part Two

Book Two
The Land of Lollipops and Suckers

Chapter 20

"Hey babe, do you remember the figure skater named Tonya Harding?"

Erin always cocked her head and raised her right eyebrow when she asked questions, no intonation or inflexion change in her voice whatsoever. It annoyed Ben, and in his humble opinion, was one of the many reasons Erin O'Connell was a terrible trial lawyer. Erin never connected with normal humans. She was more like an artificial intelligence algorithm packed into one of those mechanical animals at Chuck E. Cheese.

"Someday, someone is going to make a great game about some creepy animatronic mascots like those things at Chuck E. Cheese."

She cocked her head and raised the eyebrow. Again. "What are you talking about, babe?"

Ben was speaking out loud again, instead of thinking quietly to himself. "Never-fuckin'-mind already," he said, this time, speaking out loud on purpose, and louder than necessary.

Erin was tone deaf, which was another reason she was a terrible trial lawyer. Since she didn't connect with normal humans, it made sense that she never even realized she was tone deaf. You can't fix a problem you don't know exists. Not that humans could fix anything anyway. Humans rearrange problems. Sometimes, we decorate them in interesting ways, but humans are stubborn and limited organisms. People don't change, and people don't fix problems.

"Sometimes, we manage to unload a problem on someone else—a neighbor or coworker, perhaps—but what exists can never be destroyed. It can only change form. Erin was the current incarnation of every problem I had with the world. She represented class divide and conceit. Her existence brought out that chip on my shoulder that was the size of the Space Needle."

Ben had been rearranging and unloading that problem his whole life, but no matter how many times he dumped it off on some other dipshit, someone else would put it right back on his doorstep. Sure, it was in a different form, but it was the same old problem. At least, its current incarnation came in a pretty blond package.

Day after day, he found himself stuck in this perpetual rut of a relationship with Erin, and he wondered why he didn't just call it off for real. The answer turned out to be pretty simple. The next version of this particular problem would certainly be more unbearable than Erin, so he might as well hold on to this version of it. The next version could be a predatory landlord, another lawyer, or some asshole in a Porche. It was always just a dice role to see what version of purgatory you'd be stuck in for the next little while, and he wasn't anxious to see what sort of roll came next. Ben was a pragmatic thinker, and the proverbial professional poker player, not a degenerate compulsive gambler shooting Craps. He never doubled down on stupid, so he just sat on the pretty, but mediocre, version he had, rather than potentially ending up with something worse.

"Do you remember that skater?"

Ben knew who Tonya Harding was. Everybody in the PNW knew Tonya Harding. Everyone who grew up here anyway. She was a PNW folk hero. When Ben was little, everyone in the world knew who Tonya Harding was. Ben actually saw her a few years ago at this dive bar out in Puyallup. She was shooting pool with a lit Camel hanging out of her mouth. After she sank the Eight Ball, she walked up to the bar and got a pitcher of Rainier. Ben recognized her immediately. He started wondering if hooking up with Tonya Harding was a realistic possibility.

"Hey Tonya, what's goin' on!"

"Nothin' loser," was her response.

Then she walked back to the pool table to shoot another game with her friend.

"Yeah, I know who she is. So what?"

"Well, that skater she beat up, my parents had dinner with her parents a little while ago. My mom said Tonya Harding was from where you're from."

"What the fuck is that supposed to mean? Does you mom think Tonya is from Tacoma, or the white trash gutter?"

"My mom isn't like that. She voted for Obama."

Erin's mom may have voted for Obama, but her dad was currently heavily involved with an emerging conspiracy theory the crux of which was that Barack Obama wasn't born in the United States, and therefore, not the legitimate president. Her mom's white guilt did very little to wash clean her own family's legacy, much less the neo-racist pontifications of Erin's three-hundred-year-old-father.

"Tonya didn't beat up that stupid bitch. I wish she had. And Tonya isn't from Tacoma; she's from Portland, if that's what your mom meant. But I guess, to your uptight twat of a mother, everybody out here is just some forest-dwelling simpleton from the provincial edge of the world. I'm sure, in her little pea-sized brain, everything from Vancouver BC to Eugene Oregon is the same place."

"I'm just making conversation. You don't have to get all territorial."

"Yeah, I fuckin' do. Someday, someone is going to make a movie, or TV show, or something vindicating poor Tonya."

Tonya is the old PNW, straight out of that aforementioned white-trash gutter. She met her husband at a karaoke bar. She builds decks and does landscaping for a living. She has a criminal record. The PNW was entering its third decade of people like Erin trying to give it a Nancy Kerrigan makeover. Unfortunately for them, the weatherbeaten face of what was underneath kept peeking through.

Ben recognized all those same themes back when the Tonya thing was going down. He was a little kid, but he recognized that stuck-up, nose-in-the-air Nancy Kerrigan the second he saw her on the TV. The way she walked, like she had a stick up her ass that stunk of old money. Those judges— stodgy, repressed, proper. They exuded the same repressed New England holier-than-thou attitude that Nancy did. She even skated like she had a stick up her ass. Ben was no figure skating fan, but he was a skateboarder, and he could tell Tonya skated differently. And there it is again, provincial clashing with high society, poor with rich, blue collar with white, and so on and so forth, ad nauseum.

Ben's current Nancy Kerrigan was lording over him as he was sitting on her couch, head cocked and eyebrow raised, once again, with her best and only imitation of a human being. She was talking about something, but Ben was too lost in thought to notice. That's not true; he wasn't thinking about anything, but his brain had a defense mechanism. Whenever Erin began speaking, Ben's mind took him to the forest, to the Northern Cascades. When he went there, he ran with his spirit animal, a Timberwolf whose fur was raggedy and matted. His wolf had a busted fang and scars of claw marks running up the right side of his abdomen. He panted, tired from the hunt. He could see his breath in the cold wet air as he and his pack of wolves bore down on an exhausted elk. Erin's voice was the trigger that flipped him into wolf mode. He learned this in a guided meditation class Erin made him go to. The irony of Erin being the architect of Ben's ultimate mental escape from her was not lost on him.

Then, it all faded away. The mountain and the forest gave way to the obnoxiously-decorated environs of Erin's front room. When he saw the telltale head cock and raised eyebrow, he realized she must be asking him something.

"So, do you want to go to Red Cow for dinner babe?"

Red Cow sounds like a great place to get a rare steak. It's not. It's this pretentious little French burger place on 34th Avenue. The food is good, but the prices are insane. At Red Cow, Ben could get one good burger for like fifty bucks. For the same price at Dick's on Broadway, he could get twenty great burgers, a bunch of greasy fries, and a killer milkshake. At the Frisco Freeze on Division Avenue in Tacoma, he could get all of that, but better and greasier. Red Cow is the place where people like Erin go when they want to pretend to slum it. Either way, Ben didn't want to go up to 34th Avenue where all those dickheads were always hanging around.

"Hey, I actually have plans to go see this hardcore band with my friend."

Erin said something, but he purposely didn't listen. Whatever it was, he'd likely heard it before. She was definitely upset, and she had good reason. Ben was ditching her on a Friday, with no notice. He felt bad for a minute, until he remembered Nancy Kerrigan. Ben couldn't take an evening with his Nancy Kerrigan. He hopped in his Barracuda and roared off to go see his Tonya Harding.

Chapter 21

Ben pulled up in front of Maria's apartment. He wasn't totally lying when he told Erin he had plans to see a hardcore band with his friend. Maria was his friend, and she had been the singer of a hardcore band, and they did have plans that night. Not that Ben needed justification to lie to Erin. It was just a convenient coincidence that his cover story was almost plausible truth. Half-truths and logical inferences framed as actual facts combined to create more believable lies. It was hard to fabricate a convincing story from the ground up. It was easier to work on a lie from within an existing structure of likely, if not completely accurate, existing facts.

People, most people anyway, need to feel that they're being consistent with actions that reflect the way they view themselves in the world. The way someone views themselves is also the way they want others to see them. When a person's actions fall short of the idealized version of themselves, it causes cognitive dissonance, and of course, makes the person a bit of a hypocrite. Ben suffered no such dissonance. He'd never held himself out as chaste or even faithful, so fucking around behind Erin's back was consistent with how he presented himself to the world. As for lying to her? He lied to everyone when it suited his purposes. Again, he never held himself out as a paragon of truth, so lying was consistent with how he presented himself to the world.

"Of course, I do. Lying is a tool, and its practicality cannot be challenged. If someone accuses me of being a liar, I simply shrug and say, 'So fuckin' what?' I use what works, and most of the time, lying works. When it doesn't, abusive honesty typically does the trick. I'm no hypocrite, and I'm no angel, but I can be a nasty piece of work when it suites me to be. I'm a pragmatist, and I suffer no dissonance because I don't hold myself out to the world as something other than that.

In any case, Maria and Ben's plans never amounted to much more than ordering Thai food, complaining about work, and the inevitable hookup.

They'd been doing this for nearly a year. Not that it would have made any difference to Ben, but he didn't consider what he was doing cheating anyway. Erin treated him like a boyfriend. She routinely attempted to introduce all the conventional trappings of a relationship into their situation. She told people Ben was her boyfriend, but Ben never agreed to be her boyfriend. Erin had created an alternate reality for them, or at the very least, for herself—one where she and Ben were in a relationship and lived together in her new house in Madrona. The reality was, Ben rarely ever went to that house. He mostly stayed in his same old apartment up the road from Maria's place, and he routinely told Erin that he didn't consider what they were doing to be a relationship.

Erin believed she could just act as though it was what she wanted it to be, and it would eventually be that thing. Ben resented her for that, but he also realized she was just acting out the scenario in a way that was consistent with who she was and what she was about. For Erin, it made all the sense in the world that she could just continue to press her own agenda, and eventually, it would carry the day. Her family, her schools, and her community growing up had conditioned her to believe she could get anything she wanted if she just continued to dominate a situation.

It genuinely confused her that people in the west didn't acquiesce to their betters. It didn't make her a terrible person. She just didn't know any better. She borrowed nearly a million dollars from her parents to buy "just the cutest little craftsman fixer upper" in Madrona.

There's a dividing line in the Madrona neighborhood. It's 34th Avenue. In times past, everything above 34th was rich folks. Everything below, and right down to MLK Way, was middle or working class. MLK was where the Central District started. Erin hated that she had to drive through the Central District to get downtown. It wasn't that she was overtly racist. In fact, the inherent racism present in her was a point of great tumult within herself. The Central District, which was largely black, seemed scummy to her. There were rundown corner stores, overgrown landscaping, and busted pavement everywhere. The fact that she took issue with this state of disrepair and simultaneously recognized that it was one aspect of generations of systemic racism bothered her. To her, recognizing rundown houses as part and parcel of systemic racism, meant she had to concede some level of prejudice in herself because of his dislike of those very rundown houses. That caused this uncomfortable level of dissonance, the same sort of dissonance Ben didn't seem to suffer from.

She could have borrowed more. She could have gotten her parents to loan her enough to buy one of those big houses on the other side of the hill with a lake view. To her, buying in the part of the neighborhood that was in transition, and Central District adjacent, reinforced the story she liked to tell herself—she was a crusader of the accused and disenfranchised, never a little rich girl who was terrified of her neighbors.

To her, that craftsman was a starter house, but to the people she displaced, it was their entire world and had been for decades. Not that Erin would ever know it, but the prior owners were a black family with three school-age children. The father had lost his job at Boeing in a recent mass layoff. The father had inherited the house from his father. A developer offered him some money, a cash offer for the house. It was much less than the market value, but enough to persuade the guy to sell. That family moved to Kent, an affordable suburb. The dad works at an auto parts store up the road in Auburn now.

But to Erin, it was a starter house, a fixer upper, even though the developer had flipped the house. Cosmetically, everything was new, but it wasn't the age of the fixtures that bothered Erin. It was the quality, which is to say, the price and perceived pretentiousness of the fixtures were not up to her standards. Anything that didn't look neo-retro like the young professionals' wet dreams on HGTV had to go. She spent another couple hundred thousand gutting that newly-flipped craftsman of hers. The result was possibly the ugliest thing Ben had ever seen, and not just the ugliest house, but the actual ugliest thing ever. The sad part for Erin was that when her parents finally came to town to visit, they still checked in at the Fairmont Olympic. To her parents, the thought of staying in such pedestrian environs, made their blue blood run cold. Colder than it already was, and that's pretty cold.

Over those many months, Ben had thought a lot about that dividing line between the Central District and Madrona. He tried not to go to Erin's place at all. But after a while, he realized if he went over there once or twice a week, she spent less time at his apartment. Keeping her out of his space was important to him, so he did what was necessary to make it happen. While that monstrosity of a house she had was wholly uninteresting to him, the neighborhood itself was very interesting.

Not two blocks away from Erin's house, on Union and MLK, was a discount grocery store, Grocery Outlet. Ben knew it was there, knew what it was. He'd been in there a few times, but since he didn't live right near it, he'd never given the place much thought. Now he did. It was a little blue-collar outpost in the middle of what had become more and more hostile territory every day. The Central District was working class, and it would more or less stay that way for a few more years. The dividing line in Madrona was eroding quickly. Gentrification was in full swing for the blocks between 34th and MLK.

Ben would walk down Erin's street and see a brand-new BMW in front of a flipped HGTV wannabe house, and then see a thirty-year-old Oldsmobile station wagon that looked like someone lived in it parked right behind it. On one corner, you'd see one of those brand-new, boxy townhouses that looked like it just erupted like a new shiny, white, adult tooth into the filthy mouth of the neighborhood. Right next to it, you'd see an eroded and pockmarked little A-frame house decaying just like a rotten tooth ready to be yanked out of that same mouth.

Ben would walk over to the Grocery Outlet just to get out of Erin's house for a little while. Also, he liked to see what they had that day. Grocery Outlet was like a flea market for food. They must have had some deal to buy all the stuff that was about to expire, because everything was half the price of everywhere else, but it all was within a week or two of its expiration date.

It wasn't just that it was cheap; it was also that you never knew what you were going to find. Some days, you'd walk in there and you could get a whole case of Cliff Bars for two dollars, a bucket of ice cream for two dollars, or three pounds of steak for, well, like two dollars. Two dollars was a pretty common thing there.

At this crossroads, this blurred border between blue collar and blue blood, a polite and quiet handoff was taking place. The reverse of the white flight of decades past. Urban renewal in Seattle, gentrification. Ben fucking Erin had always been him essentially sleeping with the enemy. Ben hated hypocrisy and valued being genuine. Erin was Ben's dissonance, hypocrisy, and shame. Ben had to admit to himself, and also to the world, that he was playing a part in this process. Little by little, he was becoming the beneficiary of the rich, white welfare of that place. Down at the Grocery Outlet, he saw as many shiny Audis and BMWs as he did beat-down Toyotas and Hondas.

He didn't like what was happening, but at that same time, he was not the self-appointed spokesperson for the displaced persons of lower Madrona either. Unlike Erin, when Ben felt that uncomfortable sensation of dissonance, he always acknowledged the disconnect in values and self. He didn't like that he was helping displace people from one of the few neighborhoods in the city where they were historically allowed to live, but he knew progress was going to happen, one way or another. Accepting that discomfort, while taking note of the injustice in which he played a small part, allowed him to be a self-aware advocate in all his affairs, if not a crusader empowered to actually change anything. Understanding that your existence on this planet has negative repercussions on people, animals, and the planet itself is more than most people ever manage. Even when they do recognize their part in the wholesale injustice of existence, they mostly fill those untidy spaces in their minds with pretty, new mental furniture, just like they fill the untidy parts of their homes with pretty, new actual furniture. It was cognitive camouflage for feelings that are best left in the back of the proverbial mental closet.

Ben would have preferred for the issue to be clearer, black and white, unequivocal. It wasn't. It would have made more sense if it were just predatory, rich white people taking everything because they're evil. Erin had some cognizance of what she was doing. It was one of her redeeming qualities, but it was still only a surface-level understanding, and her willfully ignorant attitude toward contending with this discomfort made her a coward in Ben's mind. Whenever he saw a guy with a Rolex at the Grocery Outlet grabbing a case of Lara Bars, that guy was never the face of Imperial America. He was some software engineer, or a doctor, or some other white-collar stiff. It was always just some skinny geek who looked like his only exercise was clicking a mouse. He was no different than the suburban white kids listening to hip hop when Ben was growing up. It was just some guy who didn't know any better, down there slumming it like the locals, trying to fit in. None of that changed the fact that his ignorant cultural appropriation dissolved the underlying culture.

White guilt drives hapless white people to try to be the best white people they can be, and that interest routinely and ironically stoked the culturally corrosive sequence of events they thought they opposed. It's nothing new, the paradigm. The sensibilities have migrated, but the outcomes are always identical. Don't let white people get interested in your culture, your neighborhood, or your grocery store. Without even realizing it, they're going to love your culture, your neighborhood, and your grocery store right out of existence.

About a decade after that, in 2020, Ben was driving down 23rd Avenue at Union Street for the first time in many years. That corner had once been the center of a thriving, largely black neighborhood. On that day, he took note of the murals of black leaders at the corner, a corner that was comprised largely of brand-new condos with high-end commercial shops on the ground floors.

One of those little murals was painted on a metal electrical box, the kind that are built right into the sidewalk. Behind it was a PCC Community Market. It was one of those bougie-little co-op chains where they gave you the stink eye at checkout if you didn't have a membership. Everything at the PCC was twice the price it was at the QFC or Safeway, which meant it was quadruple what it was at the Grocery Outlet. Standing in front of the mural were two middle-aged, rich white ladies with masks over their faces, holding their reusable PCC shopping bags full of overpriced organic veggies, and staring at their iPhones.

He pulled out his own iPhone and laughed as he took a picture of this ludicrous scene. Clearly, victory in Central District for the invading army had been declared. You know it's over when they start painting pictures of you on your own block and naming places after displaced peoples. Ask Chief Seattle how he feels about the issue.

It was around the middle of September 2011, and Maria was eating a pint of Lopez Island Strawberry Ice Cream. At that point, Maria was his best friend. For the most part, she was his only friend. She was from a working-class family. She was an attorney and prosecutor, like Ben. And they both liked hardcore music and horror movies. It wasn't that Ben refused to leave Erin to be with Maria. It was just hard for him to do more than the bare minimum, and things were working fine at that time. It wasn't like Maria wanted that either. Maria had her own useless boyfriend, Frank. To be honest, she'd have already dumped Frank, but he was so pathetic that every time she decided to, she chickened out.

They were sitting on the couch, and Maria fed Ben some of her ice cream, then set it on the coffee table. She had on that old Black Flag t-shirt she'd taken from her ex-boyfriend and a black thong, nothing else. Ben wasn't wearing anything. She climbed onto his lap and straddled him.

"You ready for round two?"

They always went for round two. Ben only came over once or twice a week, so they always made the most of it.

"Hey, what's this on the TV?"

Maria's TV was on, and it had caught Ben's attention.

"I think it's Anderson Cooper," she said.

"No, I mean what's this story about?"

"Occupy Wall Street. There was some stuff on about it before you came over, too."

"What are they doing?"

"I think they're just camping out down there. They're mad about having to repay their student loans while the government bails out banks. Who the fuck isn't, right!"

"Yeah, but they just look like a bunch of dickheads from the suburbs. How can these fuckers be serious revolutionaries. Look at that guy; he's wearing a Land's End raincoat and hiking boots."

"I guess, dorks in Land's End coats are the type of people who get mad that the government bailed out all those banks and mortgages, but they still have to pay their student loans. People who turn wrenches, swing hammers, and pick fruit for a living don't have student loans."

"Well, nobody wants to pay their student loans back, but who can afford to just leave work and go camp out outside Wall Street for weeks on end?"

"You don't know? You practically live with one of them. Erin is who can do that. Rich kids. Duh!"

"Erin doesn't have any loans to pay off. Her parents are so rich, she's never even seen a loan application."

"So, they're not rich like Erin's family. Erin's family are the one percent."

"Yeah, but these fuckers aren't poor either. Nobody who is genuinely poor protests by camping out in a tent. That would be like starving yourself to illustrate to everyone how malnourished you are."

"They're like the top ten percent, but they're angry at the top once percent."

"And, I suppose that they want the support of genuinely poor people who are too poor to go to college and incur crippling student debt."

"Probably."

"So like, at some point, will we see a bunch of busboys and cashiers camping out to help these upper-middle class kids from having to pay back their loans?"

Maria looked up and off to the left, like a purposely tele-graphed gesture denoting her pondering an important question.

"So, do we love them or hate them?" he asked.

"Well, I hate paying my student loans. The interest rates are predatory, and the federal loan-servicing system is rigged to make sure that you never actually pay off the debt. I like the idea of not paying the loans. And it does seem like a lot of the government's money goes toward keeping rich white people on corporate welfare."

"Yeah, but are disgruntled upper-middle-class college graduates the next in line for a government handout? Or are they jumping the line, basically just asking for the same sort of corporate handout that the banks just got? The government already gave that money to the banks and mortgage people, and it's not coming back."

"So, what they want is a broader, but still pretty narrow funneling of money to themselves when there are loads of people hurting worse?"

"I think so."

"So, how do poor people factor into their platform?"

"I don't think they do, yet. But eventually, these things always create some sort of conflation that pulls in the support of people who will likely never benefit from the spoils of whatever is being protested. So at some point, you'll probably see people who actually live in tents and need money, living next to people who are choosing to live in tents and want more money."

"So, why do we care?"

"I don't think we do."

She realized she'd been grinding him the whole time. She was wet, and he was hard. They'd suddenly lost all interest in Occupy Wall Street, Anderson Cooper, and the TV. She didn't bother taking off her thong or t-shirt. He yanked her thong out of the way, and she slid down onto his cock.

Chapter 22

Ben used to hate Monday mornings. Everybody with a job hates Monday mornings, and they should. It just sounded so lame and cliché to complain about Monday morning. He was coming up on two years at the city attorney's office. That job was like a suit that looked nice on the rack, but never really fit right. It was frustrating, because you'd see it on the hanger in your closet and you'd just keep wearing it. It was a mirage. It looked so good from far away, but the reality of it was just another lung full of dry desert air and a mouth full of sand. Whenever you did put that suit on, the armholes in the jacket were too low. The seam up the butt crack of the pants constantly gave you a wedgie. The lapel notches always looked too low, too nineties. After a while, when you'd made your peace with it, you just let that suit sit in the closet forever. Since the job was just a goof, and since, on the long timeline of Ben's life, it would never be more than the ill-fitting suit of jobs, he started having fun with it.

There was an all-staff meeting that Monday morning in one of the big conference rooms upstairs. Ben never felt comfortable in those either—the staff meetings, that is. He felt very comfortable in the big conference rooms. That particular one was pretty quiet most of the time. It was in a dead hallway, on a seemingly dead floor. In fact, Ben wasn't even sure what that floor was for. It appeared more like a place to just store office junk, desks, old computers, busted chairs, whatever wasn't being utilized or was too old to be of any use to anyone.

Ben hated the staff meetings, but he loved that conference room. Sometimes, he'd go up there after lunch and sleep for an hour or two. Ben and Maria would go out to lunch about once or twice a week, and when they did, they usually went to Linda's Tavern. Ben would always get a Cowboy Burger. Maybe it was the fried egg on it, or the mountain of fries, but he was always groggy after lunch at Linda's with Maria. That, and they always drank a few pitchers of Rainier. Maria would always just do a couple bumps of coke out of the little brown vial in her car, but Ben hated using coke to get himself alert. He used to do it with meth, which was the time-honored tradition of all persons from Tacoma, but when possible, he preferred to just sleep it off.

It was after one such food and beer-induced quasi-food coma that Ben first discovered this conference room. In addition to the grogginess, the Cowboy Burger and belly full of Rainier at Linda's always induced a monster shit. That day, Ben had walked to the men's room by his office on the fifty-third floor three different times, and three different times had discovered someone already shitting there. It was a small restroom, and the only men's room on his floor. Ben wasn't a chatty shitter, or chatty pee'r for that matter, so the situation was wholly unacceptable. "The only thing worse than stewin' in someone else's stink was having to chat to them at the faucet a few minutes later.

In addition, Ben's office had historically been a nice cozy space to get an after-lunch nap. Until it wasn't. He had a very low-seated easy chair in the corner, facing away from his office door. If he closed the door, people couldn't even see him in the office through the door window. It was perfect. Back then, Bobby, this new prosecutor, had just been put in the office next to Ben's. Bobby's sole work recreation seemed to be coming into Ben's office to gossip about everybody and everything imaginable, and when the door was closed, he knocked. If Ben didn't answer, Bobby just came in.

"And what kind of name is Bobby for a prosecutor? This kid was alright. I even sort of liked him, but Bobby! He couldn't be Robert, or even just Bob?"

Normally, nobody came to Ben's office, at all. That is, except Maria, but she usually came in after work and gave him a hand job under his desk. After that day, they started making it a habit to stay late some nights and fuck on their boss' desk. Ben loved the fact that he could see residual steamy sweat imprints from Maria's ass left behind on his desk.

"Lucky him. Maria's ass smelled better than most guys' breath." In any case, Maria coming by was fine, but Chatty Bobby inviting himself in had become an issue for Ben's slumber time. Ben needed a game changer.

That day, he discovered the floor with the office graveyard. The floor where the conference room was. The conference room they were sitting in that Monday morning. That day, when he first discovered the conference room, he explored a little first. In fact, he was up on that floor because he was looking for an isolated men's room to take his post-Linda's dump. He discovered one. There was nobody on the floor, but the facilities were fully functional. He also found a couple of old ThinkPad laptops that he stole and hawked at this shady looking pawn shop down on south Rainier Avenue.

After a blissfully uninterrupted dump, Ben meandered around for no apparent reason. Like everything else on the floor, the conference room was functional and relatively clean, but uninhabited. To Ben, it was like finding money. Actually, it was better than finding money. After all, you can always earn more money, or just spend less money if you're broke, but you can't create more hours of the day to sleep. There are a set number of hours in every day, and only painfully few of them were reserved for sleeping. Not only that, but whenever something came up that required more time, that time always came out of your already insufficient sleep time. If you had to get to work early, you had to wake up earlier and lose morning sleep. If you wanted to stay out late with your friends, you went to bed late and lost night sleep. Ben had long ago decided that he would spend his life finding ways to claw sleep back from the time thieves that sought to take it. The main offender against sleep was, obviously, work, so that's where he peeled time back from most often.

That conference room had comfortable, leather rolling chairs, and they had padded arm rests. The table was at just the right height to put your head down on your hands. That first day, Ben folded up his suit jacket and put his head down on it. He slept the way he used to sleep in boring high school classes. Every minute of that sort of sleep feels like two minutes. Every minute of sleep done on your employer's time was not just sleep, but getting paid to sleep, double dipping. Needless to say, being paid to do the thing you love is every person's dream, and Ben's dream was to get paid to sleep. When he woke up that Friday afternoon, he felt refreshed. He was still slightly buzzed from the Rainiers, but in a very pleasant way. He was still full form the Cowboy Burger, but not bloated. He went back to his office and connivingly pretended to work for the rest of the afternoon.

That evening, he and Maria had some more beers after work. Ben had a half rack of Rainiers in his trunk, so they headed out to the parking garage and sat in the Barracuda, listening to *Dear You* by Jawbreaker on his car stereo. They started making out. That was inevitable. What wasn't inevitable was Maria's suggestion.

"Let's go fuck on that prick Corey's desk."

"Corey? You mean our *boss* Corey?"

Maria's skirts were always perfect fucking length. They sat right above her knees, so you could shimmy them up to get at the good stuff, but she could pull it back down in a hurry if she needed to. She always went with bare legs too. Easy access. Ben planted her squarely on Corey's desk and knocked over his desktop family photo in the process. They both looked at the photo, now face down on the floor.

"His kids are too young to watch this anyway," he said.

"Totally, now quit talking, and start fucking."

Ben blew such a huge wad that half of it landed on the carpet under the desk. He used the sole of his shoe to squish it into the carpet, thinking that would make it less noticeable, but that really just smeared it around. For the rest of the time Ben worked there, he could see the darkened discolored spot every time he went into Corey's office. Even when Corey was scolding him about something, he was always laughing inside. He'd just stare, completely preoccupied by the little stain. The little spot of cum that, even months later, looked like it never dried.

Later that night, Erin forced Ben to fuck her. It was the predicable ten minutes of vanilla foreplay, followed by her riding him in the most boring fashion imaginable. Same meat, different gravy. In order to get her off him as quickly as possible, he made the faces, and he made the noises, and he pretended to blow a wad into a tissue he grabbed out of the box she kept by her bed. That night, even if he'd had the mild level of interest he normally brought to their fuck sessions, he wouldn't have had a thing to put in that tissue. Maria had literally fucked him dry.

But that was an immortal Friday, and this was an exhausted Monday. It seemed like their Criminal Division Chief, Corey Robinson, was always talking about things Ben didn't understand at all. Ben would always look around, and think, "If I don't know what the fuck he's talking about, how do all these new prosecutors know what he's talking about?" The turnover was so severe at the Criminal Division that Ben was actually one of the more senior prosecutors, even though he'd been on the job less than two years. He wondered why all these new prosecutors knew all these things he didn't. Even Chatty Bobby made some meaningful comments. Ben literally didn't speak the entire meeting.

They kept talking about new sentencing guidelines. Ben didn't care about sentencing guidelines. Everything that happened after a jury verdict was wholly uninteresting to him. To him, the game was winning the trial. The practice, the oratory, the public stage—it was all in the courtroom, not in this boring meeting. A courtroom was a coliseum, prosecutors and public defenders were gladiators, and a trial was a match to the death. That was the noisy part, the only part that cut through the other static. Sentencing guidelines were static, and Ben wouldn't have listened even if he could. It's true that he lacked the capacity to listen, but it was lucky that he also didn't give a shit about what they were talking about.

Maria was listening, though. She really was a good prosecutor. And she always helped him with his homework, things like writing sentencing recommendations on his cases. With that comforting thought, his mind went fuzzy. It went to that place between relaxed and unconscious, that place where proximity to sleep made daydreams vivid and real dreams lucid. Ben loved that place.

Chapter 23

Erin's parents were coming to Seattle to visit. Ben said they were only coming out to check in on their investment. When she said, "What, my house?" he said, "No, their daughter. Ha!" Ben hadn't met them yet, but he had nicknames for them. He called her father "Stodgy" and her mother "Stuffy." Alternatively, he also referred to them as Thurston and Lovey or sometimes, the Howells. Then he would sing some stupid song that went "the millionaire and his wife." Erin hated that stupid song. She didn't even know if it was a real song or some stupid thing he made up. She thought he said something about some island TV show from a hundred years ago, but to be honest, she just didn't really care. What she did care about was Ben showing up for dinner with her parents. She'd made reservations at Canlis for the four of them.

Erin and her parents were sitting in her living room. It was after five, and she could tell her mom and dad were getting restless. She'd taken the day off work so she could spend it with them. She didn't pick them up from the airport because her dad preferred to have a rental car when he was out of town. They'd gotten in around noon, and they went straight to the Fairmont Olympic to check in. After that, they drove up to Madrona to see what their million dollars had purchased. Even with all the renovations she'd made, her parents were not impressed. In fact, even if she'd borrowed two million and bought one of the old foursquare craftsman houses further up the hill, they'd have been unimpressed.

In truth, the only real reason they'd come out at all was to try to convince Erin to move back to Massachusetts. Her parents were afraid that if she spent any more time in Seattle doing what they viewed as, essentially, volunteer work, the respectable law firms in Boston and New York City would lose interest in offering her a position at all. To them, doing public service for a couple of years after law school simply rounded out a resume. It gave future employers the impression that a person cared enough about their reputation to appear as though they had a soul. Erin's problem was that she really did have a soul. Those white-shoe law firms actually preferred that you have none, but the appearance of one was desirable.

At the moment, Stuffy and Stodgy were being strategic about how to broach the subject. Stodgy was looking down at his Patek Phillipe, wondering where this boyfriend of hers was. It was warm outside, and Erin's house wasn't having the air conditioning unit installed until the following week, so Stuffy was doing her best to look, well, not so stuffy. Little did Stuffy and Stodgy know that Ben was about to serve them up a huge softball. Erin had sent Ben a text forty minutes earlier, asking if he was going to meet them at her house or the restaurant. His tardy reply simply said, "Fuck no."

It wasn't even anger she was feeling. It was more like humiliation. He'd approved an invite she put on his calendar a month prior. Later, he'd tell her that because calendar invites were so voluminous and annoying, his standard practice was to just approve all invites that he received but only show up to things he felt like going to. She already knew that about him. She didn't verbally confirm with him, partially because she knew he might bail on her if she did. She knew there was no right answer with Ben. If she reminded him of the dinner, he'd blow her off. If she put it on his calendar, he'd blow it off. She knew that whatever he didn't feel like doing, he'd just blow it off.

It was so annoying because she knew he was probably sitting at the Dick's Drive-In on Broadway chomping on a cheeseburger and washing it down with a chocolate milkshake. It wasn't that he had anything important to do. It wasn't that he was working late, or prepping for a trial. He wasn't. What bothered her was that he disregarded important events in favor of childish and selfish nonsense. The other day, he had a trial starting, and he sent an email to the public defender and court staff that said he had the flu and needed a continuance until the following week. He sent the email at eight thirty in the morning, a half-hour before the trial was scheduled to start. Then he went back to sleep for three hours. When he woke up, he drove to Portland to go record shopping.

He was inconsiderate—that was beyond debate—but he was recklessly irresponsible as well. But this... This wasn't even that. This was him purposely refusing to do something, to make a point to her. This was him illustrating to her that he was perfectly willing to embarrass her to make a point. This was him laughing at her from afar as he mocked her to his friends. It was a gauntlet thrown down. It was a challenge extended. He dared her to dump him with his actions.

Erin had long known of Ben's defiant nature. She'd long endured the same defiant attitude from other Pacific Northwest natives. It caused a genuine disconnect in her brain. People around there just simply didn't comply with cordial requests. At best, they'd comply, but only in the narrowest terms possible, and only to the extent that compliance suited their own needs. Most of the time, they'd just blow you off, freeze you out, and ignore any further requests for interaction. At worst, they'd contort, bend, and fashion your request into a weapon they'd then use to cut you to ribbons later.

Ben was just such a cutter. To Ben, defiance of a request was adherence to his birthright as a free human, the offspring of the offspring of frontier pioneers. "Yeah, free to defy, free to resist, you're even free to fall in line if you're a chicken-shit conformist, but whatever." Further, any requests to do anything that he wasn't already inclined to do were seen as offensive, and the requestor viewed as a mortal enemy.

Erin was just such an enemy. She made herself so by continually asking Ben to do things he didn't feel like doing. Worse still, she asked him to do things she knew he would hate, and to interact with people like Stuffy and Stodgy, who he was hardwired to detest.

Erin, after much protest, was only able to meet Ben's mom very recently. This, despite the fact that she and Ben had been together for well over a year. She'd only been able to manage that because Ben's mother Barbara had called him once when Erin was at his apartment. He made the mistake of saying he'd meet her for lunch. Before he could hang up the phone, Erin asked, loud enough to be heard over the phone receiver, if she could come. Before Ben could react, Barbara agreed. Erin still had not met Ben's dad or sister.

Little by little, she had come to recognize that the defiance wasn't a tough-guy act. It wasn't learned. It was baked into his DNA. Ben's family had been in Puget Sound since the middle of the Nineteenth Century. What sort of miscreants and societal malcontents existed in the Puget Sound back then? Ben's forbearers. That's who. What did they believe? They believed they were the Alpha and the Omega, the beginning and the end, a closed circuit that started with what they wanted and ended with what they'd do to get it. They weren't much more than cavemen, crude and simple, but clever and efficient, nonetheless. Seattle back then wasn't much more than a bar, a whorehouse, and a boat dock.

At that lunch, when Ben got up to piss, Erin asked Barbara about his defiance. Barbara told Erin about when Ben was a teenager. She told Erin about trying to put Ben on restriction. To Erin, it sounded like some demented psychological horror movie. Barbara told Erin that when Ben was fourteen, he came home stoned an hour after curfew. She put him on restriction for a week. The next night, Ben came home at five in the morning stoned and drunk. He slept all day, missed school, and when he got up, he made a sandwich, grabbed his skateboard, and left without saying a word. He didn't come home for three days, and when she threatened to put him on restriction for a month, he said, "You already put me on restriction for a week. How'd that fuckin' turn out!"

Barbara told Erin that, after that, she knew she had no power over him. He knew if he just simply refused to obey, there wasn't much she, or anyone else could really do about it. He also knew if he actively increased the intensity and duration of his defiance that she would eventually fold like a cheap lawn chair, and she did.

Seattle had very recently become the land of lollipops and suckers, a cultural utopia, a place where offense was neither given nor accepted. Wounding another's delicate image of themselves was forbidden. More importantly, a politely phrased, politically correct request that was responsive to the fragility culture of new Seattle acted as a binding directive to anyone within earshot. In the new Seattle, you chicken-shit conformed to a bizarre perversion of democratic ideology. In Mobile, you chicken-shit conformed to a bizarre perversion of republican ideology. Ben fit into neither place, he thought independent thoughts way too often for Seattle or Mobile. He made himself an outsider in the middle of a crowd and in plain sight by thinking thoughts that never occurred to the people around him. He thought thoughts that sometimes disagreed with extremist political dogma, thoughts that scared sheep in Seattle. He made himself disliked by calling out what he interpreted to be toxic group think, and by so doing, incurred the unified wrath of the solid block of group thinkers.

The Lollipop Gang also insisted that every person was innocent and pure of heart; sleeping outside was a lifestyle choice; and personal accountability was a fascist value. Lollipop Gang mentality also dictated that recognition and praise were the reward for half measures and mediocrity. Lollipop Gang mentality did not recognize that some people are actual criminals with criminal motives; people sleeping outside was the tragic result of a failed social safety net; and some level of personal accountability was necessary for a well-functioning democracy. Nor did Lollipop Gang mentality account for the wholesale societal downward spiral that results from discarding all semblance of meritocracy.

"Lollipop culture is like when you're a kid, and the doctor gives you a lollipop for doing nothing more than sitting through your checkup. I always thought that doctor was a fuckin' sucker. Who gives away sugary treats for doing absolutely nothing? Even on Halloween, you had to put on a costume and walk around the neighborhood for hours knocking on doors. What's even funnier is that the doctor was always complimenting me for doing things I had no control over. He's like, 'Hey Ben, good job growing three inches since your last checkup.' No shit! That was a real doctor's visit I had when I was thirteen. This fuckin' dipshit literally complimented me for growing, like I had a choice in the matter.

"Man, the bar here in Seattle is so low, you can trip over it. That's Seattle in 2011. Good job on waking up and continuing to draw breath; now let us praise you. Give me a fuckin' break. What the fuck is that all about? And all the Seattle suckers cater to this fragility culture because they're afraid of being ostracized by the Lollipop Gang. Count me out. I grew up in Tacoma, the land of malt liquor and neighborhood bullies. No lollipops for me, thanks. Save that shit for the suckers."

Eventually, Erin and her parents made their way to Canlis without Ben. She did her best to frame his absence as part and parcel of his hardworking, working-class roots. She went on about what a dedicated prosecutor he was. How he was out about the city's business and preparing for an important assault trial. Stuffy and Stodgy weren't buying it, though. Even if what she'd been telling them had been true, in their eyes, that just made Ben a boxed-in civil servant, not noble. It wasn't true, and Ben couldn't have been more the opposite of boxed-in. By that time, he'd just as soon wipe his ass with the job as show up and do it properly.

After the appetizer plates were taken away by their waitress, but before the entrees were served, Stodgy got a serious look on his face.

"Erin, we think it's time for you to come home."

"I am home. I own a home. I have a job, a boyfriend, and a life."

"Erin, in all candor, I don't believe you have any of those things; not really. Your job is just a starter career, not something you do forever. And, that house... I'm sure you can sell it for what you've invested, maybe even a little more."

Stuffy chimed in, "And don't you think that neighborhood is a little, you know."

"It's a little what?" Erin said.

Stuffy was whispering, "You know, ethnic. Dark."

"No, I'm fine with that, Mom."

"Erin, your mom has had a couple of glasses of wine, but the sentiment of what she's saying is sound. I didn't even really want to park my rental car outside your house for too long, and it's not even my car. It's fine to represent them, but you don't have to live with them. There are upper-middle-class suburbs around here. You could live outside of the city where Bill and Melinda live.

"It's not just the house and the job, but what are you going to do, marry this prosecutor? You've got options at home, but who knows how long those are going to last? In five years, you could be married to the right man, be a partner at a good firm, and own a real house in the right sort of area. Are you trying to tell us that this is the life you want? Do you really want this life instead of the one you were born to have? The life that's there waiting for you? It's there; all you have to do is take it."

Most people turn out to be 'who' they were born to be, and Stuffy and Stodgy certainly fit that mold. It's funny that, way back when, Erin's forebearers fantasized about a time in the future when their descendants, or the descendants of their descendants, would want for nothing. Everybody wants that for their offspring. Everyone wants to spoil their children rotten and shield them from the pain that they themselves endured. People are selfish, and while parents certainly love their children and seek to shield them from pain out of love, it's also a selfish endeavor. After shielding your child, that little extension of you, from pain and torment, you shield yourself from a second painful childhood.

Parents do their best to shield themselves from that second childhood at every turn. An adult's experiences and ability to look back on the awkward and uncomfortable aspects of growing up means they will be keenly aware of the unavoidable pain of growing up. Because human narcissism causes parents to superimpose themselves onto the blueprint of a child, they must necessarily suffer a painful second childhood, all the while wasting their children's actual childhood in futile efforts to keep the world at bay.

Your child being bullied sets off alarm bells in your head because you relive yourself being bullied. That's what most of parenthood is. But insomuch as parenthood is a second childhood, it's a first parenthood. Vicariously experiencing what feels like a second childhood is just simply the next phase of existence for many.

Ben's dad Big Ben had one of the worst second childhoods imaginable. He buried a child. He raised another. A third was just about to enter adulthood. By all accounts, Big Ben would live to see his living children make similar mistakes as they continued to mature. *Jesus Christ, does a person ever get peace?*

In their own stuck up, prejudiced, and insular way, Stuffy and Stodgy were trying to save Erin from painful experiences that they did not want to vicariously suffer themselves. While their motives were gross, distorted, and egocentric, they were simply doing what everybody's DNA orders them to do. Human beings carry that genetic flaw everywhere with them. That is, shortsightedness. Everyone—Big Ben, Stuff and Stodgy... All people can be made to understand that attempting to spare a child from necessary struggles only creates a defective and helpless person down the road. As a parent, someday, you will no longer be around to save your child, and that child will likely be left to their own devices without the skills necessary to make their own way. We just can't help ourselves, so we cut off our noses in spite of our faces.

Erin was, more or less, who she was born to be, but unlike most of her ilk, she suffered severe cognitive dissonance about the whole matter. At some point, she did sincerely believe she would be free to return to some variety of the life she was born to have with a clean conscience. She'd done more in her years at DPD than most people ever would for the disenfranchised of society. Certainly, more than any of the people she'd grown up with. But while, once upon a time, being a public defender seemed like a calling and lifelong mission, it now seemed more like an enlistment. She'd been doing it for over four years. She was a good soldier, but it really did seem like enough to her.

At the same time, she was also hardwired to disagree with her parents, so she couldn't simply buy into their version of her life. What she imagined was more like their version with her own additions and adaptations. She didn't have to cash in her entire persona to go home. White-shoe law firms allowed attorneys to do pro bono work. She didn't have to live in Dover near her parents. She could live in Boston, Beacon Hill. She didn't have to marry some Harvard guy. She could marry Ben.

There was just one problem. She really couldn't marry Ben. Not yet. He was cagey, but she wanted what she wanted, and Stuffy and Stodgy has always told her that, with enough effort, she could have whatever she wanted. Right then, she realized what she wanted was an edgier version of what Stuffy and Stodgy proposed. Edgy, but still sort of safe. She would take high society, but the progressive flavor. She would take married life, but with the frontier guy in a flannel shirt and trucker hat, not a polo shirt and golf visor.

Thinking about Ben and how he blew her off had her fuming again, but she was starting to realize that she'd been going about trapping him the wrong way. Money didn't impress him. Society people like Stuffy and Stodgy annoyed him. The idea of a nice dinner at a place like Canlis made him hungry for a burrito from a parking lot taco truck. His pedestrian and contrarian nature was his Achilles' heel. Erin started to think she could go to work at the city attorney's office. She could be a prosecutor. She might even learn to like some of the other meaningless hobbies he engaged in. And if she didn't, she could always pretend. Women always pretend in order to trap men.

"It's the time-honored tradition of my people," she said out loud, all of a sudden.

Stuffy and Stodgy just stared at her, not sure what to say.

"Mom, Dad, I can't come back to Massachusetts right now. Why don't you two just keep my seat warm, and I'll let you know when it makes sense for me?"

Chapter 24

"Seattle Municipal Court. Trial. Day one. The rugged and handsome prosecution team sets out to keep the streets of Seattle safe." Chatty Bobby was a cheesy drama club nerd cast into the mold of an attorney.

"Seattle Municipal Court. What a fuckin' joke. Nobody calls it that either. Everybody just says SMC." Chatty Bobby was right about one thing. They were literally keeping the streets safe, but not the way you might think. It was a DUI trial. The defendant was genuinely a menace on the streets. She was a middle-aged white lady with six lifetime DUIs. This one was her third in the last five years. If Ben and Chatty Bobby pinned this conviction on her, the next one would be a felony, and based on her driving history, the next one was right around the corner. As for rugged and handsome, Chatty Bobby had got it half right. Ben was rugged and handsome. Chatty Bobby was neither.

SMC was a kangaroo court; that much was reflected in the off and wrong rulings that constantly flooded out of it. SMC made more bad law in a year than the rest of the state made in a decade. Most of it went unchallenged, as DPD and the city attorney's office lacked the people and resources necessary to appeal all of the legally erroneous decisions.

The situation had effectively created a legal silo, a place with a circular feedback loop. Public defenders, and sometimes even prosecutors, would stand up in court and argue a legal theory that had been formulated by the ideological partisan of the office tasked with formulating political campaigns into legal arguments. Once a friendly SMC judge had rubber stamped it through a ruling, it became part of the new marching orders for that office. Within a week, such a ruling would become ubiquitous at SMC.

SMC was a parallel system of laws, with exclusive jurisdiction over all misdemeanors and gross misdemeanors in the city of Seattle. At SMC, the Washington State Constitution didn't apply. As far as that goes, neither did the United States Constitution. It was more like pretend court, like a model United Nations at your high school, just a bunch of kids who don't really have any idea what they're talking about debating heavy matters to a high school teacher with only a tangential grasp of the issue.

Ben had made his peace with the fact that they were only practicing law for pretend at SMC, but unlike high school teachers, judges at SMC had real power. Even if it was a procedural mockery, and the home of fake laws, the consequences for the criminal defendants were absolutely real. They went to the very real King County Jail when they were convicted. Convicted defendants didn't serve much time for misdemeanors in Seattle, but anyone that has ever spent the night in county knows that one day in there is one day too many. Plus, even if it was just a pretend court, Ben still preferred to win.

A farce like SMC was actually just a game, and Ben was good at games. The fact that no one was really bound to making real legal arguments that were supported by some other authority gave Ben creative license to make up a lot of new rules of his own, and he did. It was pretty easy.

"First, you focus on something that's annoying you about how the court does things. Then, you imagine what your ideal solution would be. After that, you waited until you're in front of a friendly judge. If you assert your position, laughable as it may be, in an authoritative and confident fashion, there's a pretty good chance your friendly judge will rule in your favor. Boom! Mic drop. That's how you make bad law at SMC. Easy."

Today's game was voir dire in a DUI trial. It was Chatty Bobby's first trial, so he was even chattier than normal. It wasn't Ben's first trial. It wasn't even his tenth. He'd actually lost count, since his office tried so many cases. That is, prosecutors who liked trial tried a lot of cases. Prosecutors who didn't always seemed to find a way to make a plea bargain work, even if they had to bend over for the public defender to get it done. Others just found ways to rotate out of the trial units, off the front line, out of the shit, in the rear with the gear, as they say.

Even voir dire at SMC was pretend. Misdemeanor trials only allowed six jurors. It was ironic that every legal doctrine that could be discarded at SMC was, but a tiny, little statute about six jurors for misdemeanor trials was enforced absolutely. Typically, each side got about twenty minutes to perform their voir dire. In superior court or federal court, you could have a couple of hours or, depending on the court, unlimited time, but not at SMC. Twenty minutes wasn't enough time to seriously question one juror much an entire pool.

With twenty minutes, a lawyer could either try to figure out the personality dynamics of a potential jury or go after for-cause strikes. DPD attorneys always went after for-cause strikes. It was always an uneven playing field. People in Seattle—most people—were inclined to vote to acquit on misdemeanor cases. If the public defender could remove anyone who was seriously pro prosecution, nothing else mattered as far as what the personality dynamics were because they would all vote for an acquittal.

Ben never really held that fact against them. It was just how the city functioned. People decided what sort of city they wanted, and they voted with their ballots. They also voted when they came for jury duty. In day-to-day life, they also voted with their silence. Most of the time, they were right. Crimes of subsistence were not a serious criminal justice issue. People stealing peanut butter from QFC was a largely innocuous situation. But crimes of subsistence were often secondary to much more serious societal issues like addiction, homelessness, and mental health. Like the short-sighted parent that refuses to equip their child to survive on their own, the perceived future discomfort of dealing with these more serious societal issues dictates that people will remain silent, both in terms of petty crime and the underlying issues driving that petty crime. In short, we don't want to acknowledge that the underlying illness exists, so we will ignore the symptoms that manifest. For most individuals that cared about the plight of others, ignorance was the best they could muster. For society, kicking the underlying can down the road pretty much always ensured more desperate people would be stealing peanut butter next year.

Ben was born in Seattle, but he grew up in Tacoma. Where Seattle was concerned, he'd always be both looking in through a glass window and staring out through said window from the inside. He could see himself inside of it as he stared at himself from right outside. Ben had two arms—in the left, a sword; in the right, a treatise. "But you get the city you vote for, and Seattle is what Seattleites want it to be. It's mostly what I want it to be too—tolerant, compassionate, diverse. It's interesting. Nobody wants to live in some vanilla cultural wasteland like Spokane, or a racist backwater like Birmingham (Alabama, not England).

"For me, though, it hit a tipping point. Common sense ceased to be common, and unwinding the clock to illustrate that much of this petty crime was secondary to real societal ills, for which we have no solution, ceased to be politically correct. In fact, simply saying that out loud tended to ensure that the group think of Seattle would label you as intolerant and insensitive. That is, the gang would come after you, wielding lollipops and suckers like clubs. What about it?! I mean, I'm a prosecutor. And I'm not really a Seattleite, in any case. I guess, I'm not really much of a Tacomaite anymore either. I'll tell you what else I'm not. I'm not a sucker-ass member of Seattle's Lollipop Gang."

In any case, voir dire for the prosecutor was a more complex game. It was a game Ben had long since mastered. Ben won trials, despite all of the hurdles, because he'd been born with radar and a microphone. Some people could analyze the personality dynamics of a group at a glance. Others could make themselves heard, regardless of the actual decibel level of their voices. Rarely, did both gifts appear in the same person. Ben was just such a person, and that fact alone re-leveled this reliably unlevel playing field.

Chatty Bobby was doing his first voir dire. Chatty Bobby was technically the first chair. That is, it was his trial. Ben was his peer mentor, and as such, was just there to supervise. Ben was a little annoyed because he wasn't getting paid to be a supervisor. As a matter of fact, he was hardly being paid, at all. Being a prosecutor at the city attorney's office felt more like a minimum wage labor mill than a professional occupation. On top of that, sitting with new prosecutors really wasn't the peer mentor's job, but the supervisors and leads in the unit became uncannily unavailable whenever a new prosecutor needed help. If Ben wasn't Gen X, he was Gen X adjacent enough to recognize absentee parenting when he saw it. They were latchkey prosecutors, and their divorced parents spent their days working and their nights drinking at the local pub. Ben was the eleven-year-old who necessarily became responsible for making dinner for the six-year-old. The more it rolled around in his head, the more Ben realized he was more than annoyed. He was resentful.

In any case, he liked Chatty Bobby. At least, he liked him as much as any older brother can like an annoying younger brother. And he wanted to help him win, but every day he sat there in the courtroom with Chatty Bobby was another day he fell further behind with his own work. In any case, he couldn't teach Chatty Bobby to be a great communicator any more than a person could teach Tony Hawk to defy death on a useless wooden toy. You sort of just, had it, or you didn't. There were some things Ben could teach him though.

Chatty Bobby wasn't exactly killing it during his voir dire, but the public defender was greener than Chatty Bobby, so it didn't come off as awkwardly as it could have. That is, since they both sort of blew it, none of the potential jurors likely knew what a good voir dire was supposed to look like.

For the prosecutor, jury selection is one part popularity

contest and one part picking a team for dodgeball in gym class.

Chatty Bobby was awkward, that's true, but he was likeable, and he really was a drama geek in high school, so his presentation was over the top. It wouldn't have worked for everyone, but when a drama geek is being a talentless actor for your amusement, that really is their genuine self, and it could be endearing. For a second, Ben sensed the oxymoron in that thought. Being an over-the-top phony was an actor's genuine self. He'd never really thought about it like that before, but it piqued his interest, and he mentally catalogued it so he could entertain his brain with it when he was trying to fall asleep that night. In any case, it's not how Ben did it. In fact, he thought it was a little unorthodox because the way good attorneys typically connect with people is to be genuine; but it was effective for Chatty Bobby.

Picking a team was not something Chatty Bobby was going to be able to figure out on the fly. Ben had the read of people; that was a talent. He was born with it, but it was also, to a large extent, a teachable skill. Communication requires a person to convey a message to another. It requires a persuasive voice and a vulnerable ear. Figuring out personality dynamics only requires a basic understanding of human nature and an open ear. It's a one-way channel. Nobody has to find you persuasive for you to pick a winning team.

There were only three types of jurors. The overwhelming majority of them were the group thinkers. They didn't matter. They would march to whatever was the loudest drum. Ben watched Goody Randolph. "Who the hell names their kid Goody anymore?" Goody, or Ms. Randolph as she preferred to be called was a very young and inexperienced public defender. She wasted nearly all of her time on attempting to strike group thinkers for cause. Worse still, she failed to get even one juror struck for cause. Ben knew that when an attorney wasted time in voir dire talking to one of the sheep, he could beat them. The whole case is won or lost in jury selection. Sometimes, you do your best, but you can't get the jury you need, but you know why you lost. Ms. Randolph didn't even understand the rules of the game she was playing.

The only people that mattered were the leaders and the dissenters. Sometimes, a loud person can masquerade as a leader, and sometimes, a quiet one can masquerade as a dissenter, but it was mostly true that the loud ones were leaders and the quiet ones were dissenters. Ben spotted the dissenters in the jury pool right away. He, himself, was a dissenter, so he only ever had to look for the jurors like himself. You really don't want a dissenter, even one that is ideologically inclined to support your side. As soon as a dissenter becomes a leader, they find another way to dissent. They are contrarians and should be avoided at all costs.

You have to pick a leader. A smart lawyer picks the jury foreperson in jury selection. The jury doesn't know it, of course. But Ben always pinned the person he believed would be the leader, and the one who would ultimately be elected by the other jurors as the foreperson, and he was always right. "It's a science, picking a jury; maybe, a little bit an art, as well."

Ben helped Chatty Bobby get rid of two would-be leaders for the defense with for-cause strikes. He used one preemptory strike to get rid of a wickedly thorny dissenter. He used another preemptory to remove a mostly innocuous group thinker for a better educated group thinker, as educated group thinkers can often explain the scientific processes used with the blood alcohol content device. Ben didn't even bother using their last preemptory strike. Ms. Randolph had used all her preemptory strikes on inconsequential group thinkers and wounded her credibility with the jury through numerous failed attempts to strike other inconsequential jurors for cause. As far as Ben was concerned, the trial was already in the bag, so he relaxed and mostly let Chatty Bobby have a turn with the reigns.

Chapter 25

"So do you think we're the bad guys, or is it them over at DPD?" Maria asked Ben.

"Everybody is the good guy of their own story. Once they perceive they are becoming the bad guy, cognitive dissonance kicks in and convinces them that they're still the good guy because their actions were justified for some greater cause or some shit."

"So, nobody ever thinks they're the bad guy! That's crazy. What about Charles Manson?"

"Charles Manson definitely thinks he's the good guy. That guy has a messiah complex—a fuckin' huge one. Those fuckers are all like that—David Koresh, Jim Jones, all of them. To them, they themselves are not the problem. It's the big bad world, or the government, encroaching on their little fiefdoms, or some other such cultish, little beef with humanity."

"What about Han Solo?"

"Han Solo is sort of a jerk, but he's still the good guy."

"Not really. Look, you made me watch those movies, and I took some notes. Han Solo shot some green guy in a bar who was trying to collect a debt from him."

"Well, to be fair, that guy was a bounty hunter, and he was pointing a gun at Han."

"Okay, so he gouged that old monk guy in the brown robe and Luke Skywalker for all their money when they just needed a ride somewhere. And that Luke guy had to sell his car to pay for the ride."

"Luke and Ben were fugitives, and taking them off Tatooine—I imagine—was a pretty serious offense in the criminal justice system of the empire. That's not gouging; that's just being an enterprising criminal taking advantage of a situation. Also, it's a speeder, not a car. And Luke's aunt and uncle were murdered, so he was never coming back to Tatooine, so he didn't have much use for the speeder. Although, I've often wondered about his aunt and uncle's moisture farm. The lawyer in me wants to think Luke got a real estate agent to sell the farm, and a junk dealer to do an estate sale. I mean, he's the only person around that could inherit all that stuff, so he should have gotten paid, but I know he didn't. I'm sure the fuckin' government just auctioned it off after Luke never paid the property tax."

"Okay, well, Han Solo took all the money the rebels gave him and bailed on them."

"Yeah, but he came back!"

"He did? Alright, well, I really did fall asleep right there at the end. Seriously, all you guys love those ridiculous movies. I don't get it."

"Look, you have a point. Han Solo's a loner and an outlaw."

"Is that why he has that tough name"—she made air quotes—"Solo, because he's a tough loner? A tough loner like Pee-wee Herman?" She mimicked the nasally tone of Pee-wee, "'You don't want to get mixed up with a guy like me. I'm a loner, Dottie, a rebel.' But then he bailed on the rebels, so I guess he's just a loner, not a rebel."

Maria was openly laughing and mocking the movie by this point.

"Actually, that is why his name is Solo, because he's solo. He's the anti-hero. Luke is the pupil. Ben is the learned elder. Vader is the nemesis. It's pretty smart storytelling. I'm like the Han Solo of the city attorney's office."

She took another rip off the bong and started cough-laughing uncontrollably as a cloud of smoke escaped from the full chamber.

"Okay Solo, whatever. Hey Han, it's your hit. Smoke it quick before Dark Veiner attacks the confederate army with his red-light lipstick sword."

"It's *Darth Vader*, not *Dark Veiner*. And they're the Rebel Alliance, not the confederate army in the Civil War."

"And I suppose the Storm Troopers aren't Nazis."

"Actually, that one's pretty much accurate."

"Anyway, I fell asleep, so I didn't see him come back. Also, I fell asleep before the end of parts two and three, so I have no idea what happened with the little-green troll puppet guy that lived in the swamp in the second one or the teddy bears that lived in the forest in the third one.

"Jesus Christ, it's like we're from different planets."

"Yes, you're the farm boy from the farm planet, and I'm the princess from the palace planet."

"You're the one that grew up by the farm. I grew up in Tacoma. Neither of us are from the palace planet. And technically, *Empire Strikes Back* and *Return of the Jedi* are Episodes five and six, not two and three."

"Then why didn't you show me the first three first? Who shows someone the fourth movie in a series first?"

"The first three came out after four, five, and six."

"WTF!"

It's a long story, never mind."

"So, you and I aren't from the palace planet, but what about your little princess, Erin? She's from the palace planet. She's Princess Lay-Me"

"Aw, man, don't bring her up. I'm trying not to think about work."

"She's your girlfriend."

"Yeah, having a girlfriend is work, and I'm trying not to think about work. And, it's Princess Leia, not Lay-Me"

Maria was snorting and laughing uncontrollably. She'd taken her mouth off the bong mid-toke again, and more smoke was billowing into the air than was going into her lungs. It was an egregious waste of usable intoxicating smoke. When he was a teenager, Ben never would have wasted pot smoke like that. He didn't have enough money to be wasteful like that. Back then, getting good weed was like finding porn mags wrapped in twenty-dollar bills. But now, he didn't care so much. Plus, it was Maria's weed; so, he supposed, it was hers to waste in any way she liked.

"Look, here's how it is. Han isn't evil; he's just living outside the expectations of society, makin' his own way. But even though he's a jerk, he has a conscience. He has a code. He could be the bad guy, but when he steps over the line, his brain tells him he's gone from being a lovable rogue to an evil bastard, and it always snaps him back to reality. Then, he does the right thing.

"People can't be one way and perceive themselves as another. It causes dissonance, so people have to justify otherwise unjustifiable actions in order to quiet their brains. Sometimes, when something happens that is too much for your brain to justify, it sets off an alarm. People without consciences don't view themselves as the bad guys because they have no working concept of right and wrong, on account of their psychopathy. People who do, when confronted with a situation like Han bailing on the rebels, turn the ship around. For Han Solo, turning the ship around redeems him, and arguably, makes him the biggest hero in the movie because he did something out of character for him. That is, he acted in the interest of someone else, to his own detriment.

"Luke and Leia are already true believers, so fighting the battle isn't that heroic, since they were inclined to do so any-way. Obi Wan is a disciple and good soldier, so his martyrdom is logical and expected. That is, he's doing what he's trained his whole life to do. Han has to discard an entire lifetime of self-centeredness to become who he becomes. It's like Russell Crowe in 3:10 to Yuma."

"You're soooo smart, Ben. Can you please tell me more about movie-character psychology?"

Her mocking had reached peak levels.

"Also, I don't know if you're talking about the Russell Crowe movie where he's the cowboy or the gladiator because I fell asleep both times. But he is fine!"

"That's real original. You have a crush on the brooding and roguish Australian movie star. In any case, DPD thinks they're the good guys because they're protecting the accused. We think we're the good guys because we're protecting society from the transgressions of those we charge with crimes. Neither of us are actually "the good guys." And neither of us are really "the bad guys," either. You and I are prosecutors, but we're sitting here on a Friday night watching Hamlet Two and taking bong hits of weed we bought from the pot dealer that lives upstairs."

"Smoking weed isn't a crime in Seattle; not one that anyone enforces."

"I'm sure that ballot initiative will result in the legalization of weed, but I'm thinking all of the coke we just snorted will still be chargeable as a crime, and it sort of paints us as hypocrites, to some extent."

"So, good people do shady stuff; oh, well."

"Exactly, we're good people by virtue of what we do for a living. We're the "good guys," so snorting a bunch of coke and fuckin' each other behind our partners' backs is justifiable."

She giggled. "But you know those DPD fuckers are doing the same shit."

"And worse, I imagine. But again, my cognitive dissonance needs to tell me they're worse, whether it's true or not, because I need to be the good guy of my own story."

"But really, though... They're worse."

"Yeah, probably."

"So, how do the forest teddy bears and little green swamp troll factor in?"

"That's it, we're going to the video store to rent *Empire Strikes Back* and *Return of the Jedi* right now. Are you too fucked up to drive?"

"Yeah, kinda, you?"

"Yeah, probably, but it's too far to walk."

"We gonna drive anyway?"

"Yeah, I guess."

Chapter 26

en was living his life in snippets, just little snapshots of reality. It sounded so cliché to rail about Monday, he couldn't help but think about *Office Space*. He feared that if he ever said anything about the Mondays out loud, Diedrich Bader would pop out from behind a filing cabinet and punch him in the head.

Still though, it was a mostly terrible life with tiny interludes of peace and quiet. Unfortunately, on account of his tinnitus, even Ben's peace and quiet was a little louder than it should have been. When he woke up from a well-earned nap on a Saturday, the floaters in his visual spectrum panning across the white ceiling of his bedroom, his heart would skip a beat. What was it? It was an anxiety attack. It always was.

Friday night was the only time he ever relaxed. Dread for the coming work week always started as soon as he rose on Saturday and continued on through the rest of the weekend. Friday night was fun. That's why he always tried to spend it with Maria.

The rest of the weekend was all about Erin's twisted New England version of domestic bliss. "What the fuck was going out for brunch anyway? She always wanted to do this goofy-ass shit like going to the park or a museum. It was like a daytime date with someone you'd been with for a million years already. I really can't be bothered to put in that much time. Shit, I didn't want to put that much time in, even when I was first dating her. Also, somehow, I always spent Saturday afternoon dragging some heavy household adornment Erin had purchased from some pretentious showroom into her house. It's like she thought, if she just put one more piece of tacky garbage in the entryway, the house—and by extension, her life—would be complete. I'll tell you what was complete, my exhaustion from carrying heavy-ass shit into her house."

In Ben's mind, the workweek started Saturday morning. It might as well have, since the dread of Monday swallowed everything after Friday night. Time was a nemesis and a thief. When he was a kid, he read Robinson Crusoe. To Ben, the story was a dream come true. Ben daydreamed that about being on that island, no days of the week, no rudder, no foreboding of the pain to be inflicted by the modern world in the coming days.

That particular Monday was worse than most of the others. A city prosecutor was required to be present for all criminal hearings, indeed, any criminal proceeding in SMC. The city was always the charging party, so the city always had to be present. The court staff ensured the smooth operation of the courtrooms, and the judges presided over the hearing calendars and trials. Also, a hodgepodge of public defenders, private criminal defense attorneys, and pro se defendants represented those charged with crimes, but the prosecutors managed the courtroom. That is, prosecutors decided what cases to call and when.

Nobody wanted the Monday morning calendar, and since Ben was perpetually outside of the clique of trial unit prosecutors that his supervisor doted attention on, he routinely ended up with the most shit of the shit assignments. That's how he wound up being the prosecutor in Courtroom 1001 that Monday morning.

On the flipside, those courtrooms were arenas, and the attorneys were gladiators. As the only prosecutor in the room, Ben was the reigning champion, and he fought all comers. Walking into those courtrooms, surrounded by hostile defendants, apathetic court staff, and weaponized defense attorneys forged him in a way that few will ever understand. It's easy to pick a fight when all your friends are standing right behind you. In those SMC courtrooms, the gallery was routinely filled with defendants, and the jury box with their defense attorneys.

"And I fuckin' walk into the courtroom five minutes late and look at all the annoyed public defenders sittin' in the jury box. They always sit there because there's no jury during hearing calendars, and if they sit in the box, they can avoid talking to their clients in the gallery. I see 'em there, and I'm always like, 'That's a fuckin' terrible lookin' jury for the city.' None of those little pea-brained, pubescent, Ivy-League twats ever laughed. Shit, I know they're not clever. Any rich kid that goes to an Ivy-League school, clearly, lacks cleverness and originality, but they couldn't even track what was, comedically, pretty low-hangin' fruit." If that was the role the world had cast him in, Ben was happy to oblige, and he did.

So, Ben slayed them, one-by-one. In that manner, he went about the city's business, day-after-day, month-after-month, and eventually, year-after-year. He did so with a smile on his face, but never an inviting one. It was never a good-morning-it's-nice to-see-you smile, but instead, an I-can't-wait to-adorn-my-apartment-with-your-entrails-and-skull smile.

It was true that Ben generally dreaded work, and as such, dreaded Monday more than any other workday. Further, he dreaded Monday morning more than Monday afternoon. At least, on Monday afternoon, there was light at the end of the tunnel. At any given time on a Monday afternoon, Monday was only a couple of hours away from being over. Monday morning carried no such solace, just torment.

Ben loved to complain about work, but he didn't wholly hate the job either. Even a shitty Monday morning pretrial calendar carried with it some perks. For instance, he arrived at about five minutes after nine that morning. Court starts at nine, and making the judge wait on him always put a smile on his face. Also, defense attorneys that annoyed him or that he simply didn't like... He could push their matters to the end of the calendar. A prosecutor would be stuck in that same courtroom all morning doing hearings. Public defenders had dozens of clients with matters in a handful of different courtrooms on any given day, so making them sit and wait on you to call their case was always a good way to reinforce the pecking order. For the private criminal defense attorneys, spending a whole morning in a court room for one five-minute hearing took serious billable time away from other cases, so keeping them there screwed with their ability to earn fees.

Ben liked watching their bewildered little faces every time he called the next case, just hoping and praying they were next. For them, it was like sitting at the Department of Motor Vehicles, but worse. At least, at the DMV you got that little slip of paper with a number on it.

Sometimes, they got angry. Ben liked that even more. Some defense attorneys would get so annoyed, they'd actually just start interrupting between hearings, asking the judge to call their cases. Several of the public defenders that Ben didn't care for eventually just stopped showing up for hearings at nine altogether. Since they knew Ben would call their cases last, they'd just show up ten minutes before the lunch recess.

It was true that Ben was a miscreant and contrarian. The only predicate to him disagreeing was for you to take a position. For no better reason than to simply disagree, Ben would take the opposite position. The Criminal Division at the city attorney's office was a team, but Ben could never be a team player. It simply wasn't in his DNA. If the city had any fortitude whatsoever, they'd have fired hm, but Seattle is the land of lollipops. Grown-ups don't run the city, and the governing body of adolescents that pretend to can't stand up to their own employees. Ben had no respect for them because they were flaccid windbags—and of course—suckers one and all.

Because of the extreme fear and aversion that the city government had toward being perceived as intolerant, people like Ben could bend it at will. And he did. Or as Ben put it, "Those fuckers have no fuckin' balls, so I do what the fuck I please. They can't fire nobody, and even if they did, they're getting reinstated after suing the city for a shitload of money. Fuck 'em, right?"

Because Ben's supervisors thought giving him Monday morning pretrial calendars was some sort of clever and incognito way of punishing him for not toeing the line, he decided to just turn it right back on them. Prosecutors have to prepare in advance for those pretrial hearings. They have to read the case filings, police reports, etc. They have to be prepared to ask the court for sanctions and conditions of release, arraign and charge defendants, set cases for trial, and about a hundred other things.

Over the weekend, the calendar dockets change. Preparation done Friday afternoon for Monday morning is apt to be largely useless by the time Monday morning actually rolls around. It was normal to have a half dozen cases reassigned to a different court room over the weekend, and a half dozen more moved into your courtroom. The expectation was that prosecutors with Monday morning calendars would work over the weekend to keep their prep up to date or wake up at five on Monday morning to re-prep what had changed since Friday afternoon. In short, Monday morning calendars were twice the prep work, and a weekend killer. So, one day, Ben just stopped doing any prep whatsoever. He'd just show up and make it up while he was on the record in court.

That first Monday he did it, no one really seemed to notice he was completely unprepared, so he just stopped preparing for all of his calendars. That, in and of itself, cut about twelve hours out of his work week, time he diligently repurposed into napping time in his office chair or the conference room he'd discovered upstairs. He couldn't be sure if his supervisors knew he was always unprepared for court, but he suspected they knew. The funny thing is, even if they did know, it really wouldn't have made much difference. His supervisors were, likely, already aware of what Ben had more recently discovered himself. That is, SMC was a joke—a kangaroo court— run by children. At SMC, laws, rules, and authority were just suggestions, not directives to follow. Rulings were arbitrary, unmoored from reality and good sense, certainly unencumbered by existing laws. Everybody just made up whatever they wanted to do and asked a judge to rubberstamp it; and a lot of the time, they did. Ben didn't need to prepare for that, so he just made it up from that point on.

That particular Monday, Ben saw a trespassing case come up on the pretrial docket. Actually, he saw a few, but two piqued his interest. The defendant in the first one was named Buddy Gorton. For the purposes of hearing calendars, the prosecutor assigned to the courtroom handled all the cases, but based on the defendant's last name, the case was permanently assigned to a particular prosecutor. In other words, any of the prosecutors may handle any of the cases in routine hearings, but if the case fell into your alpha block, you ultimately owned it. Ben was currently the trial unit's D–G prosecutor, which meant he owned the Buddy Gorton case.

Ben knew it was mid-December, not because his birthday had just happened, which it had, but because of the weather. Ben didn't celebrate his birthday. When he was a kid, his parents made a big deal out of it, but whenever it was his birthday, he could only think about his older brother Mike. Mike hadn't died on his birthday or anything, but he was killed shortly after Ben's birthday. They'd spent the day together, that last one of Ben's birthdays before Mike was killed, so Ben's brain had stitched Mike's death to Ben's birthday.

It didn't stop people around Ben from celebrating on his behalf, though. Erin had gotten him a very expensive Brooks Brothers tie, a pair of gold David Donahue cufflinks, and an early printing of a terrible book about a prep-school twat, *Catcher in the Rye* by J.D. Salinger. Maria got him a very reasonably priced vinyl copy of the amazing *Youth Anthems for the New Order* by Reagan Youth, two Rainer tall boy six-packs, and the greatest blow job in the history of mankind. Erin had a knack for giving Ben what she wanted him to want. Maria had a knack for giving Ben the best version of anything he could ever want.

In any case, Ben knew it was mid-December because it was too cold to be outside for long without a jacket, but warm enough that having that same jacket on would make you sweat. It was too wet, as well, but that wasn't unique to mid-December. When he came into the courthouse that morning, his skin was cool and wet. He wasn't sure if it was sweat or rain running down the back of his neck and into the back of his shirt's collar. For that first hour, everybody in the courtroom was always sopping wet. The carpeted portions of the courtroom were squishy, and your shoes would slosh around in it. By the time the Gorton case was called, mostly everybody was dry, but it was that frizzy sort of dry. Freshly pressed clothes now had bumpy raindrop wrinkles, quaffed hair was flat, and the leather of men's oxfords soaked up the water like a sponge, leaving a visible waterline even after the shoe was dry. That was enough to tell him know it was mid-December, but also, the calendar of open trial dates on the courtroom wall confirmed for him, it was, indeed, mid-December.

The arrest had just happened a few days prior, and as is the normal procedure, a review and filing prosecutor had charged and arraigned Mr. Gorton. In Washington State, release of criminal defendants pending trial is the default. The only time courts hold criminal defendants without bail is where there is no less restrictive means to assure they will appear at future hearings, and/or because the court has good reason to believe the criminal defendant will commit further violent crimes or intimidate witnesses. Mr. Gorton had been squatting in a house that was in the process of being flipped—as they say—but it appeared the people financing the flip had taken a break. The house was not far from Erin's house in Madrona. For Mr.

Gorton, a partially renovated and vacant house was a perfect place to call home for a while.

Although, he was not charged with obstruction, assault, or resisting arrest, Mr. Gorton had scuffled with the police at the scene. So, even though the trespass of an unoccupied house was not, in and of itself, a violent crime, at the arraignment, the filing prosecutor had no problem convincing the judge to deny Mr. Gorton bail. Mr. Gorton had a long criminal history, including dozens of violent felony and misdemeanor convictions, most of which were from out of state. In addition, he had numerous drug-related and domestic violence convictions. On several other occasions, he'd been found incompetent to stand trial altogether.

In a nutshell, Mr. Gorton was a mess. He fit the classic stereotype Ben had become so familiar with doing this job. That is, Mr. Gorton had been in the system since his youth. He'd spent much of his life in prison or mental wards. In addition to severe mental illness, he had lifelong problems with substance abuse. Without knowing anything more about him, the fact that Mr. Gorton committed violent crimes seemed almost intuitive. In addition, he was black, from the south — rural Tennessee, to be precise — and had no education or skills to speak of. As with most of the indigent defendants Ben saw, Mr. Gorton likely never really had a chance. People who rise from adversity pretty regularly espouse that if they can do it, so can you. But there is adversity, and then there is *adversity*. Mr. Gorton was of the latter variety, and comparing that to garden variety adversity was not like comparing apples to apples. It was more like comparing apples to hand grenades.

In any case, Ben was a prosecutor, and it was his job to prosecute Mr. Gorton. Mr. Gorton has a public defender, and it was her obligation to advocate for him. She did so, poorly. Like most DPD attorneys, she was just a kid; certainly, an intelligent one, as they mostly were, but not a clever one. And most certainly, *not* a stellar lawyer. Being a good lawyer isn't just about being smart. It's no more about being smart, than being a great professional fighter is about being physically strong. That is to say, being strong helps, but professional fighters defeat opponents because they have superior combat skills. Skilled fighters defeat stronger opponents pretty routinely. For a lawyer, having a high IQ helps, but a dumb lawyer who possesses superior practice skills typically carries the day.

So, Mr. Gorton was an in-custody defendant that Monday. His public defender made an impromptu argument for release, which was summarily rejected by Judge Cahill without Ben saying a word. Despite his unfortunate circumstances, Ben would have argued to keep Mr. Gorton incarcerated. He clearly wound up in Seattle because he was migrating from place-to-place as he burned bridges. It wasn't just a trope that Seattle was a "sanctuary city." Seattle is a tolerant place, and the down and out did find their way here pretty often. It was also simply the logical conclusion to make, and what really did happen to many in the criminal justice system. Basically, Mr. Gorton was running out of places to go, so it made sense that he eventually found his way here.

When a person has completely burned out a place to the point that he will be arrested on site, he moves on. Based on the dates and locations of his convictions, Mr. Gorton had been moving on every year or two for decades, and if released, he was highly unlikely to reappear at all. In fact, it was more likely he'd be on a bus headed for Portland within a few hours of being released. Portland was close, but in Oregon, so heading there got you out of Washington state's jurisdiction. At that point, nobody is ever extradited back to a different state for something like a misdemeanor warrant. In short, getting out of the state is, effectively, getting off the hook.

All of that was apparent to Ben within thirty seconds of looking at the case filings and Mr. Gorton's criminal history. While Ben had stopped preparing for calendars, he was still very capable of synthesizing the issues in a case for a pretrial hearing fairly quickly. Nothing about Mr. Gorton's case struck Ben as being out of the ordinary, not that day, He was just some other guy charged with trespassing on some other Monday morning calendar, in some other city on the edge of the world.

The other trespass case that got his attention was the Sarah Waltham case. It wasn't Ben's case for trial. Chatty Bobby was U-Z, so it was his. It did get Ben's attention, though. He imagined that Sarah Waltham was a fairly common name. Whether you realize it or not, basically every combination of a common first name attached to a common last name resulted in the actual name of thousands of people in America alone. Christ—he thought—how many Ben Sullivans are there in America? That Sarah Waltham, that day, on that calendar, was actually someone that Ben knew.

They weren't friends or anything, but she had been in law school when he was. She went to the law school at Seattle University. Ben went to U-dub. SU was the law school that the dumb rich kids who couldn't get into an Ivy League program went to. It had the similar paradigmatic trappings of wealth and was a good place to push the inevitable underperformer from the family. SU and U-dub were the only two law schools in Seattle, and they held joint events pretty regularly. Those events were usually things like job fairs. Ben had met Sarah at one of them.

Then, he met her again at the interview for one of the internships they'd both applied for. After that, they both wound up at that same law firm internship the summer after their 2L year. They had these terrible windowless offices at the end of a dark hallway on the dead-end floor of a large downtown law firm that had a defense-side employment practice. Those two offices were square, had almost no power outlets, and were barely big enough for a tiny desk and chair. Ben was convinced that both of their offices had just been storage closets that had been converted into offices to cram interns into.

Neither of them were interested in employment defense. Ben was interested in workers' rights and union law. Sarah was mostly interested in civil liberties and social movements. There weren't a lot of civil liberties and workers' rights law firms taking on summer law school interns. Actually, there weren't a lot of civil liberties and workers' rights law firms at all, so a downtown law firm with an employment practice, even a defense-side one, was better than nothing.

Not surprisingly, Sarah had no criminal record. She had been living at the Occupy Seattle camp at Seattle Central Community College, and was one of the handful of protestors to ignore the eviction order that ultimately had cleared the encampment from the south end of the campus. Unlike Mr. Gorton, Sarah didn't show up to court in an orange jumpsuit. She wasn't wearing shackles. She wasn't escorted through the secure door by one of the marshals. That's because she wasn't in custody. Of course, there was no reason she should be, even though, according to the police report, she, too, had scuffled with police in much the same way Mr. Gorton had. Also, she was not represented by a public defender, but instead, a private criminal defense attorney of some note in Seattle.

Ben had been too preoccupied to notice before, but that morning, the gallery had filled with people—not defendants, not even other lawyers—people with signs, cameras, and microphones. By the morning recess, it had become clear that the courtroom was becoming a media event. Reporters from the *Seattle Times*, and the weekly alternative papers (*The Stranger* and *The Seattle Weekly*) were there, and at least, one local TV news crew. Ben didn't have to read the signs people held to know they were Occupy protestors.

That morning, Buddy Gorton and Sarah Waltham's cases were both set for trial, but for very different reasons. Mr. Gorton was in custody, and the longer his attorney waited to set the case for trial, the longer he'd sit in jail. For Sarah, setting the case for trial got more media attention for Occupy. Sarah's case was set for trial the first week of January 2012. Mr. Gorton's was set for the second week of January 2012.

Chapter 27

Ben always assumed all organizations and, to some extent—and for that matter—all people were corrupt. And he quite easily maintained that belief without ever seeing it firsthand. It was like Bigfoot. The forests up in the Cascades went on without end in every direction. They were thick too, vines and bushes everywhere. That uninterrupted tree canopy shielded the forest below from any ariel surveillance, and exploring those forests on foot in any meaningful way was equally unrealistic. Bigfoot was out there. Ben just hadn't seen him firsthand. He hadn't seen corruption firsthand either, until that Monday afternoon when the Criminal Division Chief Corey came into his office.

Normally, Corey would summon Ben into his office—the office with the cum-stained carpet. Corey liked summoning the line prosecutors to his corner office by having his assistant send a calendar invite for some time next week. That day was different. Corey was different, less condescending. He actually looked a little out of sorts. At that moment, Ben assumed that Corey had somehow caught wind of Ben fucking Maria on his desk. It wasn't that Ben thought Corey had any sort of James Bond surveillance cameras in his office or anything. It was more just because pretty much all of the line prosecutors knew

Maria and Ben were hooking up. To that end, Ben had been telling anyone who cared to listen about how he'd blown his load all over Corey's carpet, so he figured that it might have finally made it back to him. Either it hadn't, or Corey wasn't currently interested in confronting him about it, or demanding Ben pay for the carpet to be cleaned.

It turned out, Corey was just there to coerce him into doing something unethical. That figured. Corey was the Criminal Division Chief. That's the sort of job someone gets when they're testing out the waters for a political career. It's like proto politics. Doing something dirty for a shady city council member was just an entrance exam for Corey, the thing he needed to do to illustrate he was a team player to the city council.

That house that Mr. Gorton had been squatting in actually belonged to one of the Seattle City Council Members, Joseph Young. Mr. Young had run out of money mid-flip, accounting for the dormancy of the house when Mr. Gorton came across it. Corey knew it was the sort of case that the city attorney's office pretty much always offered a time-served plea deal. Mr. Young had strongly suggested that Corey impress on the trial prosecutor the importance of taking the case to trial and pushing for the maximum sentence. In Washington, a gross misdemeanor, such as criminal trespass was punishable by a year in jail and an $5,000 fine. Even in Seattle, politics is going to politic, so while Ben was not expecting this conversation, it made sense to him. Even more importantly, Mr. Young impressed upon Corey that, as a very liberal member of the city council, he could not be seen to be antagonizing a homeless man; but as a property owner, he expected the prosecutor's office to give him the justice he desired.

"So, you want me to carry some hypocrite's water for him?" Ben said.

"It's not unethical or anything. We can take any case to trial and push for the maximum sentence anytime we want to," Corey responded.

"Yeah, but we never fuckin' do. A year in King County because a dude was sleeping in a vacant house? Get fuckin' real, man."

"Look Ben, this is what we're doing with Mr. Gorton's case. You don't have to like it, but it's what's happening. I can assign it to someone else, but I'd rather not."

"Yeah, because if you do, the public defender will ask why you're benching the assigned prosecutor; her and everyone else."

"It's a solid case. We can move forward to trial, and we can request a year in jail. I'm the chief, and that's what this office is doing with the Gorton case."

"That's what this office is doing as a political favor for a city council member who wants to look like a social justice crusader, but act like a hang 'em high conservative?"

"Are you going to be the trial prosecutor on this thing or not?"

Ben never actually answered Corey, but instead just turned his head and peered intently into his computer screen.

After a minute or so, Corey just said, "Good enough, Ben."

Then he got up and walked nonchalantly out of Ben's office.

Ben was expecting an email by the end of the day from Corey notifying him that the Gorton case had been officially reassigned to another prosecutor, but it never came. By the end of the week, the case was still showing up in their case management program as assigned to Ben, so Ben decided to simply ignore Councilman Young's hypocritical desires and Corey's proto-political ambitions. Other than the unseemly overtures, the case was no different than a hundred others Ben had on his caseload, so he just worked it the way he'd work any other.

It was a nothing criminal trespass, easily provable, and Mr. Gorton had dozens of misdemeanor convictions from as many different jurisdictions. For a case like that, the next step was to put together a proposed plea deal for the public defender to review with her client. Guys like Gorton don't really care about pleading to misdemeanor convictions. A normal person, a person with a clean criminal record, would fight tooth and nail to keep any conviction off their record, misdemeanor or otherwise. Most people, people like Ben, whose professional livelihoods largely depended on keeping a clean criminal record, would rather do the year in jail over taking the conviction. A year in jail is just a year sitting in a jail cell, but for a lawyer, a criminal conviction on your record turns you into damaged goods professionally for life.

For a guy like Gorton, it was different. He already had so many convictions, another misdemeanor conviction wouldn't keep him from getting employment or an apartment. Any job or apartment he could get with forty-three prior convictions, he could still get with forty-four prior convictions. Ben actually envied many aspects of the existence of people like Mr. Gorton. Gorton could do and say what he pleased at any given time in his life. Because he had lost a vested interest in society at such an early age, he never had anything to protect. There was no mortgage to be paid, no car payment, no student loans, no wardrobe upkeep, nothing that normal people were required to do.

To Ben, the "normal people" deal seemed worse and worse every year. "You take on mountains of debt just to scrape by in the big city. Why? Because you don't want to be a carpenter or plumber who lives in Tacoma. Why? Because you want to break out of the caste you were born in to. Why? Because you want to have an easier existence, work less, play more. Why? Probably because you don't fuckin' realize that none of those things will fill the hole inside you. At best, they just give you a few more toys to distract yourself as you decay into the anonymous morass of nothing that planet Earth and human existence is." That's all Ben was doing. Most people never even figure that much out, but Ben was starting to understand. Understanding didn't, all of a sudden, create that illusive sense of purpose that people are always looking for, but at least, it somewhat explained why he could never feel right.

The deal was illusory in any case. Playing the game never got you there. Ben had no mansion. He had a crap apartment. Ben wasn't a millionaire. He mostly lived paycheck-to-paycheck, and he'd be paying for his education until he was an old man. Ben didn't work less and play more. He worked more than he thought any human should and played less than at any point in his life. He didn't have control over his career. He was a wage slave, working for the municipal government in the municipality where he lived. Ben wasn't even really the sort of lawyer that mattered. He effectively pimped-out his law license to the prosecutor's office in exchange for a paycheck. Lawyers that matter ran their own shops, took cases they wanted, and really did have some societal leverage. They weren't desk zombies at pretty law firms or ugly government offices.

Even though Ben was walking around apparently "free," he

was caged, nonetheless. Mr. Gorton was lying down in his bunk in King County Jail, free as a bird. For guys like him, taking the standard deal of 'plead guilty with time served' meant he was released from jail on the very same day the plea and sentencing were completed. Ben, on the other hand, would never be free.

When the prosecutor and defense attorney agree to a deal before a court calendar, the prosecutor can often squeeze a plea and sentencing onto the morning docket, and that same criminal defendant is released by that afternoon. Everybody wins. It's a depressing and demoralizing game of human inequity and suffering, but that's what a win looks like at SMC.

Ben emailed the deal to Mr. Gorton's public defender, Susan. To Ben's surprise, Mr. Gorton rejected the offer outright. At first, Ben chalked it up to Susan being a new attorney. He figured since she was fresh out of law school, she just wanted to earn her stripes by taking a case to trial. Most of the DPD attorneys were pretty cagey until they got a trial or two under their belt, but Susan didn't seem like that at all. As a matter of fact, Susan seemed a little like she was afraid of her own shadow.

One of the defining characteristics of the DPD true believers when they pop out of the Ivy-League womb is that people have been telling them they are special, unique, and brilliant for so long that they actually believe it. They will stand up in court, with no idea of what's going on, and proceed to lecture an elected judge about why a career prosecutor doesn't understand some basic point of law. They do it with completely straight faces, too. Ben used to try to figure out if they really believed what they were saying or were just phenomenal performers. He never really figured it out. He settled on the assumption that some were likely great performers, while others were probably deluded little megalomaniacs, and the remainder were definitely a combination of the two. Susan wasn't, though.

Susan had been camouflaged in plain sight her entire life. She was masquerading as the thing she was meant to be, but not the thing she was. She hid in the center of packs of self-confident schoolmates. She raised her hand only when the answer to the question was obvious or she could see someone else had already been called on. She possessed ability but lacked self-confidence. She made it through all situations by being both visible and interchangeably invisible. To say that, on any given day, in any one of the hundreds of classrooms and lecture halls she'd sat in, that any one of those teachers or professors could have easily mistaken her for any one of five other white brunettes in the class was not a stretch. In fact, she often believed if she simply grabbed a white girl off the street and paid her to go to class in her place, no one would have been the wiser, so long as that girl was a brunette. For anybody seeking to stand out, this might sound like a nightmare. To Susan this sort of selective covert invisibility was just a well-laid, lifelong survival instinct and mode of operation.

She had the pedigree, prep school, and Ivy-League under-graduate and law schools. Harvard and Yale, respectively. How original! She had the brand-new, Tom Ford, two-piece suits in Navy Blue and Charcoal Gray. She had the name, Prescott. Her particular branch on that family tree called Prescott was very long, and very thick. At least, it had been, way back where that branch started near the trunk, back when it had actually been a limb. On the distal end of it, Susan was no more than a twig that would never thicken enough to grow even one decent leaf. In fact, even her antecedent branch had failed to produce anything more than the little twig Susan was. She was an only child. The only child of a father who was an only child himself.

She was pretty, not beautiful, and she was friendly, but not personable. More importantly, she was smart and capable, but not brilliant or bombastic. And unlike her DPD counterparts, and much to her own surprise, she would eventually become a skilled and effective lawyer. While it rarely appeared to be the case around SMC, the reality was that the quiet and fastidiously diligent lawyer eventually mastered the game. While her colleagues shouted directives from soapboxes that were sequestered well inside their tiny little corner of this tiny little culture war that was taking place in this tiny little corner of the country, Susan learned how to be a lawyer.

She didn't know all that yet, but it would be the case, nonetheless. At that time, she was still trying to be what her father told her she needed to be, the standard bearer for a blunted line on the branch of a family tree bearing a name that nobody had really cared about in over a hundred years. Susan had, many times, wished to see that old money tree of Prescott fall. Its fall would set her free, and it's fallen trunk could foster new life instead of producing decay and prolonging its inevitable demise. She vowed long ago not to reproduce, largely to hasten the demise of that ugly old tree. But if she ever did, that child would not be named Prescott.

In any case, Mr. Gorton was staying put right where he was in King County Jail, and he was doing so because that's what he wanted, not because his lawyer's ego required blood in the SMC amphitheater arena. As Ben was reading the carefully-worded rejection email from Susan, it dawned on him what was actually happening. Mr. Gorton was from Tennessee. Most of his criminal convictions were in the south, southwest, or southern California. It was December in Seattle, and while PNW winters are certainly milder than say, Minnesota, they were still not pleasant. From that email, Ben guessed that Mr. Gorton had nowhere warmer he thought he could go, he lacked the ability to leave Seattle anytime in the near future, or both. If those were your options, Ben surmised, staying in county for the winter was the path of least resistance. That said, even if the city just simply dropped the charges, Ben imagined Mr. Gorton would still be elated to leave county and would simply figure out alternate accommodations for the winter. Sitting in jail was still sitting in jail, and getting out, no strings attached, was still the better of all deals, bad weather or not.

For her part, Susan was terrified of going to trial. She was actually a little terrified of Mr. Gorton, as her background hadn't given her much interaction with indigent or diverse people. Similarly, she was terrified of having to try a case against Ben, as by that time, he was the prosecutors' trial gladiator who had the scariest reputation.

Giving Mr. Gorton the time-served plea would have caused Ben quite a bit of trouble at work. He even suspected that if it had been agreed to, Corey might have caught wind of it before the plea and sentencing could take place and kill it before it could happen. Ben hoped that he'd get it in front of a judge before anyone at his office was the wiser. If Mr. Gorton had pled, by the time anyone at his office figured out what was going on, it would be too late for anyone to unwind the clock. Ben might be written up. Corey might even try to fire him—and there was a secret part of Ben that hoped for that—but either way, he suspected he'd be alright.

The prosecutors had a union, and while the city continued to categorize them as at-will employees, Ben knew enough about labor law to know that didn't jive with Supreme Court precedent on the matter, and the city was wise enough not to try to play the at-will card too heavily. If fact, in poker terms, it was no card at all, just a bluff. Even prior to any involvement of his union, he doubted the thing would have legs at all because government workers, even without unions, essentially have a property interest in their jobs and civil service protections. Also, if Council Member Young wanted to press the issue with Corey, Corey might finally feel enough pressure to threaten to expose Council Member Young for the hypocrite he was. If Corey sweated Ben about the issue, Ben could threaten to expose him and Young.

Regardless, Ben would have acted in accordance with his own code of conduct over any imposed on him by a job or even the bar association. He didn't view ethical behavior the way the bar did, or even the way Corey did. Ben neither strictly adhered to the dogma of the bar's ethical canons, nor capitulated to the demands of less scrupulous fellow attorneys. As with most situations, Ben was in the hot seat, all alone, and intent on being defiant, come what may.

Unfortunately, Mr. Gorton had forced his hand. He could have just dismissed the case. That would have caused him no more trouble than a time-served plea, but that was where that tiny inkling of being an actual prosecutor kicked in for him. Trying a trespasser for strictly political reasons would never sit right with him. But dismissing an easily-provable case, simply because a defendant had figured out how to game the system, didn't work for him either. Ben was fair and equitable—not a lollipopper—but he didn't like being taken for a sucker either. The following Monday, Ben backburnered other casework and started prepping Mr. Gorton's case for trial.

Chapter 28

efore Mike died, their mom Barbara had been a fully-engaged mother. Mike's murder had eaten his mother and father alive from the inside out. For a long time, it left them both emotionally catatonic. Back then, Ben could see them both peeking out from behind their own eyes, but their mouths were all gummed over, slathered with some sort of gluey goo forged from recent emotional distress. They'd just stare out from those person-shaped cages they were imprisoned in, silently screaming for someone to stop their suffering.

To Ben, it seemed like they didn't speak at all that year, but in reality, they must have spoken and interacted, at least minimally, from time-to-time. It just didn't seem like it to Ben. That's how memories work, especially when you're a little kid. Memories grab onto the strongest aspect of a situation, and for Ben, the strongest aspect of that time was watching, day in and day out, the deterioration of the human husks he called mom and dad.

Eventually, they both emerged from those trauma cocoons that they'd spun themselves into to stop the pain, the prison cells they had to escape to rejoin the human race. Big Ben managed the recovery better than Barbara, but neither of them were ever the same again. It would be fair to say that Big Ben and Barbara had been the "before Mike died" versions of themselves, and forever after that were the "after Mike died" versions of themselves. That latter version of Barbara wasn't cold or uncaring, but at the same time, she was never really warm or invested ever again.

A few years before Mike died, Ben began to take notice of the role that church played in their lives. He noticed it only because he had been at that age when contrarian children learn to ask the question "Why?" One word, and one word alone that, when asserted as a genuine statement of curiosity and proto dissent, forced accountability for hypocrisy from those who were the least of the lesser, right up to those who styled themselves as the most among us.

Mike's deterioration into crack addiction had just begun, and Barbara was, naturally, worried. Technically, they were all Catholics—both Bens, Barbara, even Mike. Barbara was the only one that actually went to Mass, though.

Barbara was walking out the door to get to noon Mass one Saturday when Ben said, "I saw Father Mike getting into his car when he couldn't walk."

"When was that?" Barbara asked him.

"The other day. He was coming out of the Fern Hill Tavern. I was on my bike across the street at the ampm getting hot dogs. He was drunk."

"He shouldn't do that. It's dangerous."

"If he's doing a bad thing, then why doesn't God fire him from his church job?"

"It's complicated, Ben."

"Why?"

"Because if the world could only rely on people who were

only good and never did bad things, no good things would ever happen."

"But why?"

"Because there's a whole bunch of people who do mostly bad things, and only a couple of people that do only good things. So, most of the good things that happen have to come from the actions of mostly good people who also do bad things."

"So, Father Mike is good at church, but he's bad at the tavern."

"And apparently, he's also sometimes bad when he's in his car. To be perfectly honest, a lot of the time when I'm getting host from him and I can smell his breath, I'm pretty sure he's being bad at church too."

"So, at church, he's bad and good?"

"Basically, yes. Being drunk at church is bad, and in a perfect world, he wouldn't do that at all. But he's also devoted his life to spreading the word of God, and that's, maybe, the best thing a person can do."

"But that's the hip-poc thing you and dad are always sayin' when you're watching President Bush on TV."

"You're sort of right. We're all hypocrites, to some extent, President Bush more than most."

"But being a hy-po-crite is bad."

"Ben, how many colors are in your Crayola box?"

"Sixty-four... Well, now it's like sixty-one because I lost a couple of them and broke one."

"Are all sixty-one of those crayons either black or white?"

"Of course not, there's lots of colors."

"I bet there're even a few shades of gray in there."

"Yeah, probably like three or four."

"Exactly! Gray is black and white, but neither. What about

this, do you have any reds and greens?"

"Of course."

"Do you know what color you get if you mix red and green?"

"Brown, even dumb Lisa at school knows that."

"Is brown important?"

"Of course, you can't color a tree without brown."

"So, brown is good?"

"I mean, I like trees, so yeah, sure."

"But red and green are opposites."

"Why?"

"When I'm driving you to school, what color light means go?

"Green."

"And what color light means stop?"

"Yeah, yeah, yeah, I get it already."

"Life is never just black and white, so in reality, it's mostly just gray. People are opposing and separate colors, combining to make a whole new color. Someday, you're likely to find yourself faced with the choice of doing a very important, good thing that's hard, or doing an easier but widely-accepted bad thing."

"And I'm all covered in gray and brown when I'm a grown up!"

"That's right, grown-ups are all covered in gray and brown. In fact, we're covered in them most of the time, but nobody judges you based on being awash in gray and brown. People judge you on whether you can be covered in gray and brown but still transcend them at appropriate times."

"You mean, to do like a better good, even if you're still sort of being bad?"

"Exactly."

"You mean, like when Han Solo saves Luke Skywalker at the

end of Star Wars?"

"Exactly. People will judge you based on doing the one better good at the right time, then the predictable and insignificant bads that everybody does at pretty regular intervals. Do you understand?"

"I guess, we'll find out. I mean, I like Han Solo."

Chapter 29

hatty Bobby looked scared. He was sitting at counsel table, or maybe he was sitting under it. He was slumped down so far in his chair that, for a minute, Ben thought what Chatty Bobby was doing might actually qualify as sitting under counsel table. It was his first solo trial, and only his second total. The prosecutor's office had been in a hiring crisis of sorts. Between a short-lived but very real societal malaise for the legal profession in the past few years, and an outright aversion to prosecution as a career by many recent law school graduates, the Criminal Division was a little shorthanded. In times past, a new prosecutor like Chatty Bobby would have had a supervisor sitting second chair for however many trials were necessary for him to feel comfortable sitting in the chair by himself. This was not 'times past.' What Chatty Bobby got was one DUI trial with Ben sitting second chair, and no supervisor anywhere to be found.

For Ben, Mr. Gorton's trial was the following week, and because the trial prep was so simple, he decided to spend a lot of the week sitting in the gallery at Chatty Bobby's trial in SMC 1103. He should have been doing other work, but he didn't really do much "other work" by that point. He did skip a couple of office-chair naps that week, but it was worth it. While Ben may have been a crap prosecutor overall, he was a skilled and curious trial attorney.

Every attorney plays judges, witnesses, and juries a little differently. In all honestly, most of them have no idea what they're doing. A trial isn't a crucible of learned principles designed to forge an objective and legally supportable truth at the conclusion. Trials are three-ring circuses mixed up with an underground fight club and presented like a play at the Fifth Avenue Theater downtown. The attorneys are ringmasters, used-car salesmen, and directors, all rolled up in one. Jerry Springer and Morton Downey Jr. would have been great trial attorneys.

Chatty Bobby had won that DUI trial when Ben was sitting second chair with him, or more accurately, Ben had made sure Chatty Bobby won that trial. This was different. This defense attorney, Brad Simms, was going to eat Chatty Bobby for lunch and pick his teeth with the bones. For Bobby, it really wasn't bad. Everyone had to be dismantled in this fashion once in a while; at least, at first. If no one ever took you apart in front of a crowd, you'd never learn how many things you were doing wrong. Most people never do, even after the humiliation. Chatty Bobby would figure it out eventually, Ben knew that, but it was going to be a long week for him. Still, as far as public humiliation goes, a tough trial against a tough defense lawyer is pretty tepid.

Ben wasn't there to cheer Bobby on. There was no point; he was going to lose. He wasn't there to bask in Bobby's humiliation, either. Bobby was his friend. Ben was a student of the game, the game of trial work. This Brad Simms guy knew the game. He knew that a trial was a war of attrition that was most effectively fought with manipulation and psychological warfare, not rules of evidence and statutes. As far as Ben was concerned, because the game was to play the people, rather than the actual game, he strongly believed most people would be better represented at trial by that proverbial used-car salesman than an attorney. At least, the used-car salesman understood the game that was being played. Ben was there to see if Mr. Simms had any good tools in his repertoire that Ben could steal. And he did. Mr. Simms was exactly that sort of ringmaster, used-car salesmen, and director, rolled into one, Ben had hoped to find that week.

Similar to that pretrial calendar when Ben had set Sarah and Mr. Gorton's cases for trial, the gallery was overfull with Occupy protestors and local news media. This was Seattle, and the news media was left-leaning. Even the conservative *Seattle Times* was further left than any other major newspaper you'd find anywhere else in the state. That didn't bother Ben. Ben had always leaned left politically. He grew up in a working-class neighborhood with a father who was a union electrician. Everyone in his neighborhood growing up had been Democrats, but working-class cred and union membership was no longer the purity test in Puget Sound.

The Stranger sat furthest to the left; so far so, one might say their reporting bordered on the zealous. The shout downs for not immediately kowtowing to whatever political dogma was being spewed could be brutal. If the rising fascist tide on the extreme political right wore brown shirts, so did the oligarchy of group think on the far left. Both bonked you on the head with clubs for disagreeing with them. Ben laughed silently in his head when he realized that the extreme right and extreme left were so extreme that they were basically the same ideology from different perspectives. "Seriously, when are the two of them going to realize that they're in love with one another?"

In any case, in Seattle, thinking about things and having a different opinion than the cliques of politically-boisterous thought leaders and the Lollipop Gang had become forbidden. If not, forbidden, it certainly got you the stink eye at the grocery store from any of the quasi-famous or genuinely rich Seattle political elite.

The hijacking of the democratic process, and subversion of the principle of one person, one vote, died quietly in courtrooms in Seattle; as it did in courtrooms in Fayetteville. Ben was a contrarian by nature. Until he learned how to be more measured in his responses, you could expect his reply to be the opposite of what you just said. All independent thinkers start out as argumentative miscreants. That spark of individuality and rebellion in certain people that snaps back hard at anyone foolish enough to negligently deliver a slight is what keeps the world on its toes. Experience tends to temper the crude contrarian into something more charming and effective, because everyone knows that no one ever really wins an argument. No one ever really bullies someone into submission. They just ingrain resentment into a beaten foe and turn them into a lifelong enemy who will work tirelessly to undermine you. Ben had become so tempered and, as such, effective.

By that time, Ban had stopped having arguments altogether, except with Erin. Those were unavoidable, but in the rest of the world, he was the Zen assassin. He beat you down by agreeing with you, then politely convincing you that what he had to sell was the thing you had been looking for all along. That is, the aim and substance of his rational thought process remained, but his strategy to obtain agreement had changed.

The irony was that, by engaging in rational thought and

seeking pragmatic solutions and compromises, he'd been pushed into the largest group of people imaginable. Outside Seattle, and for that matter, Fayetteville, existed a true silent majority; and they were silent. Loud voices were only, maybe, ten percent of the population. Dissenters like Ben were no more than one percent, themselves. The loud ten percent was sufficient to resonate the dogmatic ideology of extremism and browbeat the remainder of the population into submission. But that silent majority, that largest slice of the pie by far, wanted and needed rational solutions, not extremist slogans. They weren't likely to get it, not from the loudmouths anyway, and Ben wished they'd speak up, because together, they would be the representatives of a true democracy.

Extremism had pushed Ben into that moderate middle, and as a somewhat quiet person himself, he somehow became the loudest voice in a large group of even quieter people. If he could organize them, they'd be a political force that would dwarf both right and left extremism. Unfortunately, even if he could do that, he'd become the loud voice shouting political purity edicts from on high, and they'd become the next evolution of club-wielding group thinkers.

The irony of ironies. Ben realized right then what he already, perhaps, always had known. The dissenter must remain the dissenter or suffer becoming the machine.

But those were bigger issues, better suited for more serious people. For Ben, it was just another week at SMC, and the stink eye was in full effect. He didn't come to watch Chatty Bobby wither on the vine, but it's what he was going to witness, nonetheless.

The negative press, decrying the city attorney's office for prosecuting the poor downtrodden Ms. Waltham had begun before the trial, and daily stories flooded the morning editions of multiple Seattle newspapers thereafter. It was simply the case that rich, white Seattle, and its news media propaganda arms were intent on saving poor Ms. Waltham from the humiliation of being prosecuted for a crime that hundreds of indigent people in Seattle were tried and convicted for in that same courthouse every year.

Based on the outpouring of support, and outright denouncement of Chatty Bobby and the city attorney's office for having the gall to force Ms. Waltham to endure this indignity, it was clear that the sensibilities of many in Seattle were, to say the least, offended. The fact that Sarah was rich and white, as well as mainly concerned with saving herself from having to pay the bill for going to law school, didn't seem to percolate into the narrative.

"Why would it? Rich, white people showing up to save a rich white girl's bacon wasn't racist, at all. Why wouldn't the 'liberal' news media focus all of its resources on shining a light on the injustice suffered by this poor woman. When has the news media ever focused on a missing rich, white woman while ignoring hundreds of missing poor, black ones?" Ben's hyperbole aside, there was an odd fascination with this case in Seattle that January.

Ben wasn't one to judge. Law school was too expensive, and the student loan system was certainly predatory and broken. That was all the truth. And he actually liked Sarah, as a person. But at the same time, he wondered how many of those reporters would be sitting in the gallery at Mr. Gorton's trial the following week.

Chatty Bobby blew it in voir dire. The jury wound up stacked with affluent white Seattleites who were more than happy to delude themselves into believing they were striking a blow for the liberal crusade by acquitting Sarah Waltham, licensed attorney. Sarah didn't just get a jury of her peers. She got a jury of her clones. It was American justice at work. If you can afford a better attorney than all the poor people, you get higher-quality justice. It wasn't a theory. It was a fact. Mr. Simms was able to admit several otherwise inadmissible pieces of evidence and testimony because Chatty Bobby wasn't experienced enough to make the appropriate objections. Any supervisors that might have been able to make the proper objections for him were nowhere to be found.

Ben had begun to expect that it wasn't just understaffing issues; nobody at his office wanted the stink of that trial on them, so they just steered clear altogether. Ben guessed, from his superiors' perspectives, that to leave one replaceable newbie prosecutor holding the bag for the whole case was better than to taint the whole office. To Ben, that sounded like professional camouflage for cowardice on an office-wide scale.

On the other side, Mr. Simms objected to every piece of evidence Chatty Bobby attempted to introduce. He also objected hundreds of times to completely unobjectionable testimony. He didn't win every objection, but he won a lot of them—and when he lost—he still broke Chatty Bobby's flow. In conjunction with all of the evidence that Mr. Simms had gotten admitted, Sarah's acquittal was imminent. Technically, the fact that Mr. Simms had purposely admitted several inappropriate pieces of evidence and testimony was unethical behavior, but he knew nobody would be making a bar complaint. Nobody ever did.

Recency and primacy; that's what trial attorneys know

that you don't. If you're sitting in a jury box, you're being brainwashed by an attorney like Mr. Simms from the moment he first opens his mouth until the last word of his closing argument. You've been led around by the nose, like a pig to slaughter. You've been programmed to decide the case in his favor, regardless of the actual evidence. He fed you his theory of the case immediately, and he wove it into every piece of his presentation, right to the end.

It's called a theme. Mr. Simms' went like this: "You have a right to protest, but the government doesn't have the right to censor." It's simple, and it's supposed to be. Ben could have come up with something better, something like: "Her tent. Her voice. Her rights." Ben liked using the triad because human brains are designed to remember lists of three items, so tapping into that ensures your theme will be ringing in the jurors' ears during deliberations the way a bad commercial jingle does. Either way, Mr. Simm's theme, while not the best one imaginable, was, nonetheless, effective, and that's all it needed to be. And this was a criminal trial, so he only needed one person to disagree with the prosecutor to hang the jury.

In Sarah's case, a hung jury would have operated much like an acquittal. Mr. Simms knew that the city attorney's office never retried people after hung juries, so if he muddled the record with inappropriate evidence and peeled off only one juror, he'd done his job. He'd done much better than that, because an acquittal was a complete exoneration.

The master class from Mr. Simms was the witness testimony. Chatty Bobby put on as witnesses, the Dean of Seattle Central Community College and the two Seattle police officers who physically removed Sarah from the campus.

In a criminal case, the government, in this case the city of

Seattle, is the plaintiff, and the plaintiff puts on their case first. Procedurally, the plaintiff is the movant, and the party with a burden of proof. Because it's a criminal case, the government is the only entity that is empowered to bring the lawsuit (criminal charges). Most people never really think about that. Ben had never really even thought about it before he worked at the city attorney's office, but of course, it makes all the sense in the world. Otherwise, people could actually go around and "press charges," as you hear said on TV shows all the time. No private citizen can actually "press charges," not criminal ones. You can sue someone in civil court, but bringing criminal charges is strictly the purview of the government. Prosecuting a citizen and, ultimately, taking away their liberty if they are convicted can never be the job of normal citizens. If it were, people would just prosecute annoying neighbors for frivolous criminal charges just to irritate them.

In any case, the government puts on their case first. Chatty Bobby called up the community college dean. Chatty Bobby's direct examination of the dean was the vanilla boredom you'd expect from a new prosecutor and first-time witness. Mr. Simms' cross examination, on the other hand, tore into the dean for her bias and animus toward the occupiers, which was real and well-documented. She wanted them gone, and she didn't much care how it happened. It wasn't so much that she wanted them gone, either. Lots of people wanted them gone. That tent encampment was a habitation nightmare, and an eyesore. It was that she had no genuine curiosity about what they were doing, and as such, operated only from her own perspective. When people are unable or unwilling to even hear the other side's perspective, it comes through loud and clear to a jury. It certainly did when the dean testified.

Throughout the dean's, and all the other witnesses' testimonies, as well as in his opening statement and closing argument, Simms continually peppered in his theme with questions like, "You'd agree that people have the right to protest, wouldn't you?" and "You don't agree with censorship, do you? The First Amendment is sacred, right?"

Chatty Bobby's redirect did very little to rehabilitate the dean's testimony. In fact, in Ben's opinion, doing any redirect at all was a mistake because the cross examination had been so devasting to the prosecution's case. Redirecting the witness can be a powerful tool when the lawyer is skilled enough to actually rehabilitate the witness into a helpful narrative. Even if rehabilitating her on redirect were possible, Chatty Bobby didn't know what questions to ask, and the dean had gotten so wound up by Mr. Simms' cross examination that all she could do was get angrier and angrier. On redirect, she reiterated much of the damaging testimony from the cross examination. Ben knew, that's exactly what Simms had been hoping for.

"Jesus Christ, Chatty Bobby just didn't know when to stop chattin.'"

She imploded during cross, and then imploded again on redirect. Simms essentially got two cross examinations for the price of one.

The SPD officers were even worse. Seattle loved to hate the police, and Ben totally understood that. Currently, he was a prosecutor, and most of his trial witnesses were SPD officers, but he had also been a skateboarder when he was younger, and every skateboarder on this planet has had, at one time or another, a well-grounded beef with the police. It was the case that, while a large percentage of cops happened to be huge jerkoffs, they continued to be a necessary evil that society functioned poorly with, and even more poorly without. This was not garden-variety hate the police rhetoric, though. Seattle had reached a tipping point. In Seattle, the citizens didn't view the police as the dicks that periodically harassed you. They were the enemy of the people. At least, they were until someone prowled your Audi when it was parked outside your Madison Park mansion. Then, somehow they became an essential service again, at least they did for about ten minutes before you go back to hating them.

Those two officer witnesses were the worst pair you could hope to draw. One was a salty old veteran who was only a year or two from collecting a pension, and the other one was less than a year out of the academy, a short-timer and a rookie. Somewhere between about five years and fifteen years into a cop's career, they become, more or less, a good cop. At least, some of them do. These two were residing outside that bubble.

When cops are twenty-one, they're too wound up, too much adrenaline and testosterone—or estrogen, depending on the cop. Either way, for those rookies, conflicts happen often. And conflict is rarely handled in a diplomatic fashion. Old cops are no better, just different. They're jaded. Old cops don't really care if your head gets bounced off a curb, so long as it doesn't blow back on them.

Cops, some cops, who are in that midcareer twilight space, actually care, and they have enough experience to understand the futility of picking a fight on every routine call. Injured from youthful exuberance for the sport, they start to reassess. They play the game differently. They start looking for how to score points instead of how to inflict pain on the other team's players. They realize that policing is judo, not kickboxing. That is the point at which they become effective. In a more perfect society, we'd just grow cops in an incubation chamber until they were about thirty-five, and implant memories of the first ten years of a typical cop's career into their brains. Unfortunately, not only are there less and less of these midcareer cops today, but there are a lot more of the twenty-one-year-olds out on the street, too.

During their cross examinations, it was pretty clear that Officer McGavin wanted to crack some skulls, and Officer Hodges just wanted to clock out early so he could take his wife to the early-bird dinner at Denny's. For the first time in the trial, Chatty Bobby did something right, he didn't double down on what was bad testimony with an ill-conceived redirect and turn it into catastrophic testimony. Truth be told, at that point, the writing was on the wall, so doing a redirect or not wasn't going to change the ultimate result.

It was a short trial, and they made their closing arguments Thursday morning. Chatty Bobby's close, and his rebuttal, were perfectly on point for the legal issues. Chatty Bobby still thought trials were about the law. He was a smart kid, and Ben knew he'd figure it out someday, but he hadn't figured it out that day. Even with the extremely high burden that that government has to establish in a criminal case, the highest burden in our legal system, Chatty Bobby had cleared that burden by a mile. It's called beyond a reasonable doubt, and a common tactic by criminal defense attorneys is to inflate that burden in voir dire and closing argument by telling a jury that no amount of doubt is reasonable. It's a hack move, but if the prosecutor is too green to know to object to it, why not use it? It may be a hack move, but it tends to work when unchallenged.

None of that mattered, though. The officer's testimony had looked biased, that much was accurate, but it also clearly illustrated that Sarah had defied the eviction order. That fact alone was dispositive. She was charged with trespassing, and those officers had inarguably established that she did, in fact, trespass. But that didn't matter. No criminal defendant is required to testify on their own behalf, and Sarah did not. As a matter of fact, Mr. Simms didn't put on a case at all, nor is the defense required to. He simply stood up at the conclusion of the government's case and rested. In addition to the officers' testimony, photographs of Sarah standing next to her tent after being ordered to vacate (one of the only pieces of evidence Chatty Bobby was able to get admitted) further proved the government's case, but that didn't matter either. All that mattered to that jury was that one cop was aggressive, one was apathetic, and the dean was biased. The jury acquitted her in less than an hour.

Chatty Bobby was the bad guy, Sarah the good guy, and the Kool-Aid drinking masses of Seattleites read in their newspapers of the great vindication of our cultural values. That value being, helping rich kids with law degrees beat misdemeanor charges so they don't have to sit in jail with the hoi polloi.

Chapter 30

Eventually, it was becoming impossible for even Erin to ignore the fact that Ben appeared to have been slowly breaking up with her since before they were even actually going out. According to Ben, they were never really going out in the first place. Right up to the point that they broke up, he maintained that they were never actually "boyfriend" and "girlfriend." Ben no longer even bothered trying to hide the fact that he was spending his Friday nights with Maria. So much so, that on that particular Friday night, when Ben didn't answer his cell phone, Erin began repeatedly calling Maria's cell phone.

Maria was too smart to answer the phone when she saw Erin's number pop up, so she just said, "Ben, your stupid girlfriend is blowing up my phone again. Call her, already."

"My girlfriend? Salma Hayek?"

"Call Erin, white boy."

"Just turn your phone off. That's what I do."

"You're starting to bug me, Ben, seriously. Call her now."

The world is comprised of forks in the road. It's always a binary choice. Do you want chocolate or vanilla, security or happiness, tits or ass? Ben didn't care for the binary choice. He liked tits *and* ass. He didn't like rubbing his throbbing temples at the prospect of picking the left fork or the right. Ben was pretty much obsessed with the concept of a third option. If the forks went left and right, what would happen if you just trapsed off into the woods that were straight ahead?

"*Inveniam viam aut faciam.*" He wasn't speaking to Maria, but more like speaking out loud to himself, but in her vicinity."

"Don't speak that Latin nonsense at me, white boy."

He grabbed his phone, and he made sure Maria saw him grab his phone. He also quietly grabbed his wallet and keys, and he made sure Maria didn't see him grab those. He made for Maria's door. Ben pretty regularly called Erin from the hallway of Maria's building, so she didn't even give him an upward glance when he walked out of her apartment. Ben didn't call Erin. He didn't even turn his phone on. He didn't even turn it on that night at all. He did get in the Barracuda, and when Maria heard that unmistakable sound of the Barracuda's motor start, she picked up her phone and called Ben. Not that Ben heard the phone ring. It was off, so it didn't ring at all. It just went to voicemail.

"Fucking prick!" Maria said out loud, but not loud.

Ben didn't hear Maria's voicemail. She only left one. He didn't hear Erin's voicemails. She left at least eleven. Ben didn't see Maria's text. She only sent one. He didn't see Erin's texts. She sent at least twenty. What he did do was drive away, creating the third option, plowing straight ahead into the forest. At first, he didn't know where he was going, but he knew where he wasn't going.

He wasn't going to Erin's. That was beyond clear. She couldn't be broken up with by reasonable means. He'd taken all his shit with him when he left her house earlier that day, and he'd left before she got home from work. Any reasonable woman would see that as a clear indication that the—air quotes—relationship was over. Erin was not a reasonable woman.

He wasn't going back to Maria's for a while. He would, eventually, but she was going to be pretty annoyed for a few days. He could avoid her for the rest of the weekend, but come Monday, he'd need something a little more creative than just driving away from her apartment to stay off her radar. At work, her office was all of about thirty-five feet down the hallway from his. He wasn't worried too much. He knew he'd think of something. Honestly, Ben was a little annoyed at her for trying to make him talk to Erin at all. The fact that Maria never really tried to make him do anything was his favorite thing about her, and in that endeavor, on that occasion, she'd failed miserably.

He couldn't go back to his place. Erin and Maria would both be out for blood, and going there was like walking into a rabbit trap and springing it on yourself. He knew this day would come, so a few months prior, he'd started keeping a backpack in the trunk of the Barracuda that had extra clothes, deodorant, a toothbrush, and some other essentials.

He couldn't go to his parents' house. Maria would never bother his parents, but he imagined that Erin had already called their house looking for him. In any case, even if he did go over there, they'd just tell him the same thing that Maria did: "Call Erin, so she stops calling us."

He could go to his friend Josh's apartment in Tacoma, and he did. He didn't know when he set out that that's where he'd wind up, but it's where he wound up, nonetheless. He didn't call first. He didn't want to turn on his phone, so he just drove. He parked. He gambled that if Josh were headed out somewhere on that Friday night, that he hadn't left yet, and that it would be somewhere that Ben could tag along.

Josh didn't disappoint. Three knocks on the door, and Josh yelled, "Come in." He was baked. He was glued to his couch. Josh actually had the look of a guy that had been glued to his tacky Scarlet-Red couch for the past two days, but Ben figured that wasn't the case. Josh had fresh sawdust on his work boots and gritty grimy all over his face, so he knew Josh had been at work all day.

Josh worked for a living, not the way Ben did, but really, actually, physically worked. Some people didn't understand that, even though Ben worked with his brain, he had a dad who worked both with his brain and his body. While Ben was growing up, he watched Big Ben do the same thing nearly every Friday night. It would have taken only ten minutes to get into the shower and wash the day off him, but that was just another ten minutes at the end of a day that had been jampacked with a hundred ten-minute tasks—and very few ten-minute breaks. At the end of a long day, Big Ben wanted to sit in his chair and drink a few Rainiers. At the end of a long week, he wanted to melt into that chair until he passed out and Barbara woke him up to tell him to come to bed.

Josh was blankly staring at a twenty-year-old episode of *Star Trek: The Next Generation*.

"What's goin' on, Ben? I thought you were the pizza guy."

Ben hadn't been to Josh's in at least a year, but Josh just chatted at him like they'd been sitting there talking for hours. Josh handed Ben a two-foot-tall bong that was the same color as Berry Blue Kool-Aid and a Bic lighter that was the same color as Lemon Lime Kool-Aid. The bud in the bong was so sticky, it looked like someone had caulked it into the bowl using Vaseline. It took five or ten seconds to get the bud to burn, and another five or ten seconds to get the smoke all the way up the vertical chamber, but once Ben took his finger off the carb, the chamber cleared immediately, and the smoke blew up his lungs like a balloon. After he regained his ability to breathe without gasping, Ben was glued to Josh's brown-leather recliner for the next two days.

"If you're sticking around for a while, we should call the pizza place and get another pizza."

Ben nodded, and Josh tossed him a Rainier tallboy from the cooler he packed his lunch in for work.

"Let's go grab some more beers at the 7-Eleven after we eat; more weed too. The weed guy's apartment is up on the third floor."

"Totally."

The *Star Trek* episode was interesting. *Star Trek* is always interesting when you're baked. It was true that the episode was almost twenty-years-old, but it was from the last season of the series, so it was actually one of the newest episodes of the show. Ben remembered watching it on Sunday, prime time on Channel 13, back in 1994 with Big Ben and Barbara. That was during Big Ben and Barbara's cocooned and vacant phase, right after Mike had died.

Lisa wasn't around yet, or if she was, she was just an embryo in Barbara's uterus. In any case, it was just the three of them, sitting there watching TV. Barbara hated *Star Trek*; Big Ben loved it. But at that time, Big Ben got no enjoyment from it, and Barbara wasn't even present enough to be annoyed by it. Ben always sat on the floor in front of the TV. Ben's head always blocked half the screen, and Big Ben, Barbara, and Mike used to constantly tell him to move. Nobody bothered telling him to move after Mike died.

Ben hadn't seen it since way back then, and he realized, for the first time, that the guy who played Locke on *Lost* was the guest star. It hadn't seemed like the show had been off the air for so long. But Ben realized that even *Lost*, that came on the air ten years after *The Next Generation* had ended, had been over for almost two years. Back when he was little, he remembered liking that episode. There was a ship trapped in an asteroid... and Romulans...and a bunch of dead people. The Romulans sealed the Enterprise into this asteroid with this abandoned Starfleet ship. Back then, that was about all he was looking for from a *Star Trek* episode, just some cool ships shooting at each other. But that evening at Josh's, Ben started to see something different.

When he first sat down, he assumed the episode was half over. When you randomly sit down in someone's living room and start watching TV, whatever is on is typically half over; that's just sort of how live TV works. It's a bus line that started before you got on and, likely, proceeds well after you've gotten off.

But that evening, he'd only missed a minute or two of the episode. In fact, when Josh handed him the bong, they were just cutting away to the first commercial break. Ben watched the remainder of the episode in relative silence. Josh and Ben had been doing this since they were kids. Sometimes, back then, on warm summer nights, they'd be skating one of their ramps for an hour or two while the sun slowly crept down behind the Olympic Range. Eventually, one of them would break out the pipe, and even then, they often just sat and smoked without really talking. That's how it was that Friday night at Josh's apartment.

Star Trek was always making social commentary about something. Ben always thought that Gene Roddenberry was sort of a genius because he was able to force his hippie-liberal values on people in the Bible Belt by disguising his political platform as a show about spaceships and aliens. Ben knew what it was. He knew Ol' Gene Roddenberry was a professional camouflage practitioner of the highest order.

Gene Roddenberry had passed on by the time that episode was written, but weaving social commentary into those episodes had not. His handpicked successor, Rick Berman had continued Gene's vision, and that episode wasn't really about Romulans and ships stuck in asteroids. It was about obedience at odds with ethics, duty to a cause over fealty to a person, and redemption fueled by regret over a prior moral failing.

In a nutshell, Riker had been involved with an illegal exper-imental project and sworn to silence by his crooked Starfleet superiors. He had to decide if he would obey his former captain or disobey him, at great personal risk to his career. By the end of the episode, his guilt over his involvement in the deaths of the other Starfleet personnel propels his choice to act in accordance with his principles, and he is ultimately exonerated of the guilt he's been carrying around for years.

Ben always thought Riker was sort of an uptight prick, the sort of conservative asshole who puts NRA stickers on the bumper of the shuttle pod he drives to work. It was certainly the case that Ben's moral and ethical fiber was somewhat thinner than that of the duty and honor archetype that Commander Riker personified, but Ben did have a code. He acted in accordance with that code, and right at that point in time, he was being told by a superior to act contrary to that code.

He was being told to act contrary to that code to protect a

powerful person who was acting purely out of self-interest, and it crept up his ass and stayed there, the way poorly-tailored suit pants did. He didn't know what he was going to do about it, but he knew he didn't want to wait for years to get his redemption the way Riker did.

By Sunday night, Ben had very little choice but to head back to his apartment. He had no suit with him, and Mr. Gorton's trial was set to start that Monday morning. Also, if he stayed at Josh's another night, he was afraid he might talk himself out of going to work in the morning altogether. Considering how many messy ends had developed in his life over the past several months, he was a little scared that he might talk himself out of showing back up to work...ever. And that was just the work stuff. Figuring out how to deal with Maria would be difficult, but finally ending things with Erin in a way she would be forced to accept would be beyond miserable.

When he got back into the Barracuda to head back to Seattle that evening, he turned on his phone for the first time since Friday afternoon. He never read the many texts from Erin, nor did he listen to her numerous voicemails. He did listen to Maria's single voicemail, and he read her single text. He texted Maria, "Sorry I bailed like that. I want to make it up to you for real. But I have this fucking trial starting tomorrow. And I have to figure out how to deal with Erin. Can I come over Friday after work?" The thumbs up emoji popped back from Maria, and that's where they left it.

Then Ben called Erin and put it on speaker. It was about an hour drive back to Seattle from Tacoma on a Sunday night, so he figured by the time he made it back to his apartment, she'd be mostly done yelling at him. She answered, and he said "Hey." He didn't speak another word until he passed

SeaTac. He knew there was no point in talking. Any point he would make would simply be a bootlace for Erin to expand the conversation into some other tangentially-related aspect of their complete mismatch of a relationship, further prolonging the breakup.

When she'd talked herself out, and Ben was able to speak without interrupting, he gave the same lame excuse that men have been giving women for breaking up since the beginning of time. "Erin, it's not you; it's me." She blew her top again, and Ben silently absorbed thirty more minutes of yelling and crying.

He was undeterred, and unpersuaded by Erin's appeals. He'd mistreated her, taken her for granted, largely because he never really wanted to be in the relationship, in the first place. But he let it go. He'd let her believe it was going to keep going on. He was sort of a wank, if he were being honest with himself, but continuing on with it would only keep him being a wank for the foreseeable future. She was the best of what she could be, considering who and what she'd come from, but she just wasn't for Ben. It was never what Ben wanted. It was just easy to let it go on, and hard to end it, so when he said, "It's not you; it's me," he was telling the truth.

By the time he pulled up to his apartment building, it was over. He made his closing remark, which was, "Erin, I've treated you poorly, and I'm sorry I did that, but you deserve to be with someone who wants to be with you. I'm just not that person. I hope we can be friends someday. Goodbye."

Chapter 31

Councilman Young was sitting in an otherwise empty gallery that Monday, the first day of Mr. Gorton's trial. Corey popped in periodically throughout the trial. Councilman Young never came up and talked to Ben directly, but it was clear that he was there to armchair quarterback the trial and make sure Ben dropped the hammer on Mr. Gorton. Corey was there to courier messages so that the Councilman had a plausibly deniable filter between himself and Ben.

There's a lot of waiting when you're sitting in a courtroom. People don't think so because, when they're watching *The Good Wife* or *Law and Order*, they never show the lawyers just sitting around twiddling their thumbs. But at least half of the time a lawyer spends in a courtroom is just an idle wasteland of waiting.

Ben wasn't sure why people would watch those shows, anyway. *Perry Mason* and *Matlock* were the only good shows about lawyers. "Maybe someday, someone will make a show about that Saul Goodman guy from *Breaking Bad*. That would be fuckin' kewl!"

Ben always made sure to get a chair with armrests and four legs. The ones on wheels tended to roll when Ben nodded off, and the ones without armrests were difficult to nod off in at all. It wasn't simply laziness or apathy; there was a pragmatic and functional angle. Ben conserved his energy. He was like a computer going into sleep mode. If nobody pushed any of his buttons for a while, he just powered down.

That morning, the waiting didn't coax him into lethargy, and he got no sleep in the courtroom that week whatsoever. That quiet courtroom had crawled right up his ass and set up camp, even worse than poorly-tailored suit pants. The judge wasn't on the bench because they were waiting for the bailiff to bring up a jury venire. Ben kept turning around in his chair and looking at that empty gallery. It bugged him. It bugged him a lot that when he turned around, all he saw were Corey and the Councilman's faces staring back at him. It bugged him that *The Stranger, Real Change,* and *The Seattle Weekly* weren't there. Not because he craved media attention, but because, when the alternative and politically-liberal local media had an opportunity to out a social justice hypocrite like Councilman Young, they were too busy patting themselves on the back about helping a rich white lawyer avoid even one day in a jail cell.

But there was no one there to ask why a sitting Seattle City Council Member was hanging around in the gallery of a courtroom at municipal court during a trespassing trial of, apparently, no consequence. It didn't look right, and any decent reporter would have immediately asked why the Criminal Division Chief and a sitting City Council Member were so interested, in the first place. Any decent reporter would also have figured out that Councilman Young owned the house that Mr. Gorton was squatting in. But nobody gave a shit.

Ben had been observing the ease with which well-off white people presented themselves as the face of equity and equality.

That face is great at planting lawn signs in the front yards of effectively-segregated and exclusive neighborhoods. That face is excellent about espousing its well-practiced, anti-racist rants in the written word of the media, a primary tool of white supremacy. It's the face that smiles while it makes land acknowledgments to indigenous peoples, while simultaneously buying and developing the very land they are acknowledging was stolen.

He felt let down, but not nearly as much as he had when he was younger. He'd been let down so often by the ruling liberal elite of Seattle pretending to give a shit about normal people, that by the time he was sitting there at Mr. Gorton's trial that Monday morning, he barely felt it in his gut at all.

When the jury venire was brought in, Ben saw his marks immediately. He knew that most Seattleites either didn't really care about their inherent biases, as long as they weren't on display for others, or were simply in denial about their level of prejudice. Ben knew that if you presented most Seattleites with a plausible, non-racially motivated reason to convict a black man like Mr. Gorton, they'd convict. They'd convict him, even if they knew the reason was horseshit. They'd convict him, as long as convicting him didn't make them look like bigots.

It was unavoidable that, to serve justice, a prosecutor such as Ben also became a tool of white supremacy. It was unavoidable because, if Ben weren't doing the job, someone worse would. Prosecution was the natural conclusion of an ill society rife with inequality. But what could you do? Policing was the necessary evil that everyone tacitly accepted, in all of its implications, for the ease and comfort it provided. A prosecutor's office could never be staffed by purists and zealots because it was dirty work, and working in a racist system in order to produce a greater good was a dubious proposition, at best.

Doing a wrong thing to achieve a right result had always been enough justification for Ben to effectively do his job. As long as the punishments were roughly equal to the offenses, he didn't mind doing his job, but that was starting to feel like a distant memory that morning.

He picked a jury in much the same way he'd done dozens of times before. It was all about dissenters, group thinkers, and leaders. Every jury was. This jury had to be convinced that Mr. Gorton was guilty of the trespass, and that the right of the people of Seattle to be secure in their property rights was of paramount importance. In order to convict on that basis, there could be no mention of systemic racism, or societal inequality.

He spotted his leader immediately. A middle-aged black woman named Theresa. Theresa was a college graduate, worked as an account representative at a health insurance company, and was childless. Most importantly, she was politically conservative. If she were willing to convict, all the rich white Seattleite group thinkers on the jury would vote to convict, as well. In order to clear a path for Theresa to become the thought leader, Ben had to clear some dissenters out of the way. There were a couple of truly problematic free thinkers on the jury. A thinking juror was poison to a jury. A programed juror was the only useful juror.

By the time that jury had been empaneled, Susan had yet to realize that she and Mr. Gorton were nothing more than frogs in a pot of water. And Ben had just turned on the burner.

As the trial proceeded, Susan became well acquainted with the feeling of something slipping through your fingers—not, something had slipped through her fingers, but something was presently slipping through her fingers—and continued to do so. Continued to do so, and would continue to do so for some time to come. Also that, regardless of her ability to recognize that the trial had gotten away from her, she lacked any ability whatsoever to reel it back in. For her, it was a week of bewilderment. There are few things in life that so completely disempower an individual as sitting in a sinking boat. You just have to experience it, in all its terror; experience it, and accept your inability to change your fate. Impending death is scary, but the proposition of being a witness to your own slow demise is demoralizing.

Susan knew, by the end of voir dire, that she was being slowly devoured by an apex predator. Then, just as the last bit of life was draining out of her, that apex predator just stopped.

He just withdrew, walked away, disappeared. And it was over. She was wounded, only half alive, but alive, nonetheless. She didn't know it then, but her near-death experience in the courtroom became the event that turned her into the best trial attorney in her division. The crucible melts you down so you can be born again as forged steel.

For Ben, it was Thursday morning. Erin and Maria had walked into the gallery together, which was beyond odd. Around SMC, it was common knowledge what sort of case Ben was trying that week. Erin and Maria were with a man who Ben immediately recognized as the Lead Justice Reporter at the *Seattle Weekly*. His name was Jim Rogers. The trial had proceeded toward its inevitable conclusion without a hitch. Ben stood up to deliver his closing argument.

He stood there like he'd done dozens of times before. You never really convince anyone to see the case your way in closing argument. If that's what you're doing with your closing argument, you lost the trial well before that. This jury had bought Ben's "white hat" song and dance days ago. He didn't need to convince anyone. They were sufficiently convinced, but a good closing argument that re-sunk the hooks and themes he'd woven in throughout the entire trial could decrease the amount of time they spent coming to the decision to convict. All that was necessary was to give the leader in the deliberation room enough one-liners to club the group thinkers over the head with, and a conviction was pretty much always assured.

Ben started at the podium with a small stack of notes. He looked down at those notes. Then, he set the notes on the podium and walked out from behind it. He walked right up to the jury box and began to speak. It looked like he was getting ready to really speak from the heart, because he was.

Ben had a gift. He actually had several, but this particular one was extraordinarily useful for any trial attorney, even more so for a prosecutor who must establish a case beyond a reasonable doubt in order to win a trial. Ben had dramatically dropped his notes on the podium and walked up to the jury box many times. It was practiced, and it was certainly done for the purpose of creating a bond and appearance of sincerity and candor, but it wasn't just a farse either. Ben could inhabit his cases. He could speak from the heart anytime he chose to, about any subject. He could make you feel like you were the only person in the room, which he did to every member of the jury that day. He could agree with you while simultaneously convincing you that it was your idea to come to his conclusion and abandon your own.

It was a toolbox of chicanery that always worked because he made you feel like you were important, and that your decision was paramount. Most importantly, he could convince you that doing what he wanted you to do was your idea. Nobody likes to be sold, or to be wrong. Losing face is worse than having your face beaten to a pulp. "Because losing face is worse than actually losing your fuckin' face." So he gave jurors their face, and in return, they delivered him convictions. Evey good politician understands this, how it really works, with people. Used for ill, such a skillset could be the end of civil society. Used for good, such a skillset could inspire the greatest of goods.

When he sat down, Susan stood up. Her voice quivered, and he could see under her arms that she was sweating through her blazer. Most of her DPD counterparts became aggressive when they were under a microscope like the one she was under at that moment. Ben never understood why. Becoming more aggressive when you're out of your element makes you look both incompetent and scared. Susan opted to just stick with being scared, and that made her sympathetic. It was the best she could do that day, to be sympathetic. She would never convince even one of those jurors to acquit Mr. Gorton, but at least they got to see that she was a real person, not just a blustering idiot in a suit. Someday, she'd be able to use that ability to connect with people to win cases, and when she did, she'd become the scourge of the prosecutor's office.

In a criminal case, the prosecutor is allowed to make a rebuttal argument after the defense makes their closing argument. Council Member Young and Corey looked quite content as they watched from the gallery. They could see that it was over, that Ben had trounced Susan. Jim Rogers was sitting between Maria and Erin, writing furiously on a small-spiral notepad.

It was Judge Kim presiding over the trial, and she looked over at Ben and asked if the city had a rebuttal. Ben stood up and said:

"Your Honor, the city has a motion."

Judge Kim was a middle-aged Korean woman. She did a lot more watching than talking. She was an actual judge, or at least, what you'd really want a judge to be in an ideal world. Judges tend to fall left or right, and stick there like mud in the waffle sole of a work boot. Whether we like it or not, they're largely hometown referees, and idealogues. A handful, like Judge Kim, are thinkers, and kowtow to justice, not politics. Ben looked at Judge Kim and, for a moment, he could feel her reading his mind. She'd presided over Sarah's trial the week before, and he knew she was smart enough to see the friction of injustice playing out between the two trials.

"What's your motion, Mr. Sullivan?" she asked.

"The city is making the motion to dismiss the charge against Mr. Gorton with prejudice."

"That motion is granted, Mr. Sullivan."

Corey stood up in the gallery and charged up toward the bar.

"Your honor, the city is not dismissing this charge. Mr. Sullivan is in error."

"Mr. Robinson, you're not trying this case," Judge Kim said.

"But I'm the Criminal Division Chief, and Mr. Sullivan's supervisor."

"And as Criminal Division Chief, you've tasked Mr. Sullivan with trying this case on behalf of the city. Your prosecutors have discretion to try these cases, don't they?"

"I mean, of course, they do."

"And they do so in this courthouse every day without you intervening, don't they?"

"Of course, they do."

"Then why do you care so much about this particular, insignificant trespassing case?"

Corey had, likely for the first time in his life, run out of bullshit to say, so he stopped talking. Judge Kim looked at him for about ten silent seconds, and finally said, "Mr. Robinson, the court has granted the city's motion, and this case is dismissed with prejudice. Please sit down."

As Judge Kim gave verbal instructions to release the jury and release Mr. Gorton, Susan looked over at Ben and silently mouthed "Thank you." Ben barely looked up to meet her glance, simply shooting her a thumbs-up under the counsel table. As soon as the court adjourned, Corey marched up through the bar and to the counsel table where Ben was siting.

"Are you fucking kidding me, Ben? I'm going to crucify you for this, you little prick."

"Corey, you're a duplicitous piece of shit, and I imagine that will take you far in politics. Good luck. Oh yeah, also, take this job and shove it."

Corey retreated back to the dark corner of the gallery where Council Member Young was stewing. Jim Rogers was now approaching Ben. Ben looked over at Council Member Young and said, "Council Member Young, good luck with your house flip. I'm sure you'll be able to get back to work on it, now that it's been vacated."

Corey and Council Member Young quickly and quietly left the courtroom as Jim Rogers eyed them skeptically, clearly starting to put together what might be going on. Before Rogers could ask him anything, Ben said, "Jim, I've got a great story for you, but I can't talk right this second."

"I can't wait to hear it, Mr. Former Prosecutor," he said as he handed Ben his card and exited the courtroom.

"Well, I'm glad you showed up, and I can't wait to tell it to you."

Erin was still sitting next to Maria in the back of the gallery.

Ben looked at her and said, "Thanks for bringing the cavalry."

Erin said, "Anytime, Ben. I'll see you around, okay."

After that, the courtroom went quiet. Ben and Maria were alone. Well, not exactly alone. Shannon, the court bailiff was actually sitting at her desk near the witness stand, clearly waiting for them to leave so she could lock up for the day. But she was polite enough to pretend to work for a few more minutes before kicking them out in a more obvious way.

Maria wasn't in court that day, so she was wearing jeans and a sleeveless top. He looked at her, and for a minute, he saw her the way he'd seen her at that Psychedelic Razors show all those years ago.

"Shannon, clearly, wants us to leave her courtroom so she can get on the road before rush hour. I guess we're the occupiers now," he said.

"Flashback humor? Seriously, white boy?!"

"It seemed appropriate."

"Well, in any case, you certainly know how to burn a bridge behind you. What are you going to do now?"

"I don't know. I fell assbackwards into this job, in the first place. But leaving it was very much on purpose. Maybe, I could become a criminal defense attorney."

"DPD?"

"Fuck, no! Do I look like a wayward sheep to you?"

"Then, what?"

"Some of the most noteworthy lawyers in history have been private criminal defense lawyers. Maybe, something like that."

"You want to be Johnnie Cochran?"

"Why not? Somewhere out there, there's a high-profile celebrity doing something stupid right at this very moment, and they'll definitely need a charming and morally ambiguous attorney."

"You're morally ambiguous?"

"I could be morally ambiguous."

"You just set a homeless guy free in order to burn a hypocrite City Council Member."

"I don't have it all worked out yet. I just quit my job five minutes ago."

"So, are you coming over tonight?" she asked.

"About that, I'm not gonna be able stay at Erin's anymore, and considering I'm newly unemployed, I'm not gonna be able to keep my apartment. I was wondering if you wouldn't mind having an unemployed guy stay over at your place for a while?"

"Is this your way of asking me if I want to live together?"

"Is it working?"

"We'll talk about it."

"If you like that, wait until you see how I propose."

"You're going to propose?"

"I mean, not right this second. Honestly, it probably won't happen until pretty late into Book Three."

Maria smacked him on the arm and rolled her eyes. "We going to my place or what?"

Afterword

Thanks for reading. I'll see you back for Book Three, maybe.

In all honesty, I wrote *Professional Camouflage* as a goof, and as a way to process the daily annoyance and irritation of working as a municipal prosecutor. About half way through writing it, I realized that Ben genuinely had something to say. What he had to say was often sarcastic, always satirical, and rooted in absurdist angst, but it was genuine. Anyway, the secret sauce happened when I realized that existentialism and the farce of a criminal justice system we have in Seattle went together like peanut butter and jelly. I actually started planning *The Land of Lollipops and Suckers* before I finished writing *Professional Camouflage*.

I'm not sure if Ben still has something interesting to say, and when my characters run out of useful social commentary, I make them shut up permanently. Right now, I'm satisfied with the series consisting of just these two books. I think Ben has said everything he needed to, and I purposely made the ending of lollipops final enough to be the end, but open ended enough to come back with another book if it makes sense. If Book Three happens, it will be after a long hiatus for Ben and I both. He needs to find a new job, and I need to write a book that doesn't trigger my anxiety.

Also, I am not writing an Epilogue here, because I genuinely don't know if there is another book, and I don't want to stitch myself into anything unless I'm sure the series is done. If your annoyed that you don't get to see how things work out for Ben and Maria, I apologize. Like with *Professional Camouflage*, the ending comes on all at once—just like an LSD trip. Friends, editors, and random readers have commented that they feel a little gobsmacked by my endings, but that's just how I do it. Sorry. In any case, I think it's safe to say that Maria is the love of Ben's life. Honestly, Maria could do better, but at the end of the day, Ben is her lobster. Unfortunately, the fact that Ben and Maria will be together from here on out—while sweet— also presents challenges for writing another book. Without the Erin, Ben, Maria love triangle, any third book will need to carry a entire story where the love story is a foregone conclusion.

I have always thought *City Attorney's Office* would be perfect for a Nexflix series. And in true sellout fashion, I could be convinced to write a third book if one of the big streaming services wanted to develop it. Any adaptation by a large streaming service will undoubtedly discard anything clever or insightful about the series, which is kind of perfect for a meritless third installment that is nothing but a shameless cash grab for myself. I mean, Ben doesn't need to have to have anything interesting to say if he's just a twenty something pretty boy actor on a TV show. That shit will sell itself!

So, streaming people, the ball is in your court.

About the Author

I was a homeless teenager. Now I own a home. I was a high school dropout. Now I'm an attorney. I was an alcoholic. Now I'm sober. I was a kid well into adulthood. Now I'm the adult parent of kids. I was alone. Now I have people. I was a punk rock teenager. Now I'm a punk rock middleager . I was a talker. Now I'm a writer.

Keep up with me on the Bland Coffee website.

You can connect with me on:
🌐 https://blandcoffeepublishing.com

Also by Christopher J. Stockwell

A Lack of Intradimensional Sync

What's real if you don't know if you're awake? What if you are awake, but everything is unreal? Jon slips in and out of what most people accept to be their reality. he slips in and out of his own dimension, and onto the road.

Planned Release Jun 2026

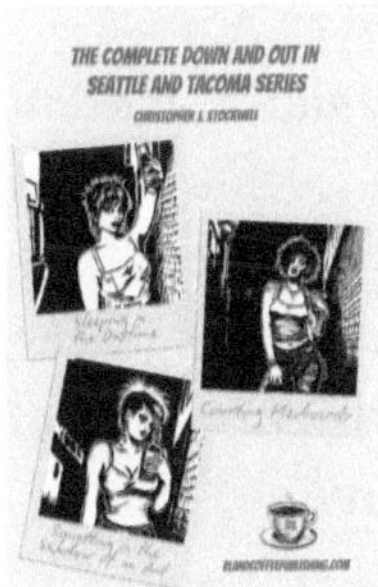

The Complete Down and Out in Seattle and Tacoma Series

The three novellas of the Down and Out in Seattle and Tacoma Series in one volume. The down and out novellas are like coke, alcohol, and cigarettes. You can enjoy them separately, but they were meant to be consumed together.

Sleeping in the Daytime

The keystone of the down and out books, a first glance at Jack. He's the car wreck you can't take your eyes off. Sleeping in the Daytime lets you see him before serious deterioration has set in. Get ready, living like Jack is a full-time job.

Courting Mediocrity

The anchor and lynch pin of the down and out books. A quiet life, in a quiet town, with sweet girl just isn't Jack's style. Continue your journey through Jack's struggles. It's half time. Will Jack pull it together, or implode spectacularly?

Squatting in the Shadow of an Ant

The coup de grace of the down and out books. What happens to a lovable fuck up when everyone else has moved on. Jack spent much of his life confined in places, but never to his own mind. This series of ends here, but where is here?

The Antagonist's Handbook

A pair of losers from the PNW start out for stardom by moving to Los Angeles. After becoming paparazzi, they soon figure out that they can blackmail celebrities into posing for their photos. Eventually, they launch their own tabloid.